T0356846

TAKING STOCK

SHANNON BAKER

SEVERN RIVER
PUBLISHING

Severn River Publishing
www.SevernRiverBooks.com

This is a work of fiction. Names, characters, businesses, places, events and incidents are either the products of the author's imagination or used in a fictitious manner. Any resemblance to actual persons, living or dead, or actual events is purely coincidental.

ISBN: 978-1-64875-619-1 (Paperback)

1

If the clothes make the woman, I was crisp, clean, understated, and brand-spanking new. Exactly what I was shooting for. From my shined and manure-free cowboy boots, my black jeans, and buttery-soft suede blazer, I looked the part of a smart and savvy cattle buyer with money to burn.

The smoke wafting from that flaming money wasn't coming from me, though, but from Aria Fontaine, the gorgeous woman with the regal bearing and flawless olive skin walking next to me. She wove through the rows of vendor booths in the noisy Expo Hall at the National Western Stock Show in Denver as if she'd never had a bad hair day in her life. Which she probably hadn't. More than a few people focused on her as she strode past in her stacked-heeled boots. My guess is she could have been ten degrees less beautiful and still commanded that notice. She had what my cool niece, Carly, would call "rizz."

Aria stopped in front of an information booth at an intersection that headed in one direction to a bank of doors leading outside and a wide central passageway running the length of the building. Across the corridor, a knife vendor called SharpCo, and a leather vendor displaying every breed of cow hide imaginable and even a few samples of fake hides no one should have created, like pink leopard skin, were set up. Jewelry, cowboy hats, boots, toys, hot tubs, and more variations of trade show treasures than I cared to itemize crowded the Expo Hall, which looked like it could cover a whole 640-acre section of Nebraska Sandhills pasture.

Aria lifted her delicate chin, dark hair dropping down her back as she scanned the hordes of oncoming foot traffic.

She'd insisted on venturing through the trade show. I'd have been plum happy to leave off this garish display of capitalism that wasn't unique to the stock show but could be found at any festival or fair where fine Chinese trinkets were sold.

I'd much rather grab a coffee to beat off the January chill and head back downstairs to the cattle barn to consider the Highland cattle we'd come to the stock show to see. I pulled in a deep breath, parsing out the earthy smells of animals, feed, dirt, and hay—my favorite perfume—from the odor of concession food and people jamming the aisle—a lot less appealing.

"Ladies. Over here. Hello." The overly friendly and boisterous voice of an older man filtered through the general chatter of the crowd and the tinny notes of country music on the Expo sound system, never loud enough to identify the song, so more like the incessant buzzing of a sweat bee.

We both glanced over at the guy waving with gusto in the SharpCo booth. He looked well past retirement age, and his thinning hair could've used a trim and wash. "Now is the perfect time to get some efficient and beautiful kitchen knives. Come on over and let me show you the Manhandler. Guaranteed to cut through anything."

Aria beamed at him as if he weren't as annoying as any carnival barker and raised her voice so he could hear her across the aisle. "They do look lovely, but no thank you."

I held back a glare but didn't give him my warmest expression, either. What marketing genius thought calling anything, let alone a knife, a Manhandler was a good idea?

He took our rejection well and spoke to a couple crossing in front of him. They didn't slow down. Maybe nothing in their lives needed Manhandling, either.

I'd been to the stock show many times, mostly down in the pens when I was younger, grooming cattle for Bill Hardy, a Nebraska Sandhills Hereford breeder. Then, I wore insulated coveralls, a wool beanie, and Sorrels.

Looking professional came with a price, and in this case, it was goose bumps.

I tipped my head to the right. "How about coffee? Or we can go downstairs and see Brodgar before we meet with Craig McNeal."

I'd been burned enough by love that I usually steered clear of romance, but all my barriers had broken down when I'd clicked on Brodgar's online profile, with all that gorgeous, wavy red hair and horns spanning the frame. He had great form, and his numbers were all good. But the photo had shown his eyes. One look was all it took for me to fall. Hard. If he'd been on a dating app, I'd have swiped right with enthusiasm.

I'd exchanged a few emails with the breeder, Craig McNeal. He insisted Brodgar wasn't for sale. I'd sicced Aria on him with all her negotiating skills, and he'd agreed to bring Brodgar to the stock show. But he made no promises to sell him. I figured as soon as McNeal met Aria, he'd be as smitten as everyone else was, and Brodgar would be on the ranch in a matter of days.

Aria pulled her phone from her back pocket. With piles of money higher than the Sears Tower in her hometown of Chicago, Aria had been raised in mansions, vacationed at the swankiest resorts, and spent her days managing her family's financial empire. She could cruise around daily in four-inch heels with the grace of a sailboat on placid waters. Today, she wore jeans, a black leather blazer, and Western boots, like a good portion of the people here, and she carried it off like a natural.

I loved Aria, but I kind of hated her, too.

She glanced at the time, then scanned the crowd again. "Have I told you about my cousin, Jefferson?"

Yikes. That's the third time she'd mentioned him. It felt suspiciously like she was a car salesman trying to off-load last year's model. "I'm just gonna grab us—"

She ignored that and kept searching the crowd. "He's presenting the cash and awards for the Charolais show, and I told him we'd meet him here."

That explained why she insisted we come to the trade show and why we were simply standing here.

She thrust her hand in the air and bounced on her toes. "Tiger! Here!"

I turned in the direction she waved to see a friendly-looking man, brown hair neatly parted and combed, button-up tattersall tucked into navy blue slacks, wearing a puffy ski jacket and looking toward us.

Aria kept waving. "Over here!" She grabbed my upper arm and swung to face me. "Jefferson. I'm so glad he made it. I can't wait for you to meet him."

I spun back to the handsome man in the ski jacket. Maybe I'd been too hasty to dismiss Aria's matchmaking without even meeting the guy. This cousin of hers was nearly as good-looking as she was.

I felt a welcoming smile form just as he averted his gaze and scooted down an alley of booths with water filters and Western art.

"Tiger!"

Before I could shift my focus, Aria gave one more bounce and launched herself into the arms of an even better-looking man. About six feet tall, he wore his more-pepper-than-salt hair trimmed neatly and was dressed in a Western-cut blazer and crisp jeans, expensive snakeskin boots on his feet. What struck me were his vivid blue eyes, the color of a cloudless Colorado sky.

His face radiated with pleasure. "Well, hi there, Turbo."

Amid the parting of a sea of schoolkids all using outdoor voices and wearing flimsy cardboard CSU Rams horns on their heads, he gave her one last hug. With an amused expression, Jefferson shuffled to the side of the aisle to make way for a concession worker wheeling a cart of supplies. It made him even more handsome. "Thanks for the ebullient hello, but we saw each other at Christmas, or were you too drunk to remember?"

She swatted him. "That was Lydia, or were *you* too drunk to remember?"

He draped a lanky arm on her shoulder. Clearly these two adored each other. "Being drunk is the only way I can survive your sisters in one room together."

"Me, too." Her good spirits dimmed almost imperceptibly before recovering and shining on me. "Jefferson, this is my friend, Kate."

Aria called us friends, and I thought of us that way, too, but technically, I was the manager of the thousand acres of Sandhills pastureland she'd convinced Troy Striker to sell her. The land abutted my two acres and tiny cottage a few miles outside of the bustling metropolis of Hodgekiss, Nebraska, population one thousand. Aria had her heart set on raising Highland cattle.

After I'd been ousted from the sheriff's office—by one vote—Aria had hired me in the fall, and I'd spent the last few months fixing fences, traveling to Highland cattle breeders to study their operations, reading up on the hardy breed, and, finally, beginning the process of building our herd.

While being as handsome as Aria was beautiful, Jefferson had a down-to-earth sense about him. There was a vulnerability I couldn't quite identify but made me want to assure him that all was well. He offered his hand, and it felt smooth and cool. "Nice to meet you. Congratulations on keeping Aria interested in a project for more than three weeks."

Aria, who only had an inch or two on my five-foot-three frame, punched Jefferson's arm. "Says the guy who constantly talks about his next great adventure as soon as he gets the nerve to quit Hansford Meats." Her eyes sparkled when she told me, "He got his nickname because he's like this cat, Tiger, I used to have. Tiger would lie around all day and you'd think he was perfectly content, then when you didn't expect it, he'd attack. Like shoot from under the couch and bite your feet, or jump on you while you're watching TV."

Jefferson glanced at me and then back to Aria, as if relishing the memory of their childhood. "And Turbo got her nickname because... Do I really need to explain?"

While still a glamorous woman, somehow Aria had taken on a childlike giddiness. "You always sucked at nicknames. Where did Pokey come from, anyway?"

A hard glint hit his eyes, then vanished quickly. To me, he said, "Pokey is my older brother, Blaine." To Aria: "Nicknamed because he was always poking his head into things that aren't his business."

Aria snapped her fingers. "That's right."

Jefferson gave Aria a once-over. "You look amazing, like a woman in love."

Ooof. That shouldn't have punched me in the gut. Aria *was* a woman in love with a man who loved her back. That was how the world was supposed to work. Good for her. And him. Damn it.

Aria hugged Jefferson again. "You're embarrassing me. Be nice."

I suspected he was usually nice. But before I could respond, I heard something that sent a chill up my neck and across my scalp. I hoped it was my sometimes morbid imagination.

Jefferson bent toward me. "Sorry, Kate. Aria brings out the brat in me."

Aria placed a light hand on my arm again and one on Jefferson's as if connecting us. "Kate's got a baseball team's worth of brothers and sisters, she's not afraid of a little teasing."

I heard the noise again, unmistakable this time. Wishing I could get Jefferson and Aria moving and put a crowd of people between me and disaster, I said, "Hey, let's get a cup of coffee."

"Kate?"

Honeydew and horseradish. I hadn't moved fast enough.

A long-fingered hand with blood-red nails clutched at my arm and pulled me away from Aria. With her usual exuberance, she gushed, "Oh my god. I wouldn't have known it was you if I hadn't recognized Aria."

If she hadn't held on, I would have bolted. I might have anyway, except a young woman pushing a stroller blocked the surest route. "Roxy." I could have asked what she was doing at the Denver Stock Show instead of being home with her husband, Ted—my ex who became my ex because he and Roxy were having an affair—and their three-year-old son, but I didn't care. And I really didn't want to engage her in any way.

Aria and Jefferson glanced at each other, then back at Roxy. Aria didn't know enough not to be her usual friendly self. "Hi. Rosie, isn't it?"

Roxy, leggy and lean, hair curled into shoulder-length ringlets and sprayed to a red-level fire hazard, batted eyes heavy with false eyelashes. She threw her arms around Aria, snugging her close to a cleavage I'd envied even before she'd snagged my husband. While I felt sorry for Aria, I felt more relieved that she was the one in Roxy's clutches and not me.

Roxy drew back. "You're a hoot," she said to Aria. She reached out to touch the silk scarf hanging loose around Aria's neck. "Oh my God. Is this Hermès?"

Aria cringed a little and, probably out of kindness to help Roxy, corrected the pronunciation of *HER-meez*. "That's right, Hermès." She made it sound like *AIR-mess*.

Jefferson stepped back and seemed to disappear next to the information booth and three metal double-doors leading outside. For such a handsome man, he was remarkably adept at slipping into the background.

People streamed in, letting in blasts of cold air. The afternoon rodeo must have ended at the Coliseum that squatted across a wide swath of concrete packed with food vendors and smells of greasy funnel cakes, ribs, burgers, and brats. From there, you had to cross under I-70 to reach the rodeo arena. The Coliseum held down the southern end of the huge complex, and the rush of interstate traffic could be heard on the trek from one venue to another.

The National Western Stock Show was spread over grounds big enough that shuttle buses and six-passenger golf carts trundled folks across the giant compound. Railroad tracks bisected the outer pens and a show ring from the rodeo arena and the various barns, arenas, corrals, and the gargantuan Expo Hall on the eastern side. The official show lasted over two weeks.

Roxy paused to give Aria a puzzled look, maybe considering the new pronunciation, then said, "I need to congratulate you."

Aria's eyes slid to me as if checking to see if we were safe.

We weren't. But "gracious" was Aria's second name, so she asked, "Congratulate me?"

Roxy gestured Vanna White–style at me. "For this amazing transformation. I've been trying to give Kate a makeover for years. I mean, she's got a decent base to work from. But she's stubborn and refuses to even try. And look at you. Only friends for a little while and already she's on her way to being attractive."

I'd tamed my chestnut curls into long waves that fell down my back, instead of the ponytail I normally scraped my wild nest into. I'd applied a bit of makeup, actually had a manicure yesterday, and wore a real outfit instead of flannel and faded denim. But Roxy making a point of it bristled me up.

When she lost her friendly smile and a hard note darkened her eyes, it was clear Aria wasn't on board with Roxy's assessment. It felt great to have someone take up for me, but the battle wasn't worth the effort, so I stepped in.

I nodded at Roxy's sequined satin duster over a short denim skirt and ankle-high red cowboy boots. "You look awfully dressed up for the stock show." I might have emphasized *awful* more than was necessary.

She glanced down at her get-up. "Oh, thank you. I didn't know if the rhinestones on the shirt clashed with the sequins on the jacket."

They did.

"But I guess I pulled it off. I'm helping out Marla Duprey in her booth. You remember Marla?"

I sifted through my memory. "Don't think so."

Roxy thrust out a hip and flipped her hair. "Oh. She went to college in Torrington when we were all there." The *all* she talked about would include Ted. "Well, she's got a high-end Western store in Casper, and she decided to set up a booth here. But you know, they're so expensive to rent, so I said I'd come help her out for free. Just a little discount on some merchandise. So, I bought this duster. Sweet, isn't it?"

Aria stared, her mouth open slightly. It took a lot to stun her, so I should have been impressed by Roxy's prowess.

"And who do we have here?" Roxy turned her full blaze on Jefferson, who had been silent and still as a mannequin.

Aria looked over her shoulder. "This is my cousin, Jefferson."

Roxy's pink-frosted lips widened, and she flicked her fingertips in a wave. "Nice to meet you, Jefferson." Before I could jump out of reach, she threw her arms around me and brought me into the smothering cloud of her perfume. "I've got to scoot. But now that I know you're here, we'll need to catch up."

As if seeing her in Grant County wasn't more than a person needed to endure. I swam away from the cloud of scent, huffing out my nose to clear it. "Sure."

She paraded off, leaving us a bit shell-shocked. But we didn't have time to recover before people in the aisle ahead of us started peeling off into side lanes, and I perked up to see what was approaching.

Ahead, the sounds of commotion settled into chanting. "Shame, shame, shame."

Placards raised above the heads and congestion of the people not quick enough to get out of the way. I caught a few with things like, "You wouldn't eat a dog, why eat a pig? Go vegan!" and "Stop Canadian goose cruelty. Don't wear down." A woman held a black five-gallon bucket and looked like she was covered in tar with a poster pinned to her declaring "Leather Is a Dirty Business." A cluster of protesters shoved our way. My hackles rose, or would have if I actually had hackles.

Aria, in her knee-high calfskin boots and fashionable black leather jacket, frowned. "What's going on?"

The protest leader was a man with a wiry gray ponytail dangling down his back, wearing what appeared to be a hand-knit sweater. It looked like wool, but unless they had a pet sheep at home, my guess was that it was made of homespun hemp over some kind of leggings that looked like mummy's wrappings, and moccasins that were probably made from birch bark. He carried a can of spray paint.

I grabbed Aria's arm and jerked her to where Jefferson stood by the doors. The young woman in the information booth, who looked about seventeen with long blond braids and pink cheeks, dropped below the counter. Across the way, the older man in the SharpCo booth started shoving cash into a bank pouch, as if afraid the protesters wanted to rob him.

Aria resisted, but I shoved her against Jefferson and stood in front of them.

Aria protested, "What?"

I held my breath, hoping we blended into the wall behind us. "PETA." I gritted my teeth against the acronym. "Or something like it." Self-proclaimed animal lovers. I didn't doubt they had animals' best interests at heart, but I wondered if they understood the compassion and devotion I felt, along with other ranchers I knew, for every one of the critters we tended in good weather and bad. Or how I'd come to appreciate Fiona, the first Highland I'd brought to the Sandhills after Aria hired me to establish and manage her herd.

I'd been skeptical about raising a breed not for commercial beef production or even dairy. More like breeding dogs or show horses. But you can't argue with the cuteness factor of the long-haired, wide-horned, stalky characters who look like they'd break into a tall tale laced with a Scottish brogue. And after research, I discovered Highland cattle could be sold for beef.

And then I'd brought Fiona home. She'd looked around the pasture with her placid eyes, then turned to me and nodded, as if it met with her approval. That's exactly how I felt about the new venture with Aria, and I forged a bond with Fiona that day.

Nor could the PETA folks know my affection for silly Poupon, my standard poodle. He couldn't replace Sarah as my best friend, but he shared my home and my life, and was a close confidante, even if his advice wasn't all that wise. And I had no prayer of keeping him off the couch. He was spending a few days with his unlikely buddy, May Keller, while I was in Denver.

Either from ignorance or arrogance—my guess was both-—a tall man in a fringed jacket and coonskin cap sauntered down the middle of the corridor with his arm draped around the shoulder of a rugged-looking woman...on a collision course with the protesters.

When the tall guy and the hippie holdover met face-to-face, the gray ponytail guy raised his can and pressed, sending a spray of crimson paint on the stripes of the racoon (to be honest, it was probably faux, or what was now referred to as vegan animal skin), down the fringed jacket, and across to the woman next to him and her leather pants.

"Son of a—" Daniel Boone launched into the guy wielding the paint, outweighing him by thirty pounds. The leather-pants woman with tats up her neck shrieked and jumped into the fray.

Several placard-waving people backed up, to be replaced with a few middle-aged men and women with cell phones raised for videos.

"Animals are people, too," was one phrase I caught as the shouting escalated and crowds clogged the lanes where the confrontation took place.

If Daniel Boone had any sense, he'd get himself out of there before anyone could ID him enough to press assault charges. Even if they'd be fined for attacking first, these activists loved nothing more than the attention litigation brought to their cause.

In the booth on the other side of the skirmish, someone let out a yelp. A guttural shout made Aria and me both lean to the right, taking in the SharpCo booth.

Someone in a black hoodie dove on top of the knife vendor's counter. The older man clutched at the bank bag and tilted backward, his mouth twisted in outrage. They wrestled with the bag that was about the size of a deflated football, each yanking backward.

Finally, the hoodie guy raised his arm and smashed his fist down, slamming the man's wrist to the counter. The vendor yelped and stumbled backward, falling and shrieking in pain. The hoodie guy grabbed his prize and lurched back.

"No. Stop!" the knife guy screamed, and a few people glanced at him, then back to the PETA-versus-Daniel Boone showdown.

The hoodie guy spun around, a blue bank packet in hand. He planted his feet, tucked it close like a Husker halfback, and took off through the melee of protesters and Daniel Boone supporters. The leather-pants woman beat on them all with a purse that resembled a saddlebag.

The man in the booth yelled, "Stop! He's got my cash!"

That's when my instinct kicked in. Which one? The law enforcement one? The helping-people one? The one who hated cheats? It's likely I always had a strong sense of right and wrong, but when Ted lied to me and had an affair, it reinforced the justice-seeking streak in me. Honestly, I was well suited to being a sheriff. It's a crying shame my sister Louise had believed otherwise and filed a recall.

With no more thought, I lit out after the thief.

Aria shouted behind me, "Wait!"

I didn't have a wait gear while I charged in pursuit.

The thief got tangled in the fight that now stretched across the corridor, slipping to his knees before jumping up and taking off. That gave me a chance to close the gap between us. While he was younger and had better traction with his tennis shoes as opposed to my slick-soled boots, he crashed into pedestrians crowding the walkway. I was able to scoot around most of the surprised people he'd knocked out of the way before they recovered.

Behind me, Aria shouted, "Stop that man. He's got my purse."

Of course, he didn't have her purse, but I had to hand it to her for keeping the image simple. Jumping into the chase and helping me made me appreciate her even more. Damn it.

I narrowed the gap between me and the wiry guy and could tackle him in another few steps. I blasted my engines, anticipating taking flight to bring him down. My mind formed the image of myself as a cheetah on the African veldt springing onto the antelope's back.

He took a sudden swerve down an adjoining aisle littered with a group of preschoolers on a field trip. Several wore little pink cowboy hats, some had straw hats, a few Rams horns. Way too many tots for the few adults herding them.

Hoodie guy knocked one over, and he bounced into another two, and the whole bunch started to topple like bowling pins.

I could only hope the chaperones would handle their charges as their cries and shrieks mingled with the rest of the noise.

He sprinted toward a set of metal doors and slammed into them, grabbed a handle, and shot outside.

I didn't slow my stride and banged into the door as it started to close. I exploded into blinding sunshine and a shock like diving into an icy lake. It took a second to figure out I was on a metal platform with stairs down to wide concrete lanes on the opposite side of the building from the Coliseum. The thief was already halfway down the stairs, and I followed, bottoming onto the ground and nearly colliding with a young woman leading a two-ton black Percheron into the lower-level stock pens. Thank goodness if I had to run into the path of a horse, it was this gentle giant and not something high-strung and prone to fits, like an Arabian.

We wound through a series of stock trailers and pickups, and he skirted behind a shuttle bus. By the time I cleared the bus, he'd disappeared.

Aria pulled up behind me. She looked right and left. "I think we lost him."

I squinted against the sunshine that seemed to burn brighter at a mile high with the mountains to the west, as if everything here wanted to be bigger and better. It had snowed the day before, but today's sunshine had melted most of it, leaving puddles and muddy spots along with the slick ice accumulating in the potholes of the blacktop. In front of the Expo building, loud music thrummed and bouncy house fans whooshed. On the back side, where we stood, livestock was led from one venue to another, vehicles idled or crawled slowly, and the stock business of the show was underway.

Aria and I panted. I had worked up enough adrenaline and energy to fight off the cold, but it wouldn't take long for the icy air to slide its way under my jacket.

Aria nudged me and flashed a mischievous grin, showing her perfect white teeth in a face too lovely for any other woman to like her. But despite everything she was and everything she owned that I would never be or own, I *did* like her. Who wouldn't want friends who'd join your posse without hesitating? In a tone like a parent who clearly sees where her toddler is hiding but wants the kid to think he's still hidden, she said, "We gave it a good effort, though—"

I snapped my head to the right. A hint of black rose above a pickup bed only a few feet away. Without a word, I sprinted toward it.

The guy in the hoodie must have heard me because he straightened before I reached him and whirled around, hell-bent on escaping.

Momentum was on my side. His foot slipped a bit, but my boots pounded on a patch of dry pavement.

With a mighty burst from my thighs, I catapulted myself toward him. My fingers clutched his hood, which fell back from his head. His jacket clothes-lined him, and he fell toward me. My foot slid, making me nearly perform the splits. Instead, we struggled for a second, then landed in a heap.

In a mud puddle.

I rolled over, getting good and coated in the icy muck, and scrambled for the loose cash bag. Grunting, he clamped down on it, pulling the bag into his middle. I fought and kicked. And he gave as good as he got, at one point slamming my chin down on the pavement. We wrestled like a Husker fighting a Buff for possession of a fumble.

I finally closed my hand around the bag just as Aria ran up. "I got him!"

But she didn't have him. The thief's rubber soles had way more traction than my boots, so he shot to his feet and clambered away while Aria stopped to make sure I hadn't broken a leg.

I rolled over to sit up and thrust the bag into the air. "Touchdown!"

Aria forced a weak smile that didn't cover her look of dismay. "I hope that won't leave a scar."

2

Something heavy plopped on the sleeve of my jacket, and I glanced down, shocked to see a blob of deep crimson spread and sink into the soft suede. I started to reach up to the sting I suddenly felt on my chin, but Aria squatted in front of me, gently swatting my hand away.

She'd whisked off the silk scarf from her neck and pressed it to my chin. "Apply pressure there and get it to stop bleeding. Then I can see if it needs stitches."

Among all her other stellar attributes that included running her family's considerable estate, philanthropy, and investments, riding a horse better than I could, and almost earning a law degree, Aria had first-responder training from that time she'd had visions of being an EMT. Aria had a wide range of interests, and some of them seemed farfetched. But I admired her energy for exploring options. Turbo, indeed.

I started to pull the scarf away. "But this is Hermès," pronouncing it correctly—take that, Roxy.

Aria brushed it off. "Too late now. I'm also worried about that jacket. I'm afraid it's ruined." She placed a hand under my elbow and, with surprising strength, helped me to stand.

I started to bend over to retrieve the money bag so she wouldn't see my gut-punched reaction to ruining a three-hundred-dollar jacket before I'd even worn it one whole day. She popped down to grab the bag.

That's when the damage to my new image became clear. I'd slid into a puddle, and not only was my jacket speckled with blood, brackish snowmelt and gravel was ground into my black jeans and splashed onto the tailored T-shirt I'd bought at a real department store and not Old Navy. The cold started to penetrate as I became aware that my head must have somehow dunked in a puddle. Cold, more ice than water, dribbled down my neck. I assumed between the blood and mud, the curls I'd tamed with the various products Diane, my bougie sister, had foisted on me would be as bedraggled as the rest of me.

Aria's cold fingers clasped mine, and she gently pulled down the scarf a couple of inches before pressing it back to my chin. "I don't think it'll need stitches. A butterfly bandage ought to do the trick. Come on."

I followed her back up the metal steps to the door we'd crashed through. We joined the flow strolling through the trade show. There must have been at least a dozen avenues lined with booths crisscrossing the hall big enough to hold half a dozen marching bands in full formation. With so much to see, hawkers and concessioners, stock trailers, equipment, tack, and every kind of toy or tchotchke imaginable, it encouraged a fine array of characters for prime people-watching. From gray-haired ladies in pink felt cowboy hats, monied people in Western chic that made Roxy look conservative, cowboy wannabes, a herd of teens in animal cosplay, and the general oddities any festival brings out, I hardly garnered a glance as I plodded toward the knife guy's booth. It wasn't lost on me that I was dotted with mud and wiping blood from my chin with a scarf that could buy a new water heater for my old cottage.

It seemed farther back to his booth than it had during the chase, and the damp soaked into me with each step. The animal rights protesters had moved on to harass someone else, or maybe, like a flash mob, had faded into the crowd.

Jefferson stood on the inside of the knife booth, his back to the corridor. Another man crowded next to him, both of them intent on the vendor, who sat in a folding chair looking pale and shaken. Aria and I leaned on the counter where kitchen knives of every size were displayed in gift boxes and wooden blocks among an array of cutting boards.

"Are you okay?" Aria asked.

Jefferson shifted to the side, and the knife vendor lifted his eyes slowly, as if it took great effort. His face looked like it had been dusted with flour, and even his lips looked bloodless. "Oh. You're here." It seemed like he tried to be upbeat, as if his salesman personality couldn't let him be defeated. "I'm surprised he got away. You were really after him. How did you get through the crowd so fast?"

Aria held up the bag. "Thanks to Wonder Woman here, you get your cash back."

A look of amazement lit his eyes. "No way!"

The other man took in my disheveled appearance and the blood-soaked scarf clamped to my chin. "Oh my gosh. You're bleeding." He yanked a crate from the back wall of the booth. "Here, sit down."

When I gave him a closer look, I realized it was that guy with the brown hair in the tattersall shirt and puffy coat. He held my gaze for a second, long enough for me to feel a surge of warmth.

Jefferson focused on the guy as if trying to figure out if he knew him. He indicated the two men. "Is this your booth?"

The older guy, who looked considerably more chipper after recovering his cash, laughed. "Oh, no. I'd never met Keith before. But I'm glad to know him now. He really helped me out while these ladies chased down the thief. I'm Ray, by the way."

Keith colored and looked away. "I didn't do anything."

Ray acted affronted. "Are you kidding? I was shaken to the core. You set me down and got me water. Watched the booth while I recovered. You're a real hero."

Jefferson's eyes shone with suppressed laughter. He and Aria exchanged amused glances.

Ray must have read their expressions. "Oh, and you two girls, too. Of course. You're angels."

While Aria gently pulled the scarf away, Jefferson introduced us all.

Aria crouched in front of me. "It's still bleeding."

Ray lifted his hand. "I don't think my wrist is broken. Just sprained." His gaze sought mine. "Thank the good Lord for bringing you here. I couldn't afford to lose that cash. But I'm not sure how I'm going to manage the booth with only one hand."

Keith spoke quietly. "I've got some free time. Would you like me to help out for a bit?"

Ray's shoulders relaxed. "God bless you, man."

Aria stood and folded her arms and frowned at me. "I think you need to go to the first aid tent."

The last thing I wanted was to have someone poke at me. "We're supposed to meet Craig McNeal in a few minutes." Seeing Brodgar took priority over a bashed chin.

"McNeal isn't going anywhere," Aria said. "We'll have time to see him."

Jefferson pulled his phone from his blazer pocket and checked it.

Aria caught the move. "When do you need to be at the arena for the presentation?"

He shrugged. "I've got time. It's not a big deal."

Aria reached for my hand. "Let's find first aid."

I pressed the scarf to my chin. I wanted to get down to see the bull sooner rather than later. "Don't you have a first aid kit here, Ray?"

He went one hundred percent salesman with a grin like a shark. "SharpCo knives are the best you can get, with an edge so sharp it'll cut a pop can and still glide through the softest tomato, so Band-Aids are a necessity."

Aria's stern look told me she didn't like my solution. She put her hands on her hips. "Fine. What have you got, Ray?"

The hide vendor in the booth next to Ray's wore a leather outback hat with the stampede string dangling below his chin. With a grizzly's build, he stood with his arms folded, scowling at us from where his and Ray's tents met.

I offered a smile, since Dad taught us all to be welcoming.

His expression didn't change. He stood still and watched us with beady eyes.

Ray rummaged around and brought out a metal box with a big red cross on it.

Jefferson gave Keith puzzled scrutiny. "What is it you do, Keith?"

Aria looked up from pawing through the first aid kit, shooting Jefferson a gaze that said he was being rude. She yanked out an Ace bandage. "Here, wrap Ray's wrist."

Jefferson accepted the bandage, and Ray held out his arm.

Keith stepped around everyone and positioned himself at the front counter. "I'm between jobs right now. I worked in a corporate finance office."

Jefferson seemed affable. "Businesses need good money folks. They're worth their weight in gold."

Aria pulled out antiseptic wipes and crouched back in front of me. She spoke to Jefferson while she ripped open the package. "Are you a solo for the fundraiser?"

Since Aria had been chirping about a charity ball on Saturday night, I knew it involved well-heeled society, ball gowns and tuxes, and a country band everyone was talking about to perform after dinner. Hosted by Hansford Meats, Jefferson was supposed to be in charge and give a keynote address. But Aria said he hated the planning, so she was helping him out.

Jefferson kept his back to her. "Nanette is visiting her sister in California. She hates the cold weather, so she left after Christmas and says she'll be back when it warms up."

From my vantage, I had a good view of Aria's snarl of distaste. That was surprising enough, but I also got a glimpse of Keith. He stared at Jefferson's back with a mixture of shock and disgust.

Probably reacting to Jefferson and not because she hated me, Aria scrubbed at my chin with all the delicacy of an indentured servant swabbing a ship's deck…if she did it with sandpaper and acid.

I winced, and she uttered, "Sorry." Then louder, "It's not a long flight. Looks like she could make it back for an appearance at Hansford's big event. It's a fundraiser for pediatric heart disease research, not a snow-shoveling contest."

An obvious undercurrent ran between them. Although Jefferson sounded casual, a tight string of tension hid underneath his tone. "I'm glad she's not here. Someone broke into the house a few nights ago. I don't want her to be in any danger."

Aria gasped and spun around on the balls of her feet. "What? Broke in? Were you home? Did you call the cops? And you're only telling me now?"

He looked over his shoulder. "I called the company security guy. They're taking care of it."

Aria handed me another antiseptic wipe to hold on my chin and dipped back into the kit, muttering curse words I assumed were about Jefferson's news. "Did you tell Aunt Eula?"

He kept wrapping Ray's wrist, and the rest of us didn't speak. "Don't say anything to her. You know how she gets."

Aria lost her annoyed look. In a mocking low voice, she said, "Son, let me build you a tower to keep you safe from the big, bad world."

Jefferson laughed. "You have your impersonation down pat."

Aria found a butterfly bandage small enough for my chin. She started to pull the wrapper off. "If you're going alone, that'll leave a gap at the head table. The optics will be bad."

Optics for a charity event? This world of theirs was like a foreign country to me. The kinds of fundraisers I'd been involved with usually tried to raise money for someone's funeral, surgery, or maybe plumbing repairs for a church. We'd plan a calf roping or three-on-three basketball tournament and hope to raise a couple thousand. Anything grand enough to be labeled a gala was out of my league.

Aria pressed the bandage to my chin, which stung from her ministrations and ached from the wound. A buzz sounded from her back pocket, and when she pulled out her phone, her face burst into sunshine. She popped up. "I'll meet you at the pens." She eased around the side of the booth, and before she was swallowed up by a family group eating turkey legs, she sang, "Glenn!"

The pain on my chin faded in comparison to the slam of a meteor into my gut.

Jefferson finished with Ray's wrist. He spun around to me, and I did my best to meet his affable smile. "I suppose I ought to make my way to the Charolais show. Got glad-handing to do and money to disperse. Can I walk you down?"

"That's the best offer I've had all day." I stuffed Aria's scarf into the pocket of my ruined jacket, accepted Ray's thanks again, and told Keith I was glad to meet him.

Keith's eyes flitted from me to Jefferson, and I had the weird feeling he didn't want me to walk away with Jefferson. Did he want to ask for my number? Did I want him to?

Before I could act on any of those questions, I found myself walking down the corridor with Jefferson. I shivered from my damp clothes and considered I must look frightful, even if Aria had done her best to clean my wound. To call me self-conscious would be like calling a ribeye a slider.

Feeling like I ought to get a conversation going, I said, "Aria's been hard at work on the fundraiser. I've had a heck of a time getting her to focus on the Highland operation."

Jefferson turned heads the way Aria did, like how lilies follow the sun. He paused for a man pushing a woman in a wheelchair, and I did, too. "I'm sorry to drag Aria away from your project, but there's no way I could have planned it. With all the typical glitter and nonsense. I'm billed as the host, but she's good at this."

"Having someone else to do the work and you get the glory sounds smart." I'd meant it as a joke, but once said, it sounded critical and I wanted to take it back.

Jefferson's heavy eyebrows dipped, but then he chuckled. "I guess so. Aria's saved me too many times to count."

I started to ask for an example, but he continued. His remarkable blue eyes flicked to me while we walked. "Aria is right."

That tickled me. "Aria is usually right. What's she right about this time?"

He quirked an eyebrow. "She's been working so hard on this gala. I'd hate to let her down by leaving the table looking like a picket fence."

I had the sudden panic he might ask me to attend. So it was almost a relief when I heard discordant sounds and movements disrupt the constant river of people.

The noise solidified to that familiar chant. "Shame, shame, shame."

My heart sank. Not again. Since my jacket was already toast, and my nerves were jittery, maybe I'd go after the boneheads this time.

The protesters made their way toward us, but unlike before, they numbered only about a half dozen, they weren't carrying placards, and they didn't seem to have any weapons. They wore T-shirts that appeared to be blood-smeared with pictures of dead animals. Basically, minus the animal graphics, they didn't look a whole lot different than I did.

Deciding I wasn't interested in another skirmish with anyone, I edged Jefferson to the side to let them pass.

The older guy with the ponytail and hand-knitted sweater scowled and chanted. He glanced our way, and his gaze traveled up to Jefferson's face. He seemed surprised and narrowed his eyes to study Jefferson, then spun around to the woman behind him, a thin scarecrow with wiry white hair and a shapeless dress, leggings, thick cotton socks, and sandals. Whatever he said made her focus on Aria's cousin.

I tilted my head to Jefferson, but he seemed interested in a booth showing off solar panels.

The white-haired woman looked doubtful, and the two protesters exchanged some words before the others in their group urged them to keep up with the shaming and marching.

We crossed the busy main corridor, and I swerved left to miss being barreled into by a tyke galloping on his red-spotted hobbyhorse. His father chased him, giving me a fly-by apology. "Sorry—runaway."

I paused to watch the kid outdistancing his father and caught sight of the aging activist couple. Another chill started from my bones and climbed up my spine and across my scalp. My teeth chattered a time or two before I got control.

The hippie dude and the white-haired woman were next to a water fountain along a wall. They huddled together in deep conversation, then popped their heads up and looked in our direction but didn't seem to notice me.

I followed their line of sight to Jefferson smiling at an attractive woman.

I looked back to the couple.

The line that ran through my head was, "If looks could kill."

3

Aria caught up to us before we'd gone far from the booth. "We've got some time before we meet the Highland breeder, I'd like to see you give the presentation to the Charolais—" She was interrupted by an anguished wail.

We all spun toward Roxy shoving through a group of tipsy cowboys. Even if it wasn't quite noon, I guessed it was never too early for a Coors. "What happened to you?" She stopped in front of me and stomped her foot and, despite the general crowd noise, I swear I heard the heel of her red ankle boot hit the ground.

"I...it..." She shouldn't be able to corner me like this. I felt Jefferson's and Aria's eyes on me.

Roxy tossed her ringlets. "You were so danged cute earlier. Now you look like you've been working cattle. Nobody's going to give you a second glance in this state. For heaven's sake, Kate. You're self-sabotaging."

"I didn't..." With Roxy, there was always the overwhelming urge to clock her right in the kisser and also the voice of Dad telling me there was no cause to be rude. It could leave me tongue-tied.

"And that tangled hair? Really? Why you don't do a blowout is beyond me. Men don't want someone who looks like a ranch hand. Didn't you learn anything from losing your husband to someone like me?"

Someone *like* her? I was about to unload on her when an arm landed on my shoulder and hugged me into a warm, muscular body. Nearly jumping from my skin, I peered my head around to see Jefferson, Caribbean Sea eyes alight with humor. "Are we still on for later?"

Roxy's jaw dropped. Grandma Ardith would have said she was catching flies.

Aria's eyes twinkled as she fought laughter.

Well, okay, I'd play along. And be grateful for it. I leaned my head into that well-toned chest. "Sure. See you later."

He caught Aria's eye with a hint of mischief and whirled away, heading down the wide corridor that would eventually take him to the double doors to the outside.

I caught a glimpse of the SharpCo booth a few yards away, and Keith's face crinkled in concern as he glanced from me to Jefferson. I had a tiny stab of regret I'd leaned into Jefferson like a flirt because maybe that look on Keith's face meant he might have had the slightest hint of interest in me. I admitted to maybe the tiniest bit of maybe, kind of, possible attraction to him.

Bah. I was making up the whole thing. Besides, the opportunity to exchange information had gone.

"Okay," Aria said. "We've got to go."

Aria grabbed my arm and tugged me into the traffic. I narrowly missed a thin platinum blonde with a dark tan and skillful, if abundant, makeup, who looked more suited to an afternoon shopping in Beverly Hills than tromping around a stock show. But it takes all kinds. She held one of those wobbly drink carriers with two cups of coffee that looked as unstable as a three-legged cow and rushed ahead of us.

Before we'd wended our way more than two booths down, Roxy attacked me from behind, winding her arm through mine. She giggled as if we were teens at a slumber party. "Oh my God, Kate. Jefferson Hansford. Don't let this one get away."

Aria looked over her shoulder at us with a wry twist to her lips. "He never said his last name."

Roxy looked self-satisfied. "Hansford Meats is a big deal. Of course I know who Jefferson Hansford is."

I tried to pull my arm from her. "Then you know he's married." It seemed possible that before Roxy had decided my husband was her destiny, she'd done some research on eligible bachelors. I didn't care enough to ask.

Aria gave a disgusted snort. "Tiger's getting divorced."

I hadn't seen that one coming. "He said his wife was visiting her sister. He didn't sound like a guy getting divorced."

Roxy jumped in. "Now's the time to strike. Before some gold digger gets there first."

Aria's nose twitched as if the whole situation stank. "He doesn't know I know, but he can't hide anything from me."

Roxy gave her an annoyingly playful punch in the arm. "Anyone can keep things from anyone if they want to badly enough."

Aria looked annoyed with Roxy, but, as usual, Roxy didn't seem to notice. "Jefferson doesn't want to tell Aunt Eula. She goes to an off-brand strict church with a Puritan streak. And when Aunt Eula is unhappy, she passes judgment with the purse strings. So, he's not telling anyone yet."

Well, if Roxy knew, then keeping it secret was already impossible. Roxy could lap any teen in a rapid text-off. Obviously, I knew about Hansford Meats, the biggest privately held meat-processing company in the world. But Jefferson Hansford? Aside from being Aria's cousin, which meant he was wealthy, I didn't know much.

Aria glanced ahead of us, and her eyebrows arched in annoyance. "But maybe the word is out."

The blonde with the coffees grew closer to where Jefferson stopped to study some Western art.

Roxy raised her eyebrows at Aria. "Oh, for sure. You need to get in there and stake a claim, Kate."

What did they see that I didn't? "Is something happening?"

Aria held up a finger. "Wait for it."

We were bulldozed by a group of teens who were concentrating on each other and not noticing anyone standing in their way, but we held our own.

"Shouldn't they be in school?" Roxy said, smoothing her duster over her hips. We scooted to the side of the aisle and returned our focus to Jefferson.

Aria muttered, "He's always like this. Never thinks anyone means him harm. When we were kids, I always had to defend him."

As the blonde came up behind Jefferson, someone behind her must have jostled her, though I didn't see anyone. She stumbled into Jefferson's back, and the coffees upended and splattered to the ground.

Jefferson spun around and reached for the woman's elbow, leaning into her and saying something. She seemed upset and slapped a hand to her forehead.

Roxy and Aria nodded at each other as if they'd won a bet. Sarcasm laced Aria's words. "Such an unfortunate accident."

"You don't think she planned that." I knew how tricky those carriers could be.

Aria laughed. "Oh, Kate. You're so naïve."

Roxy threw an arm around my shoulder and snugged me to her. "That's why I love her so much. She trusts everyone. So pure of heart."

First of all, I'd trusted my husband, who cheated on me with Roxy. So, untangle that scenario. And secondly, I was absolutely not naïve. I'd been sheriff for three years. Long enough to witness some of the seedier sides of life, such as a mother murdering her son, and a wife taking out her husband. Not that killing a husband was a bad idea.

Just kidding.

Obviously.

While people streamed around us, we watched as the blonde gave Jefferson a polite nod, and her expression looked worried before she turned and disappeared into the throngs.

"See," I said. "If she really had designs on him, she'd have stuck around and got him to buy her coffee."

Roxy and Aria caught each other's eye and burst out laughing. "Never change." Aria's grin disappeared, and she stiffened.

I whipped around to see the activist couple marching toward Jefferson. Before I could get my boots scooting their way, Aria was ahead of me.

"Shame!" The older woman pointed a bony finger in Jefferson's face.

Shocked, he took a step backward as if her finger was loaded.

"Watch out, Gwen," the old man shouted, but too late.

Aria flew toward the woman and, though she was smaller, planted her hands on the woman's shoulders and shoved her away from Jefferson.

The woman shouted, "Get him, Arlo!"

Gray-ponytail guy, apparently named Arlo, lifted his spray can, but I was on Aria's heels and barreled into him, getting a slash of red paint on my already ruined jacket. It still torqued me off. "What the hell?"

Aria kept pushing Gwen through the crowd and away from the booth. Keith appeared beside Jefferson and dragged him to the side of the corridor between two booths. He must have been watching us.

Arlo shouted at me, even though I stood two feet away. "That's Jefferson Hansford. That's Hansford Meats. You know, the plants that..." He tried to shove around me, raising the can again to target Jefferson. "...That exploit immigrants. That destroy the planet with their methane-farting cattle."

Oh. That Hansford. I pushed Arlo's arm down. "You can't go around spray-painting people." I sounded so danged reasonable when I would much rather shout at him. "I should charge you for this jacket."

Arlo drew his attention to me and the red slash across my lapel. "Leather. Have you no heart? A soul died so you could adorn yourself in their skin."

Aria had Gwen halfway down the corridor, people moving out of her way and staring. The activists didn't have a lot of support in this crowd.

I grabbed Arlo by his skinny upper arm and swung him to follow his accomplice. I'd gained some swagger and authority by being sheriff for three years, and I pulled it all up now. "You're lucky I don't arrest you for destruction of property and assault. If you and your friend leave the stock show now, I'll let you go. If I see you around again, I'll haul you in."

Arlo stumbled as he stared at me, maybe trying to decide if I really was law enforcement. I might not have been able to pull it off, but two Denver cops were striding toward us, maybe alerted by a concerned bystander.

Arlo and Gwen caught sight of them, and suddenly we didn't have to work so hard to get them heading toward the doors. We both let go and stood back while they trotted off and the cops picked up their pace following them.

Aria walked back to me, her eyes on the doors where they'd disappeared.

"Troublemakers," I muttered when she got to me.

She frowned, her perfectly shaped eyebrows lowering over her green eyes. "That's the problem, though. What if they aren't just annoying? What if they're wielding more deadly weapons than spray paint? Jefferson is vulnerable, and he never suspects anyone means him harm. I'm worried about him."

I poked Aria. "I didn't know you were related to the evil Hansford Meats."

Her mouth gave a wry twist. "Aunt Eula's grandfather was smart. Figured out how to bring the plant to where the cattle were raised. He made a lot of money."

I thought about what Arlo had said and what I knew about Hansford. "They catch a lot of heat for bad working conditions and hiring undocumented workers who won't complain about it."

Aria sighed. "A lot of those workers are grateful to be in the States and have a job. I don't know. My main concern is Jefferson. He's never been suited for a big corporation. He's too creative and sensitive. Aunt Eula dotes on Jefferson, but I think she loves Hansford Meats even more. She'd probably cut him off if he didn't work for the company."

Since I'd never had family wealth, I didn't see how getting cut off as a man in his late thirties would be a tragedy. Most people work for a living. "What does he do for the company?"

Aria maneuvered through the crowd. "He's the front guy mostly. Aunt Eula calls him the face of Hansford Meats. That's the other thing. He's really an introvert. Hates the spotlight. So, this is a hard role for him."

"There's nothing else he can do?" Seemed to me he could find another position in the huge corporation.

Aria's laugh sounded bitter. "Aunt Eula decided that's his job, and that's his job. Period."

By the time we got back to Jefferson, he seemed fine and said Keith had gone back to the SharpCo booth.

Aria frowned at Jefferson. "Maybe take a self-defense class or something."

He threw an arm around her neck and hugged her briefly. "They weren't going to hurt me. You worry too much."

She straightened her jacket. "Maybe, but we'll walk you to the arena anyway."

"Totally unnecessary, but I don't mind the company of two-thirds of Charlie's Angels."

Too bad we weren't setting out for the cattle pens on the first floor of the Expo Hall. I'd been anticipating meeting Brodgar the Highland bull for weeks. I couldn't wait to get downstairs.

But some of the shine had gone out of the stock show. Everyone looked a little suspicious. Even Keith. Was he interested in me and shy? Or had I imagined it?

I excused myself to slip into a bathroom to see about repairs. The mud hadn't dried enough for me to brush off my jeans. My hair looked like bats had thrown a party in it. I pulled a hair tie off my wrist—when you have untamed hair like mine, you keep one on you at all times—and pulled it back. My chin was still red and appeared as raw as it felt. Roxy was right, I looked like I'd been working cattle.

I rejoined Aria and Jefferson, ready to get to the business of cattle.

Thieves, gold diggers, domestic terrorists—okay, Arlo and Gwen didn't feel that threatening, but who knows what could tip them from spray paint and chants to guns and bombs? I mean, Mom seemed harmless enough... until she wasn't.

It all felt wrong.

4

The crowds thinned as we exited the Expo Hall onto a platform. Across an expanse of concrete stuffed with vendors for the food court, the interstate loomed above us, casting a shadow river to chill the area between the Coliseum and Expo Hall. Compared to the opposite side, where we'd chased the thief and where the activity revolved around livestock, this side was pure carnival. Still cold, but now a hint of a breeze made my damp clothes feel like tiny knives.

The cow barn and arena were on the ground floor of the Expo Hall, and though we could have made the trip inside, we'd need to cross the entire length of the hall to reach the stairs. Frigid but quicker, we clunked down the metal stairs to the smells of carnival food and the strains of countryfied pop music. By the time we slipped into the open barn doors in the lower-level downstairs, I was shivering like a Yorkshire terrier surrounded by Rottweilers. My hands felt like ice blocks and my feet had gone numb, but when the blood started to flow again, they'd hold a grudge for making them sprint across cold concrete in thin soles.

I stopped Aria. "You go ahead to the Highland area. I'm going to see if I can borrow a jacket or something from my brother. I'm about frozen."

She looked surprised. "Oh. Let's go back to the trade show and get you something from one of the clothing vendors."

On my best days, shopping was harder work for me than putting up a field of hay. Now I wanted to go see that bull, not decide on an outfit. "I'll grab something from my brother. He's grooming cattle for a rancher down here."

Something made her alert like a hound catching the scent of a rabbit. Normally so polite and interested, her attention switched away so quickly it made me curious. She mumbled, "If you're sure. I'll catch up to you at McNeal's pens." She was gone before I could ask what was up.

This day was getting even weirder. Thieves, animal rights protesters, Jefferson Hansford saving me from Roxy's taunts. Aria disappearing like she was on a mission. All I wanted to do was meet the bull of my dreams, look at some cute Highland cattle, and talk to Aria about whether we should use solar water tanks or put up another windmill.

I pulled out my phone and texted Jeremy, my youngest brother. He'd had some issues with me last year. Louise, my older sister, somehow convinced him I was responsible for our mother's disappearance from our lives. It's as if he didn't want to understand she'd taken off to Canada with some guy she called the love of her life—not Dad, by the way—to escape a prison sentence.

He'd always been close to Mom and missed her terribly. I understood it helped him to blame someone for all the pain.

After the recall, he seemed to come around. Not that we'd ever talked about it. We're Foxes, after all, and why bring issues into the open, when we can bury them in the hopes they'll decompose and turn into fertile soil of love and support? As it only happens in Hallmark movies.

I'm as black a pot as any of my siblings' kettles. I'm not one to dig into secrets and problems if I don't need to. Denial and compartmentalization were good enough for my ancestors, so why change the dysfunction now?

Jeremy didn't answer, of course. He'd be busy washing, blow-drying, and fluffing the red-and-white Herefords Bill Hardy was so proud of but that had fallen out of favor with almost everyone since their heyday in the sixties.

Lit with arrows of fluorescent lights, the massive space of row after row of steel-paneled pens stretched as far as I could see. Cattle of every breed from Angus to Zebu. A constant roar from shop vacs that were used as cow blow-dryers, along with a variety of speakers playing music favored by each crew of groomers, loud voices, an occasional moo, and the garbled announcements from the arena that no one could understand, all gave me that thrill of excitement from the years I'd worked the stock show as a teen. The smells of wood chips and hay, manure, wet hide, and greasy food were as comforting as the aroma of fresh-baked cookies.

I'm not saying I've got great intuition, more likely all the strangeness of the last few hours made my Spidey senses tingle even when nothing warranted it, but something prompted me to step behind the rear end of a big Simmental bull and look behind me.

Keith walked down the center of the lane as if trying to stay as far from any animal as possible. He seemed to stutter mid-step when I disappeared, then swung around to retreat in the opposite direction. He'd told Jefferson he was returning to the knife booth. I didn't know what to make of him following me down here. Maybe he wanted to hang out with Aria or Jefferson. Or he could be a scammer, as Roxy and Aria accused the blonde with the spilled coffee.

Skirting around two preteen girls leading shiny, coiffed Angus heifers by pristine halters, I beelined to where Bill Hardy usually penned up his cattle. That led me past a young family working on their prized Belted Galloway steer. The dad and teenaged son knelt by the back legs, each hunched close in the glare of a shop light, trimming the hide with electric razors. While two younger children swept up tufts of hair, a mother sat in a folding chair with a sleeping baby draped across her chest. Her face and shoulders drooped in fatigue, but she smiled at her busy family. I'd dreamed so much about my own family working together when I was younger, I could see chubby cheeks pinked with the chilly air and little fingers stroking horses' noses and bucket-feeding hungry calves.

Thirty-six wasn't too old to give up on having a baby, of course. I could always opt for being a single mother. But I wanted a partner. And damn it, I wanted one specific man.

Problem was, I absolutely needed to get over that. People had accused me of stubbornness all my life, and it hadn't bothered me. But now, I'd about had it with the way my heart wouldn't budge.

I drew in a lungful of wet cow hide, manure, and wood chips. It had been a decade since I'd been here. After I married Ted and started managing Frog Creek, I didn't need the cash infusion of the temporary job and I couldn't leave our own herd in the middle of the winter. But being down here brought back good memories.

I turned a corner and nearly ran into Bill Hardy. With a personality nearly as large as his big belly, he reared back and let out a guffaw. "Katie Fox! What are you doing in our section? I thought you were after those overgrown bedroom slippers."

Not everyone appreciated what they called "exotic breeds." Highlands were as hardy as they come and didn't need much babysitting, calved easily, and converted forage better than most. I'd done my research, and with only Fiona and fifteen other ladies so far, I was sold on them. Plus, they were undeniably adorable. "I'm looking for Jeremy. Is he around?"

Bill seemed to notice my appearance. "What happened to you? Get in a fight with PETA? I sure hope you won. Those sons-a-guns."

"They're out in force upstairs. But I got most of this from chasing a thief."

Bill wagged his head. "Whoo boy. It's as bad as I've ever seen it around here. Fritz Scoville got mugged behind the barn two days ago. What's the world coming to?"

The world had probably always been dangerous. Even folks in the Sandhills couldn't always be trusted. Another lesson I'd learned as sheriff.

Under the best circumstances I wouldn't want to chew the fat with Bill, and with hypothermia a possibility, I pushed the level of Sandhills nice and said, "Have a good one," and scuttled off before he could drag me into one of the endless stories he considered hilarious.

Jeremy was in a pen a row over from where Bill had stopped me. Probably why I'd run into Bill on his way to see his prized heifer enter the show ring. My brother and a young woman from Postville were combing and hair-spraying a red-and-white Hereford. I recognized her from watching my niece Ruthie's basketball game.

The girl would have graduated from high school a year or two ago. Jeremy was in his mid-twenties. But the flirting aroma was nearly as cloying as Roxy's perfume. While he concentrated on grooming, she purposely bumped his hand.

He grinned at her. "Watch it."

Jeremy glanced my way, and he raised his eyebrows in surprise. "Kate. You look like you got caught in a stampede."

The girl stared at me. She might remember me as sheriff, might know I was a Fox from Hodgekiss, or maybe didn't know any of that. The Nebraska Sandhills, covering more than a third of the state, had a population of less than one person per square mile. Most of us knew a good portion of folks within those boundaries, but not everyone. And it often took the younger generation a few years of adulthood before they widened their horizons and noticed other generations outside their families.

I wasn't in the mood to make small talk. "Do you happen to have any extra clothes here I could borrow?"

He crinkled his forehead, considering, and a memory of him at about five years old and me at fourteen came to me. I'd been playing in the backyard with him because he'd been so cute when he asked me to be the monster and chase him. I slipped and ended up splitting the crotch of my favorite jeans. He had the same look then as he did now as he took in my condition and tried to figure out how to fix it. Then, he'd run to his bedroom and came back with his favorite teddy bear. He'd handed it to me and said, "My new jeans ain't big enough for you, but if you hug Beary hard, it'll make you feel better."

He couldn't know how happy I was to have him back in my life and on my side. Even if he couldn't give me a new three-hundred-dollar jacket and Beary was long gone.

He tipped his head toward a duffel nestled in the wood chips in the corner of the pen. "There's a clean hoodie in there."

"I love you the most." I stripped off the blazer and rummaged in the duffel for the navy hoodie. It hung to my thighs, and I rolled up the sleeves while I watched him comb and spray. "This feels like heaven."

He spared me an up-and-down. "Gotta tell you, it doesn't look very professional."

That was probably okay since I didn't feel all that professional anymore. I smoothed my ponytail.

He spoke over his shoulder. "Have you seen Louise yet?"

My stomach dropped. Louise was our older sister, the one who'd instigated the recall vote against me. We'd supposedly made our peace, but Louise was like a new pair of boots: stiff and prone to cause blisters. "She's here?"

"Brought Mose and Zeke down here earlier. I'm telling you, those two are worse than ferrets on crack."

I laughed at that. Mose and Zeke were my ten-year-old nephews and two of the most entertaining people in my life. If I had to corral them, I might find them more frustrating than funny, but they were Louise's problem, and the more mischief they created for her, the more I liked them.

I wasn't thrilled about seeing Louise, but as Grandma Ardith often said, you couldn't swing a dead rat and miss a Fox.

After letting him get back to work and flirt, I passed a giant concrete room with hoses and warm water. A stock show shower room where three young people in rubber boots sprayed cattle and scrubbed them down. Those kids would be as damp as I'd been, and I only hoped they had someone like Jeremy to lend them something warm and cuddly.

I hurried on my way to meet Aria at Craig McNeal's pens. The bull I wanted was special, and I'd heard McNeal was a tough negotiator. Even though Aria didn't seem to worry about the cost of anything, I took pride in being a frugal manager. Thinking about cutting a deal for the best breeding stock, I turned into the Highland area and nearly ran into a kid leading a black Angus steer.

I apologized and backed up. To make sure I wasn't stepping in the way of someone with livestock, I looked behind me. All the cuddly warmth from Jeremy's hoodie vanished and a chill hit me when I noticed Keith's back as he rushed into another alley.

5

The hairy red cattle wore halters clipped to a rail, noses facing a solid wall. All three cows were clean, brushed, a bushy fluff of bangs between horns that jutted about a foot from their foreheads, looking ready for the arena.

A burly man maybe about Dad's age, with a white mustache and ruddy complexion, poked at the rear of the bull that was clipped next to the groomed cows. "Git yer arse off the coos."

His Scottish accent was like sunshine in the dreary cattle barn. A small banner hung on a pole declaring this McNeal Highland Cattle, but I didn't see Aria anywhere. I was curious about where she'd hightailed it off to.

The man faced me, folded his arms across his barrel chest, and lifted his chin, as if inspecting me with sharp gray eyes. He waited for me to speak.

At his cold-as-concrete countenance, I hesitated to offer to shake hands. "Mr. McNeal? I'm Kate Fox. I called you last month about Brodgar."

I couldn't see his teeth because the mustache hid them, but I assumed he broke into a grin. "Oh, aye. I recognize the voice but didn't expect such a wee lass."

At least, that's what I thought he said as I translated the thick accent. I rested my hand on the unkempt bull. "This isn't Brodgar, is it?"

His eyes glinted with humor. "And you know yer cattle, I see. Noo. This ain't my man, Brodgar. He's out back. I dinna want ta let all the igits see 'im. If I'm gonna let him go, it's gotta be to a good home, not to some igit."

It seemed an honor he didn't consider me one of the igits. "Have you seen the ranch owner? Aria Fontaine? She was going to meet me here."

He probably started to reply, but at that moment all sound muted for me. All sights, smells, everything faded into nothing, and it's doubtful my heart kept beating or that I drew breath. That moment lasted forever and was gone in the blink of an eye as I struggled for composure.

McNeal spun around so quickly it was as if he thought he was being attacked. He swung his head back to me, then behind him again.

That's all the time it took for Glenn Baxter to go from impersonating a marble statue to walking toward us again.

I blinked hard and patted the bull's hairy butt, pretending to study his composition. Inside, I was doing my best to silence the clanging alarms, the rush of blood so loud it drowned out the roar of the cattle barn. This reaction definitely had to stop. I was a grown woman who'd been in gun battles, had my life threatened, killed, and been the target of killers. I could manage my own heart, for the love of cheese. I refused to allow it to ambush me.

McNeal didn't show Baxter the hesitation he'd had with me. With a jovial note, he said, "Craig McNeal. You lookin' fer me?"

Shoving all those dangerous feelings back into the vault in my heart, I lifted my head, hoping like hell my face looked as unconcerned as the hairy heifer in front of me.

Baxter's face, the one I saw most nights when I closed my eyes to sleep, seemed flamed with heat, despite the barn's chill. He took the hand McNeal offered. "Actually, I'm looking for my fiancée. She said she'd be down here."

McNeal stood back. "Looks like ya found her."

Both of us fell all over each other with a stuttered string of denials. "We're not," I started.

"She's not," Baxter said.

"Aria. She's the... My boss. The fiancée. I mean." If a blazing meteor crashed through the roof and vaporized me, it would be a mercy to everyone.

Baxter closed his eyes for a two-count, then turned to me with those brown-flecked golden eyes. "Hi, Kate. How are you?"

"Good. Good." How lame. Stupid. Awkward. Here he was, right in front of me. The man who'd cast out all the longing and emptiness I'd felt most of my life. Then I'd made a mess of it all by accusing him of something he'd never be capable of. I mean, any therapist worth their salt would tell you I was afraid of how good we were together and subconsciously lobbed a grenade into something so right. Anyway, he'd left me with gaping holes I had no clue how to shore up. And here I stood, swimming in a sweatshirt ten sizes too big, my hair scraggly, and a bloody bandage on my chin. I wanted to disappear. "You?"

The color in Baxter's face hadn't faded, and he didn't take his eyes from my face. He pointed to his chin. "What kind of trouble found you this time?"

"Bantamweight division finals."

His lips twitched, then he looked skeptical. "More like flyweight."

McNeal didn't turn his head as his gaze bounced from Baxter to me and back again. He looked amused but acted all business. "Well, you'll want to see Brodgar, then."

A squeal of delight cut through the strain. "Glenn!"

Baxter's head snapped up, and his eyes, so much like a lion's, lit up. He opened his arms, and Aria slipped into them. She threw her arms around his neck and planted a kiss on his lips before stepping back. It wasn't a passionate, no-one-in-the-world-but-us kiss. Almost worse. A casual kiss that said they had plenty of time to be alone together later.

A slow leak of acid dripped into my stomach. This was my problem, and I needed to fix it. *Look at the two of them. They are sleek and beautiful. They could run the world. They are the perfect couple. Compatible, in love. Everything you could never be. Let it go.*

This sad refrain, played on repeat in my head daily. At some point, I'd get the message. I believed I would. I prayed I would.

Aria turned her winning light on McNeal. "I'm Aria Fontaine. I'm so glad to meet you and to see your cattle. Kate and I have talked a lot about the right bull to start our herd. We've asked around, and your name comes up over and over. You're the whole reason we're at the stock show."

He preened a little, his gray eyes bright with pleasure. "As I was tellin' Katie here, Brodgar is out back. I gotta warn you, though, he's not so easily won over by a pretty face as I am."

I warmed at him calling me Katie. Only my family and people who'd known me forever used that nickname.

Aria looked torn. "I really hate to do this. But I've got something I need to take care of. Can we meet later?"

Huh? I'd been looking forward to this for weeks. Brodgar was sure to be in high demand. I wanted to snatch him up before someone else got a chance. What was suddenly so important? Did it have something to do with why she ran off earlier?

McNeal shook his head. "Got the steer show later."

"I can take a look at Brodgar now." I was as excited to meet this bull as I'd been to go to homecoming with Danny Duncan my junior year. And that's a whole lot of anticipation.

Aria's beautiful face wrinkled up with frustration. "The heifer show starts soon, and I was hoping to catch that. Besides, I want to be with you when we see Brodgar. I really need to take care of this now, though."

Her money, her passion. How could I steal her joy? At least she planned on going to the heifer show. "Sure." I gave Craig a questioning look. "Tomorrow?"

"I can meet with ya in the mornin', but I'm not gonna hold off introducin' him around if I get a thought ta."

Aria bounced on her feet as if trying to hold herself from bolting. "Give us a chance to look at him before you sell. I'm sorry, I just can't do it now."

Baxter hadn't said anything. In fact, he'd slipped behind Aria as if making it plain she was in charge.

While it should have made it easier for me to forget him, I remained acutely aware of him, as if he vibrated with a special frequency my cells detected. Impossible in the barn with all the animal, wood chips, and feed odors, but I smelled his warm, spicy Baxter scent. My heart seemed to find the rhythm of his and beat in sync. I refused to look at him.

Craig seemed as charmed with Aria as most people. He tossed his hands up in surrender. "Try to make it early, is what I'd ask."

Aria nodded at him. "First thing. I promise." She grabbed Baxter's hand and hurried away. After a few steps, she stopped and spun toward me, a look of determination wrinkling her brow. "Come on, Kate. I need you."

6

I gave one longing look at the barn doors behind McNeal, where I assumed Brodgar waited, and like an obedient puppy, I followed as Aria and Baxter held hands and rushed down the hay-strewn alley amid the hubbub of fans, blowers, music, and people. The double-wide barn doors were open to the concrete lot outside, and Aria pulled Baxter into the freezing afternoon.

The sun still stabbed its high-altitude brilliance over the front range, but it brushed the mountain tips to the west. Snug in Jeremy's sweatshirt, I barely felt the cold until it sank slowly through the fleece.

Baxter stopped and pulled, gently yanking Aria back to him.

I couldn't hear what he said to her, but she listened intently before glancing over her shoulder at me and holding up a finger to indicate I should wait a minute. She leaned toward him and tilted her head to his face, her hair falling down her back.

He wasn't a big man, but he needed to bend slightly to put his face close to hers. The air around them seemed to create a bubble for the two of them only, shutting out everything and everyone else but them. Their eyes met and I turned away, trying to focus on a Longhorn bull being led past, or the mule with a woman dressed in formal dressage on his back. Anything except Baxter and Aria about to share a kiss.

Aria bumped my arm and surged past me, heading to the stairs leading up to the trade show. "Let's go."

"Where?" I trotted to keep up.

Baxter strode a few feet ahead of us, his steps fast and hard, as if irritated.

Over her shoulder, she said, "I need to talk to Jefferson." We waited for a pickup pulling a stock trailer to idle by in front of us.

Aria considered me from the corner of her eye. "You know about the fundraiser at the Brown Palace on Saturday night."

I doubted she'd forgotten she'd mentioned it to me several times. Bringing it up now sent a shiver of apprehension down my spine. She'd had me meet cattle breeders who were more hobbyists than hands-on. They had luncheons instead of noon dinner. I'd managed to not embarrass myself and knew what fork to use. Aria said it was part of the business of raising purebred exotic breeds. I'd managed fine in those situations, but if she wanted me to talk cattle at something as fancy as a gala, I had some serious doubts about that.

"It's kind of a big deal for Hansford Meats. Aunt Eula especially."

We entered a door at the far end of the trade show and took a left toward the arena. Crowds thinned as we passed through double doors.

"Hmm." I tried to make the sound as uninterested as possible, not as panicked as I felt. Rich people and their rich friends getting together in expensive clothes to sip champagne and chat about their rich interests—or at least, that's what I imagined—sounded like torture to me.

We trudged from the pens into a series of alleys on our way to the arena. "Glenn and I are going. Jefferson shouldn't go alone."

Baxter snapped his head away as if irritated by what she said.

Did I imagine it, or was she studying me for my reaction? Hopefully she couldn't see the flames leaping from my gut about to singe my throat. "It doesn't look like any more snow is predicted until Sunday, so you ought to have a good night for it." We threaded our way along the gloomy passage.

"Aunt Eula can be daunting, and if Jefferson tells her about Nanette, he's going to need some support. I was thinking maybe you could go, too."

No. No, no, no. "Oh, you know, it's just. Well, I'm staying with my sister Diane. And she's been after me to visit for a long time, so I think I really should hang out with her. I'd hate for her to feel like I'm taking advantage of her."

Baxter's face was set in stone, and he looked everywhere but at us.

We were coming into the arena. Entering from the hallway brought us to the top, with a few trade booths along the wide upper corridor, and the seats cascading to the show ring below. Only about a fourth of seats in the stands were occupied. A few people meandered away after the Charolais show, and a few more entered to watch the Highland heifers who would be up next. With his duties of handing out checks done, Jefferson climbed the stands heading toward us.

Aria's gaze pinpointed him, and she spoke without looking at me. "Oh yes, Diane. Glenn introduced me to her last summer. She's going to the fundraiser, too."

Of course, Diane, some international investment strategist bigwig with one of those banks conspiracy theorists say run the world—and who knew what else she dabbled in?—would be attending a bazillion-dollar-a-plate charity event at the Brown Palace.

Aria kept talking. "Glenn and I and your sister. We'll move her to the head table. You'd have a great time. No awkwardness of being on a first date or anything. Jefferson will mostly be schmoozing and giving a speech."

Baxter kept his face stern and pointing straight ahead.

Jefferson recognized us and waved, his face breaking into a happy expression.

Sure, none of that awkwardness, just the special hell that comes from hanging out with a man who upended my heart so all the emotions roiled like they'd been tossed into a flooding river and made it hard for me to even breathe when he was in a five-mile radius. And that wasn't even hyperbole. "I'm not much for formal events."

Aria nodded in understanding. "I know. I really hate to put you in this position. I'll have my personal shopper pick out a couple of dresses for you to choose from. But Jefferson is kind of lost right now, and it would help me out to not have to worry he's going to fall apart. I know it's asking a lot."

He didn't seem fragile to me. She stopped, knowing when to cut the sales talk and let the mark dangle.

Jefferson made it to the section below us, but before he could climb upward, he was intercepted by a tall older woman wearing one of those Western polyester pants suits they favored in the seventies, complete with pointy-toed cowboy boots. She wore steel-blue hair in the same style as Queen Elizabeth, with two waves on either side of her forehead. A man with her looked reminiscent of Jefferson, but the white had made a bigger advance on his hair than with Jefferson's. He carried an air of gloom around him.

"Oh, shit," Aria said. She shot away from us.

Baxter and I gave each other a questioning look and followed.

By the time we got there, the man was scolding Jefferson. "You're the face of this company. You can't swagger in anytime you want and keep people waiting."

The older woman, who looked pasty and rigid and like she might have been a stern old woman since battling her way out of the womb, pursed her lips in a wrinkled face. "He's right."

Aria flashed her most winning smile. "He was on his way in plenty of time. But there were activists on the prowl upstairs. They targeted him. A nasty scene."

Aria grabbed my arm. "Isn't that right, Kate? We had to keep them from getting to Jefferson until the cops showed up."

Baxter's alarmed face focused on me before shifting to Aria.

"They were bent on causing trouble," I said, not knowing what to add.

A few people nearby found seats in the arena. It wasn't well lit in the stands, since spotlights shone on the dirt-covered ring where a few of the hairy heifers emerged. We didn't need any more females this winter, but I couldn't help being distracted by their general cuteness.

The woman, who I'd already guessed was Jefferson's mother, Eula Hansford, reached out a long arm and cupped Jefferson's cheek. That stony face melted into a maternal mask of concern. Her eyes were the same striking shade of blue as her son's. "My dear, that's terrible. You must be a wreck. Maybe after the gala, you and Nanette should take a week off. Go someplace warm and relax."

The other man's eyes were the same vibrant blue as Jefferson's and Eula's. But his glittered with what appeared to be malice. He had to be

Jefferson's brother. "We have the annual board meeting on Sunday. I think Jefferson's trauma isn't too acute that he can't attend that."

Eula studied Jefferson's face, and he gazed back with a child's trust. "I'm okay, Mother. It wasn't a big deal."

Eula stood straight and assessed Jefferson. "I definitely want to hear your PR report at the board meeting, and I don't want to wait until next quarter. There's room to expand our efforts. But if you feel overwhelmed, say the word and off you go."

Eula leaned over and pecked Aria's cheek with a dry kiss. "Always nice to see you, dear." Without acknowledging the rest of us, she strode away.

The man's smile was so far south of sincere it could cause frost bite. "You got her again, Tiger."

Aria blessed him with a quick hug, as if ignoring all tension. "Kate, this is my cousin, Blaine Hansford. Blaine, this is my friend and ranch manager, Kate Fox."

Blaine's pursed lips looked much like his mother's. Prim and judgmental. "Pleased."

Pleased? Now that was some old-fashioned pretentious response. "Nice to meet you," I answered, mostly to his back since he stomped away.

Aria took hold of Jefferson's arm. "I need to talk to you," she said.

He started to protest, but she said, "Now." And away they went to an empty section several feet away from us.

Baxter pulled his phone from his pocket, held it up to his ear, and said, "Yes?" He turned his back to me and bent his head in a conversation.

The group of heifers were led out of the arena, and another set of six entered. There would be multiple categories. One after another, all looking similar to an untrained eye.

Just as Aria started launching into Jefferson, I caught sight of a sprinkle of sequins and red ankle boots.

7

Cupcakes and concrete. Roxy. Didn't she have to work at the fancy Western-wear booth? Out of seven hundred thousand people who attended the stock show every year—I'd read that figure online, and it stuck with me—how was it she found us?

"Here you are!" She squealed as if astounded.

I stepped out of reach of an incoming hug. Honestly, she was like a dog who wanted to slobber all over you even if you'd only been gone a few minutes. Not Poupon, of course.

Jefferson's blue eyes focused on Aria, and then he gave her a skeptical frown. I hadn't heard what she'd said, but since he faced us and his voice was loud, we heard clearly. "Calm down, Turbo. You worry too much."

That caught Roxy's attention, and she flipped her head to watch the exchange that, from body language, was serious.

We could only see the back of Aria's head, but she jerked it to the side as if annoyed, and then back the other way. She said a few things I couldn't make out, but I had no problem hearing: "She's dangerous. Do I need to remind you?"

Roxy nudged me and tilted her head their way with an exaggerated "Wow" expression. I pretended not to see her. She poked me and whispered, "What's going on?"

Jefferson frowned. "You're paranoid."

Roxy chirped out at me, "I thought you were going to see a bull. I know that could take you hours because you're so obsessed with all of that stuff."

Baxter hung up and turned around. His face softened, and he gave me a half smile. "You did seem pretty pumped about it."

That set me off. "Craig McNeal is probably the premier breeder of Highland cattle. He's not keen on selling Brodgar, so we need to convince him the Sandhills is the perfect place. Brodgar is obviously special to him, and Craig wants to know he'll be happy."

Baxter watched me with amusement. "I'm not sure I've ever seen someone this excited to view livestock."

I could barely contain myself. "I was in Montana last month to see a bull. He would be fine. There wasn't anything wrong with him. But then I saw pictures of Brodgar, and I just had this instant connection. I can't explain it."

Roxy clucked. "If only you'd spend the same time and energy on dating sites as you do cattle sites, you might actually find someone."

Baxter's jaw tightened. "Kate doesn't need a dating site. If she wanted to date, she would."

Roxy shone back with a fake grin. "Oh, for sure. I mean, you and Aria could probably set her up with lots of eligible men." She elbowed him. "That cousin of Aria's, for starters."

Cream and crackers. I said, "And Brodgar has great numbers. His sire is Curaidh, who's known for throwing calves with great birth weights. His dam is one of Scotland's most sought-after cows. But all of that is beside the point."

Baxter grinned. "Okay, Flicka. Try to contain yourself. It's just a bull."

Roxy tried to be part of the conversation, but neither of us looked at her. "Kate is so weird about livestock. I think being a rancher is great, but that's not what's going to bring you true happiness. On their deathbed, no one ever said, 'I wish I'd spent more hours in the calving barn.'"

"Just a bull?" I countered to Baxter. "That's like saying your son is just a kid. Wait 'til you see him."

Aria and Jefferson rejoined us. She and Baxter shared a nanosecond gaze of greeting that made them both a little more glowy.

Jefferson wore a frown of concentration on his face, not hurting his stunning good looks, though.

Aria held up her phone to indicate she'd had a call. "I've got to go. I need some documents I left in my room."

Baxter glanced from me to her. "Weren't we getting lunch after the heifer show?"

Aria didn't seem at all sorry to cancel their plans. "I can't. I'm really sorry, Glenn. It's this new project. It's taking a lot longer than I'd anticipated. We're dealing with so many different ministries and officials, it's making me nuts. But, I swear, it's all going to be worth it." She explained to me and Roxy. "It's a water desalination system in Chile, and we're using a new material to evaporate and collect the water. If it works, it has potential to help a lot of people, and not incidentally, make a lot of money."

Jefferson lifted a hand as if displaying Aria. "And this is why we call her Turbo."

Baxter questioned her. "Don't you have a project manager taking care of the details?"

She stashed her phone in the pocket of her leather jacket. "I had to fire her. She wasn't up to the job. Until I get someone else in place, I need to be available."

Baxter wound his cashmere scarf around his neck. "She wasn't willing to work twenty-four-seven like you do?"

Jefferson nodded agreement at Baxter. "Right?"

Aria playfully grabbed Baxter's chin between her thumb and forefinger. "Says the man whose doctor has to tell him not to work so hard."

Wait. Baxter's doctor was concerned about him working too hard? I studied Baxter's face, noting his pallor and the smudged circles under his eyes. It surprised me I hadn't noticed it before, probably because I was too busy trying not to notice him at all.

He seemed fine with the change of plans. "If you're sure, I've got some work I can do. I'll meet you at the hotel later."

They shared a quick peck, causing me to turn to Roxy to avoid watching.

She adjusted her cowboy hat and watched them leave in opposite directions. "That's the trouble with women these days."

As if Roxy wasn't a woman these days.

Jefferson gave her polite attention.

But I didn't comment because I definitely didn't want to hear Roxy's assessment of anything.

Didn't stop her. "They take charge like that. Doing business and firing people and things and making money. It emasculates men."

Before I could ask her to explain that bit of wisdom—which I wouldn't have anyway because the explanation might nauseate me—something barreled into my belly. Then I was hit with another bomb.

"Boys!" The bellow came from behind me. My loving sister Louise. That meant the missiles attacking me were Mose and Zeke.

"Casa Bonita. Casa Bonita." The boys started chanting, causing more chaos than Gwen and Arlo's group had earlier. They wore crisp jeans a little too big, because Louise bought jeans they would grow into as they faded. Of course, this late in the day, their knees were dusty and the hems caked with mud. The ubiquitous cardboard CSU Rams horns circled their heads.

Louise huffed up to us, arms full of jackets, bags, and water bottles, despite the bulging pack strapped to her back. Of course she'd be worn out.

Anyone would be, trying to keep up with Mose and Zeke at the stock show, even if her daily routine included wrangling these scallywags. She took care of a busy family and volunteered all over the place, not to mention doing her darndest to bring our family together. She ranked about 6.8 on the Richter scale of annoyance, but she meant well.

Whatever problems we'd had in the past, and believe me, we had plenty, I was determined to remember Louise was my sister, and as Dad had raised me to believe, family is important. Louise was responsible for me being foisted from a job I'd grown to really like, if not love, and that I believed I was suited for. But, thanks to Aria, I'd landed in a great position that might even be better for me.

Roxy stepped back, hands up, as if afraid Mose and Zeke might splash on her. They hugged me, still chanting, "Casa Bonita. Casa Bonita."

Jefferson looked bemused as he watched the boys rattle me. Louise grabbed Zeke by one arm and yanked him away. "If you don't straighten up, I'm taking you home right now."

Mose gripped me harder about my stomach, but his chant quieted. "Casa Bonita. Casa Bonita."

Zeke knew better than to resist his mother. They might be like fleas in a hot skillet, but if Louise could get close enough, she had ways of containing them. He whined in his ten-year-old squeak. "But you said we could go to Casa Bonita."

Despite the doughy quality of her face, Louise managed a Mother Look heavy with threat. "I said if you behaved." She turned her headlights on Mose. "Let go of her."

He unlatched immediately and stood at attention.

Roxy's nose twitched in disapproval. "I'm just glad they didn't do this earlier when you looked so good. Now, with the dried mud on your jeans, you can't even tell they smeared chocolate all over you."

Louise frowned at my chin as if I'd done something to offend her. "What in the world have you done now?"

Ignoring their judgy attitudes, I clapped a hand on each twin's shoulder. "Jefferson Hansford, these are my nephews, Mose and Zeke. Short for Moses and Ezekiel."

Roxy, probably wanting to make sure any rich man took notice of her, placed a hand on Jefferson's arm and flashed one of her coy faces, stopping shy of batting her eyes. "See, the Fox family has all these naming things. Louise names her kids from the Bible, and Kate's parents used the Best Actors and Actresses winning the Oscar the year they were born."

Jefferson responded with a simple "Oh" to Roxy, then turned an amused face to the twins. "Going to Casa Bonita, huh? What's that?" Hansford Meats was based in Greeley, less than an hour up the road from Denver. Jefferson knew about Casa Bonita.

Zeke sounded close to hyperventilating. "It's so cool! Like cliff divers and Black Bart's Cave and all this—"

Mose jumped in, "And gorillas. And sopaipillas—"

"Boys," Louise commanded, and they fell silent.

I finished for Mose and Zeke. "And the worst Mexican food you've ever eaten."

Roxy's lilting voice accompanied her leaning into Jefferson in a way that showcased her cleavage. "It's schlocky and for kids. I'd never go there, but it's famous in Denver."

I hadn't heard Roxy use *schlocky* before, but maybe she pulled out her Yiddish to sound worldly.

Together, Mose and Zeke rattled off their disagreement in a jumble of words that included *cool* and *awesome* and *fun*. Mose ended by turning to me. "Mom said you'd go with us. And Aunt Diane and them. She said it was family fun night."

I glanced at Louise, and she didn't seem at all sheepish. She planted a hand on her ample hip and thrust her chin at me. "You love Casa Bonita, and it'll be good for the family to do something fun together."

I held up a hand to stop her. "I *loved* it. When I was ten." I indicated the twins.

Louise huffed. "Fine. I get it. But if I have to go, you have to go, too."

I opened my mouth to say they weren't my kids. But then, my nieces and nephews meant the world to me. I'd done a lot of the raising of my oldest niece, Carly, while her mother was sick and after she passed.

I hesitated. I might love them with all my heart, but Casa Bonita? That was a whole other level of devotion.

Louise pounced despite Jefferson never saying he was planning to go along. She sounded like an over-excited TV announcer as she addressed him. "You're gonna love it. A not-to-be-missed Denver experience. Iconic."

I tried to let Jefferson off the hook. "You don't have to do this. It's..."

Jefferson had the same rascally gleam in his eyes as the twins. "You couldn't keep me from someplace with gorillas, cliff divers, *and* sopaipillas."

After declaring she'd never set foot in Casa Bonita, Roxy tried to backpedal. "It really is fun just because it's so over the top. When are we going?"

Louise did her Louise routine. "We're going home tomorrow, so it has to be tonight. And we'll go early to beat the crowds. We need to stop at Diane's to get her and the kids—Jefferson, was it?—can meet us at the restaurant." She grabbed Zeke's arm again to tug him away.

"Should I go with Jefferson?" Roxy asked.

Louise considered her for a second, gave me a quizzical look, then said to Roxy, "You're coming with us?"

Roxy let out a *pfsht*, as if it was obvious. "I need to make sure Kate wears something decent. I guess I'll ride with you guys. I can get Diane's address from Kate."

Mose and Zeke let out a shout and took off in a dead run down the aisle. One left his Rams horns behind.

Louise set her chin. "Oh, Lord. There's a mechanical bull." She marched after them.

The boys slipped through a group of cowboys, and I thought I caught sight of Keith again. When I zeroed in on the cowboys I thought he'd been behind, he'd disappeared. I'd really let myself get spooked and was seeing boogeymen everywhere.

Not to mention boogeywomen, because there was no mistaking that overdone blonde who'd dropped the coffees. She stood at a tack booth on the top level of the arena, holding a snaffle bit I'd bet she wouldn't know how to get into a horse's mouth. She looked down at it when she caught me focused on her.

8

Roxy watched the twins with a disapproving frown. "I'm not going to let Beau be that out of control."

She'd been parenting for three years and so far hadn't impressed me with her skills. So, I kept my response of "Good luck with that" to myself.

My focus remained on the Barbie who'd juggled her coffee. She targeted Jefferson with a laser look of a predator, and I jumped the fence from thinking she was innocent into Aria and Roxy's pasture of seeing her as a woman with a plan.

Roxy was busy asking Jefferson inane questions. It sounded like flirting to me, but she probably couldn't help herself.

I wanted no part of this, especially if Roxy was imagining herself as my wingman or something similar. Pointing a few rows above us, I said, "I'm going to watch the rest of the Highland heifer show."

Jefferson tipped an imaginary hat toward me. "Until tonight, then." He bounced down the stairs toward the show ring.

Roxy looked shocked to be standing alone and spouted to no one in a tone steeped in importance, "I've got to get to Marla's booth."

The current group of cattle was being led from the show ring when someone plopped in the seat beside me. Aria let out an exhale that said she'd been on the run. She pulled up her phone and punched at it, more perturbed than I'd ever seen her. She typed at a pace that rivaled Roxy's, and without looking up said, "I was waiting for an Uber when I remembered the heifer show." This scattered version of Aria was something new. I felt bad for her, but it was kind of nice to see her less than perfect.

Ten docile cows stood in the arena, haltered and sweet, trainers standing at attention holding their leads while the judge, a lean woman in black Western dress pants and jacket with a black flat-brimmed hat, clutched a clipboard and walked around each animal.

Aria growled at her phone and, with a tense face, used both thumbs to type a long response. When she punched what must have been "send," she muttered at me. "This plant is going to be great, but it's pulling me in twenty directions right now. I need someone I trust to take the reins."

I knew she juggled several projects, but I'd hoped the breeding operation would have her whole attention this weekend. Not only was she distracted with the fundraiser, she was getting a new business passion off the ground. It wasn't the same feeling as when I'd discovered my husband had cheated on me, but it had that flavor.

"It's hard to find someone I have as much faith in as you. And if I don't find someone I can rely on, this project will be impossible." Aria turned her full attention to the arena, and her eyes sparkled like a teen's eyes at a Taylor Swift concert. "They are adorable. Look at that."

Traditionally, Highland cattle were shown in their natural state. Sure, they were bathed and fluffed, but their trademark tresses were left long and unruly. The trend now was to cut and coif. Sort of like the difference between a Bichon Frise in the show ring and your grandmother's Lhasa Apso who was six months overdue for the groomer.

I wasn't all that impressed with the shaved and overly manicured cattle. But then, I'd refused to have Poupon groomed in the traditional poodle do. To my mind, the wild hair was Highland's trademark. "I think they ought to leave them unshorn."

Aria elbowed me. "Of course you would. You like everything authentic, no pretense." She teased, but I wondered if there wasn't a note of annoyance in her voice.

A minute ago she seemed to be riding Jefferson about something. What was bothering her so much today? Maybe she was as jumpy as I was after all the ruckus of thieves and protesters. "Don't you?"

Her gaze still on the fancy heifers in the show ring, she said, "Of course. Obviously when they're on the prairie, they need all that hair, and I love their wild, rock star look. But glamour has its fun side, too."

I couldn't help a guffaw, and I elbowed her back. "I get it. Selling me on the fundraiser again."

Her pixie mischief shone on her face, a relief after her uncharacteristic agitation. "Come on. It'll be an experience. You've met Tiger, and you know he's nice and not bad to look at."

"Yeah, but the dress and shoes. And what about makeup and this mop?" I flopped my ponytail up and let it drop.

She surveyed me with an expert's eye. "Leave it to me. I'll make this as painless as possible."

I frowned at her, letting her know I wasn't sold.

She quit with the pitch and grew serious again. "Look, I'm worried about Tiger."

She'd said that before. "He seems fine."

The cows were led from the arena, and another class entered, looking much the same. I pointed. "That dark one is from Starlight Farms. That's where we got Fiona."

Aria beamed at the coiffed critters. Then her face darkened. "You never know what's going on with Jefferson. Aunt Eula can be a tyrant, and when she's disappointed, she can withdraw anything from money and privileges to affection. Blaine tries to keep on her good side, but he never seems to get it right. Tiger learned to charm her. That happy face is sheer survival."

I'd grown up smack in the middle of eight other siblings. I knew a thing or two about keeping my feelings to myself. "Why are you so worried?"

She swiveled toward me. "Jefferson's wife, Nanette, is nothing but a conniving opportunist. They have a prenup, of course. But she's going to want more than that. And Jefferson is so trusting. I could guarantee she was behind the break-in at his place."

No matter why it's happening, divorce is the death of dreams. You always start with the hope of a happily ever after. Struggling through the death throes is awful, and drawing the final breath, though it can be a mercy, is tough. "Even if he gets taken financially, I wouldn't call that a dangerous situation."

Aria's eyes flashed. "Just now Jefferson told me when he tried to talk her out of leaving him, she tried to stab him. She ended up slashing his tires to keep him from following her. She's vindictive, mean, and probably deranged."

This didn't sound like a playground I wanted to swing in. "If he's worried, why doesn't he hire security?"

She kept her eyes on the cattle, seeming to take in everything about them. "The problem is that he's not worried. Women flock to him, and he's got no defense against them. You saw how he was with that woman who spilled the coffee. He's handsome and rich, and all he wants is someone to love him. He needs looking after."

I stated it as plainly as I could. "Are you trying to set me up with your married cousin so I'll protect him?"

She waved that off while she watched the judge move from one heifer to the next. "Not at all. But I'd like the head table to be full, and having you around might keep the vultures at bay. And maybe keep Nanette at a safe distance."

I gave her a questioning cock of my head and waited for her to explain.

She looked away, clearly uncomfortable, then back at me. "So, yeah. Nanette is back. She's trying to squeeze more money from Jefferson. I looked into getting a restraining order against her, but so far, she hasn't really done anything that warrants one."

"Threatening him with a knife and slashing tires isn't cause?"

An angry gleam lit her eyes. "Nanette claims *he* had the knife and slit his own tires and blamed it on her. I guess the judge agreed with her because, of course, men are always the aggressor."

"If they had a prenup and she gets a settlement, then why would she come after him?"

Aria nodded as if I'd hit the right button. "Exactly. A normal person would leave it at that. The settlement is more than generous. But Tiger has this big heart, and he feels guilty, and Nanette knows how to work him. I'm afraid he'll cave and give her anything she asks for."

She'd quit watching the cattle, which was fine because we weren't here for heifers. We needed a bull, and there was only one I was interested in seeing. My clinging to a sense of monogamy was annoying.

Meddling in other people's lives was something I tried to avoid. "Jefferson is an adult. He might not always make wise decisions, but I don't think it's a good idea to make them for him."

Aria nodded agreement. "Normally, I'd say the same thing. But in this instance, Jefferson needs protecting."

Jefferson was part of a hugely successful business. Or, at least that's how I always thought of Hansford Meats. "I'm sorry that he can be manipulated, but people need to live their own lives and make their own mistakes."

She spun toward me. "I agree. But to a point. Nanette is dangerous, and Jefferson is gullible."

I wondered if she overreacted, and it must have shown on my face.

"You know, when I met her, I really liked her. She and her sister grew up poor. But she was sweet and seemed to really care about Jefferson."

"But?"

She shook her head. "Not long after they were married, Jefferson got drunk and told me she had a dark side and got violent."

"That's not good."

"I was skeptical, but then she tried to turn me against him. She told me he abused her. And that's when I realized she's a psycho."

"Really?"

She tapped the armrest between us. "At first she was affectionate and trusting. But then, I suppose her true colors came out, and she got tough and hard. I've done my best to get Jefferson to change his will, but he insists on keeping Nanette in it. He won't believe me that she's dangerous, even though I showed him the report."

"Report?"

A sheepish dip of her head showed a little embarrassment. "What was I supposed to do? He wouldn't believe my intuition. Nanette has a history of crime."

That didn't sound good. "What did she do?"

Aria looked away. "Shoplifting, mostly. But that's only what they caught her for. She saw an easy mark in Jefferson and went for it. She's psychotic. I mean, why else would she file for divorce, then decide she wants to stay married? She's hatched a better plan."

I understood wanting to protect people you love, but I thought maybe Aria was a little over the top on this one. "What plan is that?"

She turned to me as if wanting to convince me. "If he dies, she's in line for a fortune."

"You don't think she's really plotting to kill him, do you?"

Aria lifted her eyebrows in a way that invited me to think about it. "If something happens to Jefferson before the divorce, her future gets a whole lot brighter."

I gave her a skeptical frown. "Murder is a pretty drastic step."

She leaned in to me. "I saw her. Here."

"Nanette?" That sent a chill up my spine.

"I didn't catch up to her, but I'm sure it was Nanette. I'm telling you, Kate, that woman is scary."

9

My older sister Diane had negotiation skills that could create world peace when she had the mind to use them. She must have been highly motivated because somehow, she'd managed to get her two kids and Mose and Zeke all into Louise's Suburban, leaving me to ride shotgun with her in the sleek Mercedes. While Louise took off with the kids, I threw Jeremy's hoodie and my jeans and T-shirt into the washer. I bet on Diane making up for the delay.

We zipped in and out of lanes on Colfax heading west to the Pepto-Bismol-pink palace that was Casa Bonita. In the dashboard lights, Diane looked elegant, even though she'd shed the power suit she'd worn to work and now wore a sweater, jeans, and riding boots. She had the money and confidence for any manner of self-care regimens that pulled, tucked, injected, highlighted, and dissolved to leave her looking wonderful with seemingly no effort. She and Aria probably had a profusion of treatments most of us knew nothing about.

Diane jerked to the right to slide between two giant SUVs. "We're meeting Jefferson Hansford at Casa Bonita?" That was the fourth time she said it; each time sounded more disbelieving.

I gripped the door handle and the console, even though neither would help me in the fiery explosion that she was sure to create with her crazy driving. "He seemed taken with Mose and Zeke."

She glanced at the rearview and gunned the little rocket into another lane, eliciting a honk. "Yeah, but. No one *willingly* goes to Casa Bonita. Especially someone with enough money to buy twenty restaurants with gourmet chefs. The food there is worse than prison slop."

I dabbed at my chin where Diane had changed out the butterfly bandage. It was tender and, last time I'd looked, red as a baboon's butt. "No one goes to Casa Bonita for the food."

She slapped the steering wheel and squealed. "Oh. I know why he's going. Jefferson Hansford has a thing for you."

"You're delusional. And PS, he's married." My abundant and irritating family loved to remind me I should try dating again. They knew about my failed marriage and humiliation on that front, but they didn't know who had really shattered my heart. Still, their advice wasn't wrong.

I fought against the memory, but I've got to hand it to myself: When my brain landed on a powerful image, it had the strength to follow through, no matter how much I fought it.

Three years ago now, could have been a lifetime or twenty minutes, how fresh it felt and how impossible to ever get it back. The fireplace's glow cast the tiny cabin in cozy shadow as we drank a wine that tasted like the mysteries of life wrapped in smooth liquid gems. Those eyes, so much like a lion's, darkened with desire as Baxter leaned in to kiss me.

We'd started our relationship with me suspecting him of kidnapping my niece Carly. But for the next two years, we had spoken on the phone nearly daily as we tried to find her. Each conversation had brought us closer as we revealed ourselves little by little.

Finding Carly coincided with us admitting our true feelings and committing to finding a way to merge our disparate lives. And we'd shared that night. That one magical, wonderful night.

But when I'd had suspicions Baxter might be a killer, it had driven the stake through the newly awakened heart. The warmth and safety of his gaze had turned glacial. And ice that hard and thick wasn't likely to melt.

And now Baxter was engaged to Aria. Two people who meant so much to me. And it sliced into me like a rusty steak knife.

Whipping through traffic, Diane warmed to her idea. "No. This is great. Just what you need. A romance with a super-wealthy man. He'll show you what you've been missing. Get you over your stubborn idea about staying in the godforsaken Sandhills wasteland."

I glared at her. "That is offensive on so many levels." Not the least of which was the fact that I'd dived off the cliff of a relationship with one of the richest men in the country. And it wasn't his money I missed. The Sandhills and tending cattle came the closest to filling the emptiness. "Might have slipped your notice that he's married."

She teased me as if we were still kids sharing a bed in that freezing upstairs room. "Ooooh. Hit a nerve. As for the marriage thing, it's over."

I slapped my palm on my thigh. "How do you know these things?"

She grinned at the windshield. "Don't ask, and I won't tell."

"When it comes to my life, stop finding out things."

She gave a noncommittal lift of her eyebrow. "Still, it wouldn't hurt you to indulge in a little romance. Or let's just call it sex. Have some fun, Katie. Think about it. Why else would Jefferson Hansford go to Casa Bonita?"

I would have poked her but didn't want to distract her from piloting. "You loved it as much as the rest of us."

A smile tugged at the corner of her mouth. "Remember when Michael and Douglas snuck behind the waterfall and tried to climb up the cliff because they wanted to dive?"

"And Dad caught them right before the gorilla threw them out."

She laughed. "Gorilla! What is the deal with a gorilla running around a Mexican restaurant?"

"Makes no sense. Maybe that's the point."

She sniffed. "I was so pissed because I was working through my weight in sopaipillas, and we had to leave."

"Hope Mose and Zeke are better behaved."

Diane darted into the parking lot. "Don't count on it."

Louise had left a good twenty minutes before us, but I was sure it'd take her a while to catch up. Maneuvering her Mom-mobile through rush-hour traffic wouldn't be anything like the guided missile Diane managed.

Casa Bonita had started out as a department store but was transformed in the early 1970s into a weird Mexican-themed quasi kind of amusement park that served cafeteria-style enchiladas and tacos. An eighty-five-foot domed tower rose into the night, and a fountain splashed, despite the winter air. The allure of Casa Bonita started before you ever got inside, with the tower and a statue of an Aztec ruler with gold leaf. As we made our way across the parking lot, a black Lincoln pulled up to the mock plaza in front of the fountain, and Jefferson unfolded from the back seat.

When he caught sight of us, he made a goofy face and raised his voice, "Are we ready for fun?"

Before I could answer, he bent down and offered his hand to someone in the car.

Maybe Aria and Roxy wouldn't have been shocked, but it surprised me when the platinum blonde coffee-spiller from the stock show emerged from the Lincoln.

Diane muttered, "Who's the bimbo?"

The car drove off, leaving Jefferson and the blonde waiting for us.

I started first. "Diane, this is Jefferson Hansford." To him, "And this is my sister, Diane Fox."

Jefferson shook Diane's hand with enthusiasm. "Aria has only wonderful things to say about the Fox sisters."

Diane raised her eyebrows at me, and I got her telepathic message of, *Not including Louise.*

"And this is Sandi Peters." Jefferson lightly touched the blonde's shoulder. "Diane and Kate," he said to her.

Sandi's teeth were as white as a snow bunny, which was what she made me think of with her tiny nose and beady eyes. Cute, but in an artificial way I couldn't quite place. "You all are so good to invite me to join you. It's really so kind." She had a squeaky voice, kind of like Dolly Parton's laugh.

Diane's face muscles made the appropriate assembly for a smile, but it didn't come together. "The more the merrier, I always say." Except, she'd never said it with conviction, and she didn't now.

Jefferson rushed in. "Sandi came to the stock show with her sister. But there was a family emergency, and her sister had to hurry back to Montana, and Sandi got stuck here alone. She's never been to Denver, so I thought it would be a shame if she never visited Casa Bonita while she was here."

I was saved from needing to answer when a wild rumpus of nieces and nephews surrounded us. Mose and Zeke had Kimmy and Karl start in on their irritating chant, and they circled us like Indians attacking a wagon train in a spaghetti Western. "Casa Bonita. Casa Bonita."

Diane raised a perfectly manicured finger and didn't say a word.

Kimmy, a year older than the twins, and Karl, younger by a year, froze. They didn't appear to even breathe or blink.

Mose turned curious eyes to Diane. "What?" Zeke bumped into Mose, gave him a shove, and then realized something was up and focused on Diane.

Diane slowly retracted her finger. "No one goes through those doors unless they can act like civilized human beings."

Louise caught up with us, lugging a backpack bulging with coats and who knows what else. "I don't know how you deal with this traffic every day. I'm stressed out. Kate, you're driving home."

"She's with me." Diane spoke with such steel in her voice that anyone who valued their life wouldn't argue.

Louise was undaunted. "You're not the boss." Guess regular rules didn't apply to sisters.

I held my hands up as if I had no choice.

Louise glanced around. "Where's Roxy?"

"She texted that she had to work the clothes booth tonight." It was news good enough it almost made up for my busted chin.

Diane raised her arms to herd the kids toward the door. "You will *not* act like a troupe of hooligans."

At least for now, Diane seemed to tame them.

But she couldn't control the whole world, as became clear when a chant of "Shame, shame, shame" rose from nearby, drowning out the fountain's burble.

"Speaking of hooligans," I said, and tried to hurry everyone along.

Louise gaped at the hippie couple from the trade show as they advanced on Jefferson. They wore the same garb of rustic clothes, but their placards had changed from animal rights to human rights. There were only Gwen and Arlo shouting and holding up signs that said *Capitalism Sucks!* and *People Aren't Illegal!*

I nudged Louise forward while Diane shot poison darts with her eyes and rounded the kids toward the door. Sandi scurried after them.

Jefferson stood beside me as we brought up the rear. We turned our backs on their shouting. "How did they know we'd be here?" he said.

The man yelled at us, "Your wealth can't protect you."

I cranked my neck to look at Jefferson. "Mose and Zeke were shouting it to the rafters. Anyone within a three-acre radius would know we were heading here tonight."

Jefferson winced. "I'm sorry. I should have been more discreet."

I thought about Aria's worries. "Does this kind of thing happen a lot?"

He had the innocent look of a child. "Not really. Sometimes. But I've done some interviews about the charity event, and the stock show had a special on the news, so maybe I'm a little more visible than normal."

Gwen shrieked right behind us and waved her poster made from heavy cardboard and stuck to a stake. She startled me with how close she'd gotten without us noticing. "You're a monster and deserve to die!" She swung her placard at Jefferson, sideswiping him across the cheek.

"Hey!" I hadn't expected her to physically attack, and I acted on impulse gleaned from years of defending myself from sibling ambushes. I jumped in front of Jefferson and shoved her.

Arlo threw his sign down and started for me.

Jefferson stood to my side with his hand on his cheek, looking stunned.

I took a step forward and braced myself, ready to defend us. In my calmest voice, I said, "Really? You want to fight this out here?"

I wasn't sure what stopped them. Maybe I still had a whiff of sheriff authority clinging to my tone. More likely, it was the herd of a multigenerational family migrating from the parking lot and a few of them pulling up phones aimed our way. Arlo grabbed Gwen's arm as she launched herself at me, pulling her back.

She whirled on him, glanced at his face, and stopped fighting him.

When she turned back to us, her eyes were accusing, and her voice and face venomous. "Watch your back." I'd rarely seen so much hate. "Karma's a bitch."

10

Arlo pulled Gwen away, and I snatched Jefferson's wrist to walk him past the fountain and through Casa Bonita's ornate wooden doors.

The rest of the gang waited inside, and Louise immediately organized us into the serving line to order from a short list of flavorless dishes, all with beans and rice on the side. From experience, I knew the food tasted a lot like old-time TV dinners, all mushy, bland, and in weird shades of orange.

We settled into the second story of the multitiered, dimly lit dining room festooned with twinkle lights and decorated with fake palm trees. The smell of chlorine and the rush of a thirty-foot waterfall accented the less than high-class ambience. It was only slightly less chaotic than a battlefield. An arcade, gift shop, and video game room filled nooks and crannies in walls made to look like cliffs and jungles. Facades made of adobe walls, doors, and windows, with fake flowers and greenery snaking everywhere, gave the impression of a quaint Mexican village. Western gunfighters, mariachi bands, and señoritas with flowers in their hair roamed the passages along with harried servers carting drinks and food.

The earlier incident didn't seem to affect the kids. They hadn't seen much of it, and the excitement of the immersive venue with the roving performers sucked them in. Louise appeared tense, but then, when didn't she? Diane had the strained look of a soldier between battles. Maybe she was thinking of work, maybe the encounter irritated her, or, more likely, she hated Casa Bonita and was biding her time.

Aside from a red spot across his cheek where the poster had struck him, Jefferson seemed to shuck the whole unpleasantness and was bantering with Mose and Zeke like any other ten-year-old. Maybe with a mother like Eula, he'd never had the chance to act like this. And despite all their warnings, once inside, Louise and Diane didn't demand Sunday school behavior.

Sandi tried to join in, but fart jokes and super-hero references didn't seem to be her thing. Her glistening red lips held a pleasant, if confused, smile, and the humidity from the waterfall drooped her curls.

We were stretched out at a long table with waterfall views, and before Diane was halfway through her first margarita, the cliff divers began their routine. The cliff for the divers was modeled after one in Acapulco, and the pool was fourteen feet deep. All so very exciting...when you're ten.

I sipped a beer and worked my way through the enchiladas, mushy beans, and bland rice. All the hot sauce did was add heat, not flavor.

The boys and Kimmy could barely contain their excitement. Mose tugged on Louise's arm. "I ate two tacos. Can I go to Black Bart's Cave?" That had always been my favorite place when I was their age. So many twisty, dark passageways. And you never knew when a gunslinger might pop out at you. Or even Black Bart himself.

Diane sat at the head of the table, her untouched plate pushed back and two margaritas in front of her. Kimmy and Karl flanked her, both of them picking at their tacos. Louise and I bookended Mose and Zeke, with Sandi and Jefferson taking up the other side.

Sandi nursed a white wine. Who orders wine at Casa Bonita? Jefferson had opted for a root beer, which seemed equally weird.

Diane set a red flag upright on the table, signaling we needed the first of our endless sopaipillas. Seems like every culture has their version of fried sweet bread, from donuts to funnel cakes.

Sandi's enthusiasm felt a little stale. "Isn't this fun. It's so family oriented."

Louise clamped down on Zeke's shoulder and held him to his chair. "Eat a few more bites, and then you can go."

A mariachi band wandered to our table. Three older men with black mustaches and two young women, all wearing white pants, red sashes, and sombreros, brass wailing, fiddles humming, and two men opening their mouths in a Mexican harmony.

Diane didn't need words—Spanish, English, or Elvish. Her glare said it all, and the band sidled away at a much faster clip than when they arrived.

Meanwhile, amid the bedlam, a young woman performed an elegant swan dive from the top of the cliff to the *ahhs* and applause of the diners.

"How can you eat that crap?" Diane curled her lip, giving a head jerk at me and my plate.

I gulped my beer. "My last meal was an English muffin at your house this morning." I pointed to Louise's plate. "She's eating it, too. Why don't you pick on her?"

Diane set her empty margarita glass on the table and picked up the full one. "Louise is just happy to have someone else cook for her."

Louise swallowed a mouthful and grabbed her soda. "And that's the truth."

"Mooooooooom," Mose and Zeke whined in unison.

As if releasing hounds, Louise lifted her hands. "Go. But stay out of trouble."

Kimmy and Karl both sat up and trained their eyes on Diane, more disciplined but no less canine. "I will not put up bail money, so you'd better behave." Diane actually smiled at them as they flew from their seats, hot after Mose and Zeke on their way to Black Bart's Cave.

Sandi raised her voice so I could hear her. "Do you have kids?"

Louise swallowed fast and answered for me. "She's a wonderful aunt to her nieces and nephews."

Aw, that was nice of her to say. Except...

She kept talking. "And she really should have some of her own. You know, she's not getting any younger. But she needs to find a husband first, and so far, she's not trying very hard."

There might not have been much spice in my enchiladas, but I had a sudden flare of heartburn.

Diane held her margarita an inch from her mouth and paused. "Louise, shut up."

"Well, I..." she stuttered.

Even if I doubted Sandi's sincerity, I welcomed her kindness in shifting the conversation. She turned to Jefferson. "How about you?"

He was inching his chair from the table. "Not yet. But someday, I hope. I mean, how much fun would it be to bring your own kid here?"

"Exactly," Sandi agreed, though I wondered if she hadn't manipulated the whole conversation to let Jefferson know she'd be the perfect mother for his future children.

Much to her disappointment, I was sure, Jefferson stood up, and before leaving the table said, "I'll go and check on the kids. Make sure they're not getting into mischief."

Diane considered her quickly disappearing margarita. "Knock yourself out," she called after Jefferson.

I shoved back from the table, and Diane raised her eyebrows at me suggestively. "Lots of secluded passages in this place. Which direction did Jefferson go?"

"Going to the bathroom," I said in my deadest deadpan.

Louise reached for the last sopaipilla at the same time as Diane. I flipped up the red flag to signal the server they'd better bring more before the guns came out, and went in search of the women's room.

The restroom lights seemed garish after the dim restaurant. The door behind me didn't bump closed before it swung open again and Sandi popped inside.

"Oh." I hadn't known she followed me, and I tried for something friendly to say. "Kind of dark out there, huh?"

She stopped in front of the mirror and checked her hair, patting it smooth, although I couldn't see anything out of place. Her makeup looked fine, and even though I caught a whiff of flowery perfume, she pulled out a tiny bottle and dabbed more behind her ears. "Your family is so fun." Bless her heart, she tried to sound sincere.

I really did need to pee and had no interest in bonding with Sandi. She might be the gold digger Aria and Roxy imagined, or she might be perfectly innocent. Call me judgmental, but Sandi and I weren't cut from the same cloth. Mine was flannel and denim and hers was all pleather and fluff, and I didn't see that we'd find much in common.

"They can be a lot." I backed up and pointed to a stall. "I'm just gonna, you know."

She washed her hands. "Oh. Sure." But she didn't stop after I'd slid the lock and sat in the stall.

"Do you know Jefferson well?" Her squeaky voice echoed against the tile.

The door opened, noise from the restaurant, the mariachi band, festive voices, maybe the pop of fake gunfire, then the soft bump and relative quiet resumed.

What would happen if I didn't answer? Really, some moments in a person's life should be private. Now that someone else had entered, could I keep quiet?

The stall next to me opened, and someone entered. The smell of stale cigarette smoke curled under the metal wall separating us.

Sandi pulled paper towels from the dispenser. "Okay. I'd better get back."

It would be polite to respond but, come on. I was busy with my alone time. A few moments later, after I was finished and washing my hands, I was still irritated.

A door behind me banged open, slapping the wall, and a woman slinked out. Trim and dressed entirely in black, in clothes that snugged to her compact frame, she clipped to the sink in knee-high boots.

Her black hair was one of those super-short cuts that you knew had to be professionally touched up every week or two, and she wore large silver hoops with diamond chunks. Her makeup looked subtle but was probably a function of several dozen different steps, like what my nieces watched influencers perform on YouTube. All in all, she straddled goth and elegance in an impressive way.

She bent over the sink and reached between us to the soap dispenser. She caught my eye in the mirror. Hers were vivid lavender, and I wondered if she wore colored contacts. They were remarkable against her pale and flawless skin. Her voice was deep. "Is that munchkin a friend of yours?"

That brought a bitter taste to my mouth, and not simply because I was shorter than Sandi. If this pale vampiress were one of my nieces or nephews, I would have quashed that talk immediately. Since she was a stranger, and I'd already tackled a thief and wrangled some activists today, I wasn't in the mood for another skirmish. I met those violet eyes with a disdainful expression.

She shut her water off and flicked her hands in the sink and chuckled. "Okay. Sorry. But is she? Your friend?"

I kept washing my hands.

"Okay, so what about the guy with you? Are you, like, a thing? Is she boning him?"

Maybe Aria was right and women everywhere wanted Jefferson. I grabbed a paper towel from the dispenser and, without looking at her, dried my hands and headed for the door. "Have a nice night."

"Rude." Her laughter was harsh and mean before the door closed on her.

Trying not to be rattled by the woman who'd seemed threatening somehow, I returned to the table where only Louise and Diane sat in front of a basket of sopaipillas. Diane held a pitcher of honey over a bit of the puffy bread. "These are deep-fried death, and I can't stop eating them."

I helped myself to one and dribbled honey on the warm greasiness. "Margaritas and sopaipillas. How do you keep your girlish figure?"

I caught sight of Mose dashing from a dark passage toward the arcade, Kimmy in close pursuit. The rest of the gang could be anywhere.

Louise smacked her lips over the last bite of a sopaipilla and stared longingly at the basket. "I shouldn't."

Diane raised her dripping sopaipilla and pointed one finger at Louise. "You shouldn't. On the other hand, it's not every day you get to Casa Bonita."

Louise took another one but set it on her plate and stared at it. "Remember how Mom loved these?"

Dang. She had to bring that up. I slid my plate away, sopaipilla untouched.

Diane licked her fingers and smiled. "She could eat a whole basket by herself, totally oblivious to what we were doing."

Louise poured honey. "I'll bet that's the reason you love them so much. You're trying to get closer to Mom by filling up on what she loved."

Diane smirked at Louise. "Or maybe everyone on the planet loves fried bread and honey. You need to quit watching all those daytime shows."

I fought the memory of Mom, maybe sitting at this same table. The sheriff chasing Black Bart up the cliffside, shouting and shooting. Susan sleeping in a baby carrier near Mom's feet. I'd been at the arcade and was on my way back to the table for a soda. Mom and Diane sat at the table together, eating sopaipillas and laughing at something. They looked so happy. I hated to intrude, so I went to the gift shop, feeling happy for Diane. When Mom was with us, no one could make you feel more special. Now the memory pinched in all the wrong places.

Louise sat up straighter. "You can learn plenty on a variety of subjects by watching talk shows. They have experts on as guests."

"Like who's sleeping with whom in Hollywood and the latest diet fad Gwyneth is into." Diane laughed.

That was mean. I faced Diane. "Not everyone wants to be a corporate bigwig who goes to their own trainer, has a personal shopper, and hasn't cooked a meal in five years. There's value in being a mother and home-maker, and you don't need to put Louise down all the time."

Diane and Louise stared at me as if I had turned green and grown leaves. I froze and imagined we looked like some distorted painting, maybe a Picasso of *The Last Supper*.

Then we all laughed. It might have been the best moment I'd spent with my sisters in a decade. I wished the rest of the family could be here. We needed more times like that.

Of course it didn't last long. Louise leaned in. "What should we do about Deenie Hayward?"

I held up my hand. "Whoa. Dad is happy. Leave it alone."

Mom's defection had detonated a bomb inside of Dad. It had taken a couple of years for any of us to gain equilibrium, and I'd worried he'd never get traction. But he'd somehow found a special friendship with Deenie, and she seemed devoted to Dad, was friendly, loyal, and cheerful. I really liked her, mostly because Dad had come back to life when he was around her. After Mom's treachery, making him smile seemed a miracle.

Diane looked mildly interested. "Why? Is it getting serious?"

Louise fidgeted in agitation. "People are talking. Her car is parked in front of his trailer a lot of nights. A *lot*. And, you guys, she's only a few years older than me."

Diane sat back and picked up her empty margarita glass. "He's a grown-ass man. Why shouldn't he have some fun? Kate could take some pointers from him."

Louise seemed on the verge of tears. "I'm raising children in that town. Do you know how hard it is to teach them right from wrong with that going on under their noses?"

"Deenie and Dad aren't doing anything wrong. Leave them alone." I stood up. "I'm going to check out the gift shop."

Kimmy and Karl wandered up to the table and slid into their chairs. They grabbed sopaipillas without saying anything.

Diane pushed Kimmy's blond hair back from her face. "Where did you lose Mose and Zeke?"

Karl answered for them. "They wanted to find the way to the waterfall."

Louise dropped the Deenie line and sunk her teeth into this news. "Where? Why didn't you come get me right away?"

I cast around the darkened room filled with families, the mariachi band strolling, a young man with a cowboy hat and shiny sheriff star, and, oddly, a person in a gorilla suit. They'd been doing this schtick since the seventies, so who was I to question their aesthetic? In one corner where a fake casita opened into an equally fake cobbled path, someone spun around and slipped out of sight. He seemed familiar, and it took a moment for me to place him.

He wore the same tattersall shirt. Keith. That seemed unlikely. I had to be mistaken. There had to be tons of middle-aged men with that same build and neat hair and similar clothes. Aria had me feeling paranoid about Jefferson.

Diane started laughing. "Déjà vu. Michael and Douglas all over again."

"This isn't funny." Louise was on her feet.

Kimmy, who inherited the regal bearing of her mother, had a way of speaking to Louise in a polite way, but with a hint of condescension. "Jefferson was with them, so I assumed he had it under control."

I'd only been around Jefferson for a day, and I suspected he had more of the ten-year-old in him than adult. Why else would Aria be so worried about protecting him?

"Where did they go?"

Karl pointed to Black Bart's Cave, and I started that way. "I'll see what I can find."

Louise followed on my heels. "I'm going to tie them to their beds for a week and give them prison rations."

She wouldn't, of course. But they'd know they were in trouble when she got hold of them.

The dim tunnels forked, and Louise started down one way. I took the other. She let out a bellow, "Moses. Ezekiel. You boys get out here, now."

I figured that would send them scurrying my way. I moved down the dim passage, squinting for sign of a doorway.

In a few minutes, I found what I was looking for. I supposed fire laws kept them from locking a door hidden behind a fake cave wall. I opened it to a gloomy corridor with a cement floor and scuffed walls. I had two choices and picked left. Treading softly, I listened for the miscreants.

I hadn't gone far down a narrow hallway when I thought I heard shuffling noises in the other direction. I'd barely started that way to investigate when a bang and crash sounded, followed by high-pitched screams that could belong to two boys. More yelling and grunts.

Once a sheriff, always a little nuts. I was running toward it before I'd given it a thought. The clatter of footsteps came toward me, and suddenly a figure emerged from around a corner up ahead. I raced toward the door where I'd turned left. Whoever it was reached the door before me and slipped out. They could fade into the crowded restaurant in no time. It seemed clear that anyone fleeing like that had a story to tell, and I darn sure wanted to hear it.

I was about to take after them, but the noises coming from the other end of the passage spiked into my veins.

11

"Oh no!"

"What are we gonna do!"

"Get him out!"

"I can't. He's too heavy."

Obviously, it was Mose and Zeke. Their back-and-forth was full of panic. And these were kids who'd nearly set a pasture on fire and burned down the town. They'd been in a cave collapse. They'd been lost countless times, and the most fear I'd ever witnessed from them was when anticipating punishment from their mother. This sounded serious.

I clattered down the hall. "Zeke, Mose! Where are you?"

"Here. Over here. Hurry."

I slid into the small room and assessed the scene as quickly as possible. A narrow pool lapped at one end. An electrical panel was on one wall. Shelves with stuff I took no notice of. Mose and Zeke knelt by the pool. They were more in the water than out, all four of their arms sunk, their faces and shirts wet.

A heavy orange extension cord was plugged into an outlet across the room, and it was stretched toward the pool. As if someone had thought about trying to electrocute whoever was in the pool.

This had to be where the divers swam after their daring antics from the cliff. A narrow opening at the other end of the room must be where they climbed behind the waterfall.

"Jefferson," Zeke huffed out.

Oh. My. God. He must be in the water. And all three were at some risk of electrocution. I grabbed the cord and tossed it away, then slid to the edge of the pool.

Mose and Zeke each grasped one of Jefferson's arms, but his head dangled face-first in the water.

I grabbed under his arms and threw myself backward. He slid most of the way out of the water, and I lunged forward and grabbed his belt loop and yanked again. The boys and I were able to pull Jefferson out and turn him over. His hair flopped over his forehead, and his eyes were closed.

I wondered about CPR or wedging him on his side so he could spit up the water, when he heaved and started to cough. I tugged his arm and rolled him on his side. His jeans and shirt ran with water.

He coughed more, then moaned.

"Jefferson, can you hear me? Are you okay?"

Mose and Zeke stayed on their knees, eyes round and scared.

Jefferson opened those killer blue eyes and placed a well-manicured hand on his forehead. "Yeah, I—" He coughed again. "I'm...ow!"

I moved his hand and leaned in to investigate the red lump growing on his forehead. "What happened?"

He pushed himself to sit up, still holding his head. "The boys. We, um..." He paused. "Well."

Mose patted Jefferson's back. "Dude. You were awesome."

Zeke nodded with such enthusiasm, I was amazed his head didn't snap off. "Totally. Like Wolverine. No. Batman."

Mose spoke so fast I had a hard time understanding him. "No, like Superman."

"Whatever, dude, you were awesome."

Jefferson gave them a weak grin. "I don't feel awesome. More like he got the better of me."

I put a hand under his arm and leveraged myself backward to help him sit. "Let's start at the beginning."

Mose and Zeke had the quivery look of kids on the verge of panic. Zeke said, "We're okay. So is Jefferson. So, like, you don't need to tell Mom, do you?"

I shot them the look that told them they were already screwed.

Jefferson said, "I got curious about where the divers go behind the waterfall. I shouldn't have let the boys come with me."

I allowed a smile. "Nice try."

He let it go. "Okay, well, so we came in here. I thought it looked really dangerous for the divers, you know? Electrical panel right next to water. That could be a problem. I thought we should report it to...maybe OSHA? But then we heard someone coming."

He seemed confused, had to be cold. I knew I was, and my clothes weren't nearly as soaked as his. But he wasn't wrong about the electrical panel on the wall only steps away from the pool. I knew a thing or two about water and electrocution, since I'd investigated a murder with a center pivot irrigation system last summer. OSHA should be alerted.

I waited, and he didn't go on. "And you thought you'd talk to them about the...danger?"

Mose said, "No. We didn't want to get in trouble, so we hid. Jefferson told us to go up the stairs."

Zeke said, "But Jefferson, like he totally stayed behind to protect us."

"And then," Mose took over, "we hear this noise, and it sounds like grunting or something."

"So, we came back down to see, and there's Jefferson fighting with this dude in a ski mask. But the dude, he's got, like, a gun."

What? "Are you sure? A gun?"

Jefferson wrinkled his forehead as if trying to remember. "Yeah. He had a gun. Big."

"I didn't hear any shots," I said.

"No," Mose yelled. "Jefferson was fighting with him, and then he pulled back and whacked Jefferson in the head."

Zeke was equally loud. "And Jefferson fell down. And the dude shoved him into the water."

"And he was getting the extension cord."

"And we couldn't let that happen, so we, we, we..."

"Yelled."

"And then the dude took off."

"And we had to get Jefferson out of the water."

"And..."

"WHAT IN THE EVERLASTING HEAVEN IS GOING ON HERE?"

12

Maybe it was only Mose and Zeke in trouble. And Jefferson, too. But Louise spiked fear so deep into my bones I froze for a few seconds.

She plowed into the room.

At the same time, a young woman surfaced in the pool. She popped her head up, took one look around, and said, "You all can't be in here."

Louise gave the diver a quick glance. "Oh, don't I know it." She grabbed for the closest kid, latched onto his arm and pulled, shoving him toward the door. One more lunge for the other twin sent him scrambling after his brother. It reminded me of a YouTube video of a mama bear herding her cubs across a busy Yellowstone highway.

The diver climbed from the water, hugging herself for warmth. "I mean, this is restricted."

Louise spared some of her wrath for the diver. "Then the door should have been locked."

I tried to sound in control of the whole mess. "We're on our way out. So sorry for any bother."

Jefferson looked confused as he stared at Louise, the welt from Gwen's placard faded but replaced with a thin trickle of blood mixing with water on his face.

Louise pulled out her lethal pointer finger and jabbed him in the chest.

"You should be ashamed of yourself. What were you thinking letting these two urchins get back here? You're the adult."

He gave her a look of pure innocence and contrition, accented by his expressive eyes. I sure would have fallen for it. "You're right. You're right. I'm sorry."

But Louise was not having it. She lasered him with the mother of all Mom Glares. She shot her palm down in dismissal and trudged after the twins, who no doubt were already back at the table with their hands folded in their laps.

Sandi met us as we emerged from Black Bart's Cave. She reached up to touch Jefferson's face where a lump had formed already. "Oh no. This is awful. The kids said you were brave."

"Is everyone ready to go?" I asked, ignoring her fawning.

Sandi cheeped, "Oh, the manager asked us to leave. Well, not really asked. He said if we weren't gone in five minutes, he was calling the cops."

Fair enough. We caught up with Diane and Louise and all the kids out front by the fountain. Louise had a hand on each of her son's shoulders. They looked straight ahead, stiff at attention. Maybe they were frozen from their dousing in the pool.

Kimmy and Karl didn't make direct eye contact with Louise, maybe afraid they'd get caught in unfriendly fire.

The arctic air hit my damp clothes, and my teeth clacked. "Let's get going before we ice over."

Jefferson shivered and held up his phone. "Turns out their claims are true. It's waterproof."

The boys started to giggle until Louise clamped down on them.

Diane stood in front of the fountain with a look of barely contained mirth. "And now you know why I agreed to dinner with the family at Casa Bonita. Best entertainment I've had in a long time."

"I'm going to take Jefferson to the emergency room and get his noggin checked out," I said. "Diane, you'll have to ride with Louise, and I'll take your car." Guess I had a little of the bossy sister in me, too.

Sandi lined up with Jefferson. "I'll go with you."

Diane exhaled. "My car only seats two. We'll drop you at your hotel, honey."

Sandi opened her mouth, maybe to protest, then closed it in a pout. "I'll call an Uber."

Pale and listless, Jefferson bent to talk to Sandi. "I've got your number. I'll call you tomorrow."

Not if Aria had her way.

Sandi said, "Of course. You should get that looked at. Don't give me a thought. You take care of yourself." She turned from him, but she wasn't quick enough to hide the venomous glint in her eyes as she passed me.

An ER is never a fun place, and I should have been glad we were in the suburbs and not downtown, where there might be more injuries from violence, but the one nearest Casa Bonita was busy enough. I'd blasted the heat on the way there to stave off hypothermia.

A kid with a broken arm sniffled and squeaked in one corner while his mother rubbed his back. He was way braver than the middle-aged man with a full beard and man-bun who groaned and held his stomach. Another cluster or two of people had ailments that weren't apparent.

I checked us in and sat down to wait, gritting my teeth against the chill from damp clothes. "I'm going to text Aria and let her know."

Jefferson's head had stopped bleeding, but he sported a considerable goose egg. Washed out and wobbly, the aqua of his eyes had deepened, and a shadow of dark whiskers made his face look pale. He had to be even colder than I was. "I wish you wouldn't. She and Baxter haven't been together in a few weeks, and she had reservations at Rioja. There's nothing she can do for me."

I punched her number. "Yeah, but I don't want to face her later when she finds out I didn't contact her. She might have me beheaded."

His laugh was weak. "You're right. I don't want to be responsible for your murder."

Aria's response was immediate and exactly what I didn't want to hear. She was on her way.

After I hung up, my curiosity got the better of me. "How did it happen that you and Sandi met up again at the stock show?"

"Again?" He looked confused.

"When she dumped her coffee, Aria said it was a ploy to get you to notice her. And now I'm wondering if she was right, since somehow, Sandi ended up having dinner with you."

He brushed that off. "Aria is too suspicious. Always was. It wasn't anything planned or nefarious. I saw her when I was leaving the stock show. She looked upset, and I approached her. Not the other way around."

I couldn't hide my amusement. "Exactly as she'd appear if she wanted you to help her."

He looked up at the ceiling in mock exasperation. "She's a nice girl having a bad day. No big deal."

We were still in the waiting room thirty minutes later, not as wet but every bit as chilled, when Aria stormed through the doors. "Jefferson!" She hurried over in her strappy heels, clingy red dress, and some kind of brocaded wrap that had openings for her arms but no real sleeves. On me, it would look like something Grandma Ardith created from upholstery scraps. On Aria, of course, it looked chic.

I held my breath when the door opened again, expecting Baxter and not wanting to react inappropriately. Even taking that precaution, I still had to look away after the first glance.

He wore a black suit and the snowiest shirt I'd ever seen, and a wine-red tie with a discreet pattern. A tie. If men in the Sandhills wore ties, they were usually bolos. But really, ties were as uncommon there as a polar bear in Jamaica. The smattering of gray at Baxter's temples made him appear even more distinguished. He looked sleek and handsome and as comfortable in those evening clothes as he had in his jeans. He scanned the waiting room. Did his gaze pause ever so slightly on me?

He pocketed the key fob and walked over.

Aria squatted in front of Jefferson, her dress gracefully covering her knees. She glanced up at Baxter. "Can you do something about getting a doctor to see him? I'm sure he's been concussed."

In the time we'd been here, they'd called in the kid and an older woman. The man-bun guy still groaned and rocked. I figured we'd be here for another few hours before they got to us.

Baxter held out his hand to Aria, and she placed her delicate fingers in his and allowed him to help her stand. They seemed to not even notice the touch or the act of kindness, as if it was a perfectly normal thing that happened every day.

Their briefest touch or tender glance made me feel like I swallowed rocks.

She perched on the chair next to Jefferson and leaned forward, lasering his eyes with hers. "Tell me what happened."

Maybe he'd been trying to be stoic with me, but with Aria, he seemed almost fragile. He started to tell her the story.

Before he finished, Baxter returned. "Okay. You can go in."

What? Power, money, influence? Magic. Glenn Baxter had started life without much, but he'd figured out how to bend the world to his will.

Aria helped Jefferson to stand, and he leaned on her slightly. She must give him comfort and support because he hadn't leaned on me at all.

The moaning guy gave an outraged groan. He jumped to his feet and limped to the intake desk, still holding his stomach. "What the hell? I was here before that guy. Clearly, I'm in a lot of pain. *A lot.* I demand to be seen."

I felt bad for the guy. Truly. Even though I figured he was exaggerating his pain, which made me disdainful because I'm a Fox and a Sandhiller, and we minimize and hide our pain. All of it. Even the kind that corkscrews in our souls and makes it hard to breathe. Still, I was grateful for whatever strings Baxter had pulled to create Jefferson's miraculous admission beyond the wall.

Aria and Jefferson walked through the door held open by a young guy in a white lab coat clutching a tablet. I intended to join them, but when I got to the doorway, the guy said, "Only one other person allowed in."

Oh. No. That left me in the waiting room with Baxter. He hadn't sat down but stood in the space between two rows of chairs.

The intake woman spoke to the man-bun guy. "I'm sorry. We're short-staffed, and we need to triage our patients. You'll be seen as soon as possible. Please take a seat."

"This is bogus," the guy said. He stomped back to his seat along the wall and plopped down to resume his rocking and moaning.

All the while this went on, I stayed near the door to the exam rooms, wondering what to do.

Baxter sank into the seat Jefferson had vacated and tipped his head to indicate the chair I'd occupied previously. With no other option short of running into the parking lot, I walked over and dropped next to him.

He inhaled and let it out, clearly as uncomfortable as I was. "Aria tells me you've got a few cows and are making progress on getting the place all fixed up."

Safe subject. I did my best not to look into his eyes. They had a way of cutting right into me. Even when we used to talk on the phone and I couldn't actually see them, I could feel their intensity. "I'm disappointed we didn't get to meet Brodgar today."

He'd shaved since I'd seen him at the stock show, and I fought the desire to place my palm against his warm face. Why couldn't I stop this idiotic and inappropriate urge?

A smile teased his lips. Damn it. "I know why you and Aria get along so well. Both of you get an idea in your heads and you're off and running, and I don't have a prayer of keeping up. All she could talk about for the last week was this Brodgar bull and how you thought he was perfect. And then, when she's seconds away from seeing him, something else comes up."

We had more in common than that. Apparently, Aria and I shared our loyalty to family and our need to protect them. "It had something to do with Jefferson's ex. Aria is worried about him."

Baxter glanced toward the exam rooms. "Jefferson?" He gave me a skeptical frown. "That man can take care of himself, I'd say."

"What makes you say that?"

He gave a subtle shrug. "Aria and I met him and Nanette for dinner last summer. It wasn't anything blatant or anything. Jefferson ordered escargot, then made fun of Nanette because she wouldn't eat them. Later, he and Aria were teasing, and it kind of seemed like Nanette was uncomfortable, so I struck up a conversation with her."

It would be like Baxter to notice something like that and try to help.

"I told her I grew up on the wrong side of the tracks and would rather have a hot dog than caviar. We had a friendly conversation. I liked her."

"So what about Jefferson?"

Baxter frowned. "At one point, Nanette laughed, and it drew his attention. He didn't seem to like that, and very shortly after that, he wrapped up the evening and they left."

I thought about it. "That doesn't mean anything. Could be a million reasons for them leaving, or only that it was time."

He chuckled. "The facts don't cover the feel. Like, Jefferson didn't want anyone to be better liked or get more attention than him." He shook his head. "Might have just been me."

"Well, he did get clobbered and dunked into the pool at Casa Bonita." I explained the earlier happenings.

"That doesn't make any sense," he said. "Why would anyone go after him in a public place like that? It would take some planning. Seems like there'd be easier ways to assault him."

"That's what I've been wondering." We started to pick apart the incident, losing that awkwardness between us as we brought up motives and discarded them. As time went on, our theories got crazier, involving aliens from a planet run by cattle who wanted revenge for his meat-packing business, or a government plot to assassinate Jefferson because he was a double agent for the Chinese. Baxter wondered if the Mafia put a hit on him because Jefferson got into gambling debt.

It felt so good to laugh with Baxter. I managed to forget our past, the mistrust, the pain, the loss, and enjoy this isolated moment. He must have done the same.

The boy emerged with his arm in a sling, and the man-bun guy finally got his turn behind the door. And we slid from talking about Jefferson to a new documentary series on the origins of food that Baxter was considering airing, and had just ventured into discussing my niece Carly, who he'd taken a keen interest in mentoring, when Jefferson and Aria appeared.

Jefferson looked worn out. A white bandage covered the swollen wound, and he lagged behind Aria like a retired greyhound. She pulled her wrap close around her, looking serious. "The doctor said it's not bad. Maybe a mild concussion, but she's not even sure of that, She said he needs to rest, but someone should stay with him for a while. So, I'll hang out at his hotel tonight."

Jefferson frowned at her. "No way. You haven't seen Glenn for weeks. Stay with him. I'll be totally fine. It's probably not even a concussion."

Aria tipped her head back, a few strands from her updo escaping. "I'm not taking any chances. Quit being such a pain in the butt."

I stepped forward. "I'll stay with Jefferson. It'll be a good excuse to get out of bunking at Diane's with Louise and her crew."

Aria considered me. Then studied Jefferson, and finally locked eyes with Baxter. The worry and stress drained from her face, and color rose in her cheeks. She reached out and took both my hands.

The move unnerved me. I barely hugged my siblings—and even then, only in cases of extreme emotion. None of us Foxes are touchers, except Louise. I couldn't deny it felt nice to have the kind of friend who felt the urge to connect. A stab of guilt hit me when I thought about my lifelong best friend, Sarah. Since kindergarten we both took pride in our tough, stoic manner. There was no one I trusted or loved more than Sarah. But a girl could have more than one close friend. I just never did before.

Aria's smooth, cool hands gripped mine. "You're the only person I trust to keep an eye on him. I don't know who attacked him at Casa Bonita—"

"Bad Bart," Jefferson and I said together.

She huffed in annoyance. "Right. Anyway, I know you won't let anything happen to him." She poked Jefferson in the chest. "And you get some rest. The doctor said it's the best thing."

"I'll get the car," Baxter said.

"Me, too." I followed him into the cold night. He went one direction, and I took off in the other, trying not to wish we were leaving together.

13

Jefferson pulled up directions to The Four Seasons on his phone, and it somehow linked to the panel on Diane's Mercedes. The marvels of having the latest and best of everything. He rested his head on the seat back while I drove through dark, empty streets, wondering how someone with a savings account in the five digits—which I thought was pretty nice, by the way—was driving this new luxury vehicle heading to the ever-lovin' Four Seasons Hotel. This was the kind of fancy that inherited wealth could afford. Unless you were Glenn Baxter and created your own because you were brilliant and hardworking. Or someone like Diane, who knew things.

At a stoplight, I picked up my phone and found Diane's number, putting it on speaker. It rang three times, and Louise answered. "Is Jefferson going to be okay?"

Jefferson leaned in. "I'm fine. Don't worry."

If I'd have wanted to talk to Louise, I would have called her. "Why are you on Diane's phone?"

"I *said* get your teeth brushed and get to bed. *Now.*" And that's why I hadn't called her to begin with. One reason, anyway. To me, she said, "Diane is upstairs with her kids, and when I saw it was you on her phone, I picked it up."

Some Foxes' boundaries were firmer than others. I'd say Louise's were porous. "I'm going to spend the night with Jefferson at his hotel."

Louise drew in a sharp breath. "Alone? Do you think that's wise?"

Jefferson wrinkled his forehead as if trying to understand the question.

That Louise would find me staying unchaperoned in a hotel room with a man—even though I was in my mid-thirties and this obviously was not a romantic tryst—didn't faze me. "Just let Diane know I'll drop off her car in the morning."

"Well," said in that judgmental tone that made me want to slap her, "I'm just glad you weren't on speaker and the boys couldn't hear that." Which must have reminded her of the hellions. "I mean it. You get upstairs."

Jefferson winced. "I hope you aren't too hard on the boys. It was my fault for not stopping them."

She hmphed. "That's honorable of you. I might have been easier on them, but they tried to blame you for them being back there. So, they're going to shovel the Long Branch sidewalk, Olin Riek's driveway, and Beverly's walk for the next seven snowfalls over two inches." Beverly was their neighbor, and Olin Riek was probably a random pick since there were an abundance of elderly folks in Hodgekiss who could use help with shoveling.

As Dad always said, hard work never killed anyone.

Louise bellowed, "Don't make me come up there." I hung up to her next threat.

I spared a few moments on the way from the ER to the hotel to consider valet parking. I knew enough to assume there would be someone there to park Diane's car. No one in the Sandhills ever dealt with valets or a concierge. Where I came from, you took care of yourself. To take it up a notch, I usually did ranch work on my own, so I'd figured out lots of ways to use leverage and work-arounds to get the job done single-handedly.

Logistics of the bougie life aside, I turned my thoughts to the eventful day behind us. The agitators at the stock show and again at Casa Bonita. Missing my chance to meet Brodgar. Seeing Baxter and all the turmoil that created inside me. And finally, the strange attack on Jefferson and who could be behind that.

I pulled into the hotel. A cute twenty-something with long blond braids peeking out of a Four Seasons ski cap opened my door and welcomed me with her clear hazel eyes. She asked our room number, and her eyebrows twitched a bit when Jefferson said we were on the sixteenth floor. I handed her the key fob, and that was that.

We were nearly to the front door when the valet shouted, "Ma'am?"

It took a second before I realized that meant me. Ma'am. Really? I turned to her while Jefferson continued into the hotel, probably not aware I'd stopped. I smiled at the valet when she trotted up to me holding out a gray leather tote. "Did you want your computer? Most people don't like to leave them in the car when it's this cold."

It was late, so I hoped that meant Diane wouldn't need it tonight. I'd drop it off tomorrow. "Thanks."

Anticipating stepping out of the frigid night into a toasty lobby, I let the doors whisper open. But as soon as they spread wide and I focused on a glass-encased fire across the lobby, yet another surprise awaited me.

Jefferson stood by a potted tree, his shoulders drooping in fatigue, maybe pain, the bandage a white flag on his pale face, wearing a weak smile.

In front of him, with her back to me and her unmistakable platinum waves, was Sandi. Her hair hung down her back as she tilted her head to him.

It was well after midnight, and the whole day squeezed in on my head, as if my skull had shrunk or my brain had swollen. I let my boots make a loud thudding across the tiles in the quiet of the lobby.

Sandi jumped and flipped her head toward me. She slapped a palm against her sternum. An area, I was not surprised to notice, that was nothing but bare skin. She'd obviously freshened up after our dinner at Casa Bonita, new makeup, a different outfit sporting a flowing red top with a dipping neckline. With a voice like a squeezy dog toy, she said, "Oh, my goodness. Kate. I didn't know you were here." The *oh-my-goodness* sounded like something she'd picked up in an effort to appear demure, not a phrase that came naturally to her.

"It's pretty late. What are you doing here?" I admit, my tone wasn't the friendliest.

She let out a bubbly burst and said, "What are the chances, huh? I have a room here and, you know, I couldn't sleep. So, I came down to see if there was a snack bar or something, like they have at some places, where I could maybe get some Tylenol PM or something."

Okay. The gift shop had closed hours ago. Sandi was lurking around the corner from the front desk, where they might not notice her. And I strongly doubted she could afford this place.

Jefferson blinked tired eyes. "I'm sorry you're not able to sleep. That's the worst."

I wasn't buying her story, even if Jefferson appeared to. "And did they?"

She gave me a questioning look.

"Have something for insomnia," I said, my voice flat.

She looked a little apprehensive, but she beamed a smile at Jefferson. "No. But I thought I'd pace a little, just to wind down. And surprise! Look who showed up. Like I said, what are the odds we're both staying at the same place?"

My chips were on Sandi finding out where Jefferson was staying, and she'd been avoiding staff and security until he returned. She'd "accidentally" run into him at the stock show, then oddly wrangled an invitation to dinner. And now, at the exact time he'd stumbled home, she happened to be in the lobby. I watched Jefferson, assuming he'd been the object of gold diggers before and he'd recognize the ploy.

Maybe he'd been knocked too hard on the skull. Maybe he was too tired to put it all together. Who knew? He had a distracted, lost look on his face, those killer peepers a bit vacant, and his lips turned up, but not a real smile.

I tugged Jefferson's arm and directed him toward a bank of elevators. "I think you need to rest."

Sandi fell in with us. "It's crazy how you were attacked at Casa Bonita. I'd be happy to come up and keep you company. They always say not to let someone who got hit on the head go to sleep. I'm not tired at all, so I could stop you from falling asleep. That way, Kate could go home."

Not the least bit subtle. "We'll be okay." We stepped into the elevator, and I glanced at the controls. "Jefferson, we need your key card to access the penthouse."

He fumbled in his back pocket and pulled out his wallet, handing me the soggy thing. "It's in there. I can't look for it."

He canted toward the back wall, chin hanging to his chest.

I found the key card, swiped it, tapped sixteen, and looked up.

Sandi stood in front of the closing doors. That perky, elfin face a mask of rage, her green eyes shooting death rays at me.

14

I had been expecting a plush room with classier furniture and art than I was used to in a Holiday Inn Express. But I wasn't ready for the one-bedroom presidential suite. Floor-to-ceiling windows looking over the city and a view of, come sunrise, the front range of the Rocky Mountains.

"I'm sorry," Jefferson mumbled as soon as we shut the door. "I really need to lie down."

I set his wallet and Diane's computer on a hallway table. "Go ahead. I'll come in a few minutes and check to make sure you're breathing."

He plodded through the slate entryway and took a left to what I assumed was the bedroom. Illuminated by the city lights, the suite's living room glowed. A leather sectional faced the windows, with metal-and-glass tables accenting the tasteful area all tied together in grays, beiges, and an occasional black. The suite had more square footage than my cottage on Stryker Lake. And the view from the windows was awe-inspiring. It was so far out of my normal life, I felt like I was in a movie. Who wouldn't love this?

But it didn't have the sound of frogs croaking near the lake. You couldn't wander outside in the summer buck naked and collect dew on your toes as you checked the garden. And if you wanted to compare the winter land-scape, there would be a thick layer of snow, sparkling as seven-minute frosting, with only one trail of a rabbit's triangle prints to mar the surface. The stillness so dense it pressed against your chest.

I wouldn't turn down a weekend in a room like this. But I wasn't built to live locked inside for long, even if there was only a pane of glass between me and the outdoors.

After a time, I pulled myself away from the spectacular view and checked on Jefferson. He was breathing deeply and evenly. All seemed fine. I wandered through the suite, which not only had the spacious living area, but a good-sized kitchen with a refrigerator and oven, and, to my astonishment, a private workout room with a treadmill and some kind of weight machine with pullies and foot presses.

I helped myself to a Pellegrino—pushing past the Sandhiller in me who said tap water was plenty good enough—and made my way back to the living room. A cozy blanket draped over the back of a chair, and I claimed it, shed my boots, and cuddled onto the sectional, watching the twinkle of the city before my eyes dropped closed.

I came to with a cheery light glowing from the windows. I grabbed my phone and was surprised it was after eight. For me, that felt like midday. I should have been grateful we had west-facing windows so the sunrise hadn't attacked me. A rustle from the kitchen made me sit up and squint into the dim suite.

"Good morning," Jefferson fairly sang from the kitchen. He poured Pellegrino from a bottle into a crystal glass as he walked into the living room wearing gym shorts and a Colorado Rockies T-shirt. His legs were long and well toned. In fact, he looked muscular and pretty darned attractive.

I sat up and swung my legs to the floor, swiping the blanket from the couch so he could sit. "You sound perky."

He took a long swallow and set the bottle on a glass end table, hanging on to the crystal tumbler. "I've always been one of those people who don't need a lot of sleep." He slapped his free hand on the top of his head and rubbed, making his hair stand on end, and dabbed at the bandage. He looked wildly handsome, even if I couldn't drum up the enthusiasm Diane would want.

I pulled out the hair elastic, smoothed my rat's nest of brown curls and scraped it back into a ponytail. "How's the head?"

He polished off the rest of his water. "It's sore if I poke it, so..."

"Don't poke it," we said together and laughed.

He indicated my face with his water glass. "How's your chin?"

I ran a finger on the bandage, feeling a little tenderness. "It's fine."

He poured more water. "I ordered room service, and they're sending up a toothbrush for you. I was going to have them deliver something from the dress shop, like yoga pants and fleece or something, but then I thought you might want to pick something out."

The toothbrush was thoughtful. It had been a while since anyone had taken care of me. Considering my mother, my ex-husband, and most of my siblings, the last one to really look after me was probably my oldest sister, Glenda, who passed away ten years ago. "Thanks for your thoughtfulness, but I'll head back to Diane's." I hesitated. "After breakfast. I never got a sopaipilla last night."

As if I'd called the genie into existence, there was a knock at the door, and Jefferson jumped up to answer. A lanky young man in a short-sleeved white shirt that billowed from his skinny torso, and black pants two inches too short, wheeled a cart to the dining table and set dome-covered dishes on the surface. Smells of bacon, maple syrup, fresh bread, all warm and savory, made my stomach sit up and beg.

I stood and stretched, thanked the server, and waited while Jefferson ushered him out.

With a clap of his hands, Jefferson hurried back to the table. "What are you waiting for?"

Surprisingly, after the trip to the penthouse, everything was warm, even the glistening scrambled eggs. The bacon was perfectly cooked without being too crisp. Four kinds of fresh berries, warm croissants, hot coffee and cream.

We loaded our plates. "I didn't know what you liked, so I stuck to the basics. But there's French toast, and I can order a frittata or yogurt or muffins. Whatever."

I spoke around a bite of bacon. "Breakfast for me is usually peanut butter toast or oatmeal, so this is amazing."

He reached for his phone. "I can get you steel-cut oatmeal."

I held up my hand. "This is more than enough. Thank you."

We ate and marveled as the sun highlighted mountains, snow-topped brilliance against sky the blue of Hansford eyes. When I couldn't eat another bite, we took our coffees to the couch.

We'd delayed the discussion long enough. "Aria is worried someone is out to get you." I avoided her theory about his wife.

He winced. "Our Aria. She's so perfect she has no reason to worry about herself, so she's always hovering over me."

He laughed after he said it, but I wondered if it didn't carry a little bitterness. "She might hover, but last night proved she was right. Who do you think was behind it?"

Jefferson scoffed. "It was an accident. He didn't see me standing there, picked up the broom to clean something, and swung it around. And then he panicked and ran out."

I cradled my cup. "That seems unlikely. The twins said he had a gun and was coming for you. Even you said he had a big gun."

He did a double take as if I were nuts. "I said that? I don't remember any gun. I'll bet the twins let their imaginations run wild, and I was so out of it I agreed with them."

"The question is who wants to harm you."

He stared at the mountains with eyes filled with sadness. "I honestly don't know. I've never wanted to hurt anyone. My whole life I've tried to do the right thing."

I supposed most people tried to do what they believed was right. Even Mom, misguided as she was, justified her actions. "Has the right thing done damage to anyone?"

He dropped his head to the side and kept his eyes focused on the mountains. "Depends on your point of view. Blaine doesn't think I'm working hard enough for the company, even though I'm good at being the public face. My wife isn't happy with me because I work long hours and can't spend more time with her. Mother never wanted me to marry Nanette, so I've disappointed her, as well."

That was family, and I knew enough to know family can be more dangerous than anyone. But there might be more. "What about in your capacity as spokesperson for Hansford Meats?"

Jefferson's smile was sad. "I mean, sure. We employ a lot of workers in dangerous and pretty unpleasant jobs. They're paid well and aren't forced labor, but there's always someone not happy with that situation. So, I guess they might see me as the evil one. Then there are vegans who believe the slaughter of animals is murder."

The coffee was so smooth and delicious, I sipped and talked, "Have you ever thought of doing something else?"

He had that adorable childlike manner to him that might make people want to help him out. My brother Jeremy had the same quality. "Oh, yeah. I'd love to run a company of my own. But Mother and Blaine don't think I am capable of that. So they gave me this job they think is fluff. But they don't know the skill it requires. If I left, they'd find out."

The high-altitude sun lit up the mountains, showing the ruggedness that earned them their name. "You only get one life. Seems like you should do what you feel passionate about."

He sipped his coffee. "Yes, but family is important."

Sure. That had been my mantra since I could remember. With my big nuclear family, and being related to most of the county either by blood, marriage, or emotional adoption, my obligations ran deep and wide. "I understand doing what's expected. But sacrificing your career isn't the same as going to baptisms and birthday parties."

He stared at his coffee cup, now only holding a cold sip. His shoulders slumped, and with a far-off look in his eye, he said, "I couldn't abandon Mother. Her whole identity is Hansford Meats. She never took my father's name and insisted Blaine and I be given her last name so we could continue the legacy. If I leave, there won't be anyone around her except Blaine. I'd always hoped Nanette and I could give her grandkids."

Jefferson had some things to work out. Maybe knowing a little about my upbringing would make him feel he could talk to me. "Mom and Dad didn't pay that much attention to us kids. Dad was away working on the railroad a lot. And Mom was probably bipolar. I thought I was fine with that because I knew they loved me. But as I got older, I suspected I needed to deal with my past."

His eyes were on me as I spoke, seeming to take in everything. "You're so close with your sisters. Maybe if you'd had attentive parents, you wouldn't care so much about each other."

Weird how he came up with that after dinner at Casa Bonita when we'd picked at each other, and later the phone call when I'd actually hung up on Louise. "Up until three years ago, I'd have agreed with you. And I do love my brothers and sisters. But we've had some major ups and downs since then."

He focused harder. "Really? What?"

It would take a month of Sundays and too much effort to fill him in on Mom's past and her fleeing the country and the part I played, and how Louise had overreacted and filed a recall against me. And before that, the incident in the Wyoming mountains that resulted in Diane's ex-husband's death. Something I'd also been involved with, and again, not responsible for. Then there was the whole episode of Louise lashing out in a way that crushed Dad, something I had a hard time forgiving. "A lot of misunderstandings. But we're working our way through them."

He stood and reached for my empty cup. "You've got a bunch of siblings, though. I've only got the one. We were close when we were young. Blaine, Aria, and me. To me, Blaine was so smart and cool. Everything I aspired to be. I really miss him."

I wanted to ask what had happened, but I'd opened the door for him, and if he didn't want to tell me more, that was okay. "No one knows us like our brothers and sisters. Not even our parents. I can almost think their thoughts. Maybe that's why I feel so compelled to help them when they need it."

He filled our cups, adding a dollop of cream to mine, just as I'd done earlier. "I'd go to the moon and back for Blaine. But he doesn't want anything to do with me now."

Something about him made me want to reassure him, like I always wanted to do to Hugh Grant in his sweetest roles.

"And now Nanette wants a divorce." He set his cup on the glass table and plopped next to me. "I keep losing all the people I love."

That started me counting. Beginning with my oldest sister, Glenda. Then my divorce, which might seem for the best now but at the time was devastating. Then Mom. I pushed aside thoughts of Baxter. "Divorce is tough."

He rubbed his head again, disrupting his already messy hair and setting it in a new direction. I supposed more women than just Sandi would love to smooth it for him. "Nanette." He sighed. "Aria never liked her. She always thought Nanette only wanted my money. But she didn't know Nanette like I did. So sweet and gentle. She pampered me and made me feel like the only person on the planet."

Maybe the tough part of the divorce was that he didn't want it. He seemed to want to talk, so I asked, "What happened to end things?"

His face hardened as he stared at the mountains. "When Nanette and I got married, Father was still alive, and he enjoyed the glad-handing part of the business. I was mostly in marketing, and that gave me a lot of flexibility. We could travel and go out. We had so much fun. But then Father died, and Mother begged me to take over being the front man, and I got tied down. I don't blame Nanette for wanting someone who could be with her more."

He shifted his gaze to me. "I miss her, though. She loved to dance. Used to drag me onto the floor all the time. Even at home. Nothing felt as good as her in my arms. Now all I've got is Blaine riding me all the time and the stress of trying to keep Mother happy." His hands clenched on his thighs.

"Aria mentioned you have a board meeting tomorrow. Your mother seemed willing to give you some time off. Maybe this would be a good opportunity for you and Nanette to spend some time together, see if you can still work things out."

His jaw tightened. "I hate those things even more than fancy fundraisers. It'll all be over soon, though."

I didn't know what he meant by that, but my heart twisted at the pain in his face. "I've got to meet Aria at the stock show soon. I'd better get to Diane's and clean up before heading there."

He jumped up. "Of course. Give me a minute to shower, and I'll be ready in a flash."

"You're supposed to rest today, remember? I'll drop by to check on you after we see Brodgar."

He was on his way to the bedroom. "I feel fine, and there's a reception for large donors at the stock show. I should be there to represent the company."

I held up my hand. "Oh no. I can't let you do that. Aria would kill me."

He spun around before he got to the bedroom door. "She's got to stop treating me like a child. You don't have to wait for me. I can get a car to the stock show."

I smiled at him. I kind of liked a take-charge Jefferson. I flicked my fingers at him. "Go. I'll wait."

Diane texted to say she didn't need her laptop and that she'd taken a rideshare to work and I was welcome to use her fancy wheels all day. Despite the brilliant sunshine and blue sky, the temps weren't expected to rise above twenty-five, so I loved the heated seats and steering wheel. I was sure great wealth came with its own sled of problems, but it had a few perks I didn't mind.

We didn't spend more than a few minutes at Diane's since it doesn't take me long to get ready. Showered, clean jeans and sweater, warm canvas barn coat and only slightly damp curls—because drying my hair led to uncontrolled frizzies—I joined Jefferson as we entered the Expo Hall. He was headed to a reception area, and I wanted to get to the pens.

Before noon, the aisles weren't too crowded yet. The animal rights activists didn't seem to be lurking; a few rambunctious school groups drifted around wearing their Rams horns. The air smelled like kettle corn with just the light and pleasant whiff of cattle. And maybe I imagined that last bit because I knew underneath this wonderland of commerce, an array of animal pens blossomed. I couldn't wait to get down there and meet Brodgar.

Without giving it any thought, we strolled past the SharpCo booth. Keith stood at the counter engaged with a couple wearing felt cowboy hats and scuffed boots. He glanced up and tapped a finger to his forehead in salute, his eyes resting for a bit on me, his smile deepening. Then he resumed slicing a tomato, keeping up friendly banter with the couple. He seemed shy normally, but could turn on a salesman's charm.

Ray stood at the rear of the booth, arms folded as he watched Keith. It didn't appear that he'd washed his hair since yesterday, and the Ace bandage was still wrapped around his wrist. He spotted us and broke into a smile. "Praise the Almighty, look who's back." He squinted at me, inspecting my chin where I'd removed the bandage. "Glad to see you're healing up." Then he opened his mouth in exaggerated shock when he got a good gander at Jefferson. "But what happened to you?"

I started to say he'd been attacked, but Jefferson spoke over me. "Walked into a shelf."

Keith snapped his head from the customers and inspected Jefferson, an unreadable expression on his face. He glanced at me and quickly transformed into his amiable smile. I couldn't tell what he thought about Jefferson's injury. He turned back to the customers he'd been chatting with and swiped their card in a mobile device, all the while extolling the Manhandler's benefits. He placed several knife boxes into a bag for them.

Ray shook his head in wonder. "I consider myself a good salesman, but the Lord has blessed Keith here with a Midas touch."

Keith's cheeks colored, and his dimples deepened. "My father was in sales. Darned good. He taught me a lot, and I worked my way through college selling a dozen different lines. But my career was accounting and finance."

Jefferson sounded slightly condescending. "I'll bet you killed it there, too. We're always looking for good people in finance. Send me your résumé."

A darkness tinged Keith's face. "Oh, no. I'm retired now."

"Retired?" Ray sounded surprised. "You're so young. What, did you make too much money?"

Keith's friendly expression looked strained. He glanced quickly away from Jefferson. "Something like that."

"Hello, hello!" A zippy greeting made us all turn as Roxy sashayed toward us. And I don't use that term lightly. She wore a bubblegum-pink miniskirt, a black leather bolero jacket with fringe nearly as long as the skirt, white knee-high cowboy boots, and, I kid you not, a pink felt cowboy hat with a tiara on the brim. She held a lidded cup of coffee, the sipping hole rimmed in sparkling pink lipstick. She looked like cotton candy dipped in mud.

Jefferson blinked rapidly as if searching for something to say. Keith looked as if he held back a laugh. But Ray didn't have trouble coming up with something. "You gotta have confidence to pull that off, little lady."

Now, normally I'd want to punch someone calling me a "little lady." And I might take offense to what sounded like an insult about my outfit.

But not Roxy. She struck a pose with her hip thrust out. "My mother always said, it's all about the attitude." She fingered the tiara. "I wondered if this might be over-the-top, but I thought, 'It's the stock show.' Right? And if you can't wear your finest here, where can you?"

The wilds of Borneo? I could only hope.

Before anyone could muster a response, Jefferson took hold of my arm. "We should get to that meet-and-greet or we'll miss out on the best pastries."

While a pastry sounded unappealing after our big breakfast, and making a beeline downstairs was more in my mind, I appreciated Jefferson getting us out of there. "Good seeing you again," I said as we walked away.

Too bad we weren't lucky enough to shake Roxy. Again, she looped her arm around mine like we were third-graders at a picnic. "Marla's booth is this way. You can tell me what happened at Casa Bonita while we walk."

I didn't say anything but attempted to pull my arm free. Which meant Roxy clutched tighter. I could deck her and run away, but that might cause more commotion than I wanted to mess with. Before I changed my mind and balled up my fist for my swing, we reached an area at the end of the Expo Hall where the floor tile had been replaced with fake turf and was surrounded by a log fence. A bar with a neon Coors sign took up the back wall with a buffet of pastries and coffee lining it.

"Here we are," Jefferson said and seemed to morph immediately into everybody's best friend. His smile widened, and he made eye contact with everyone he passed. His posture and movements became vibrant. It had the feel of a cartoon where a beam of starlight hits a character with an angelic *ting* and they transform like magic.

He walked into the opening of the log fence to a group of businessy types, and their greetings crescendoed. "Did everyone here get the Hansford duffel?"

A few people looked confused and shook their heads. Jefferson crooked a finger toward an attractive woman with an official lanyard. "Grace, didn't we get those shipped over?"

The woman looked miffed. "Of course. They're behind the bar." She waved at a few younger people who looked like assistants. They scooted behind the bar and brought out several large cardboard boxes.

People at the reception acted like they do everywhere swag is handed out. They crowded around to get their stock show duffel bags. Honestly, the bags looked like good quality, and since they were oversized, I wouldn't have minded one myself.

Roxy pulled her neck in and widened her eyes in an *are-you-getting-this?* kind of look.

And yeah, I was getting that the little boy had disappeared into this slick captain of industry. How many personalities did Jefferson have bottled inside?

15

Roxy and I stopped outside the log barrier, mesmerized by the way Jefferson seemed to work the crowd. Behind the group growing around Jefferson, Eula and Blaine held white coffee cups and watched.

Eula wore the same pants suit as yesterday, the beige blending with her skin and her gray hair still like a helmet. I wondered if she was like my aunt Hester, who had a stash of money because she'd never spent any. She could afford nice clothes, but couldn't, for the life of her, understand why anyone would waste money on new things when that one Sunday dress of hers worked just fine for all weddings, funerals, and baby showers.

An indulgent smile on Eula's face saved her from looking like a corpse. She thrust her cup at Blaine and walked our way with an attitude that said her task was done.

Blaine only glanced at her before turning his attention back to Jefferson with a slight tick of his nostril, as if smelling something off. I didn't need my undergraduate degree in psychology to figure out Blaine didn't have a soft spot for his brother.

Eula stepped from the reception area into the thoroughfare near Roxy and me on her way out. But she stopped and squinted at me. "You're that friend of Aria's, isn't that right?"

In her laser beam, I felt like Mose and Zeke cornered by Louise. I wondered if I ought to stand at attention, maybe even salute. "I manage her Highland operation."

She flicked her gaze to Roxy and immediately dismissed her. Roxy didn't utter a peep, maybe frozen in fear of this daunting woman.

Eula studied me with a nearly imperceptible nod. "Jefferson told me you stayed with him after the attack last night."

When had he spoken with his mother? Maybe while I was showering. "He insisted he felt rested enough to attend the reception."

Eula's face softened as she located Jefferson laughing with a few people wearing lanyards and looking official. "You wouldn't be able to hold him down if you'd wanted to. My Jefferson works too hard for his own good." She inhaled and focused back on me. "At any rate, thank you for staying with him."

The way the words seemed to have nothing to do with what she was thinking felt disconcerting. I felt like a heifer in the show ring with Eula scoring me on her own set of criteria.

Blaine came up behind me. "If Jefferson had told us he was going to be here, it would have saved us a trip over. Shall we go, Mother?"

Eula didn't take her eyes from me; she had the look of a scientist studying a cell under a microscope. Was she waiting for me to divide? "He never said he wouldn't be here. I wanted to lay eyes on him after his attack and make sure he's fit."

Blaine didn't actually growl, but it looked like he wanted to.

Eula wrapped up whatever internal exam she'd put me through and spun around without another word. She marched off with Blaine a few steps behind.

Roxy exhaled with passion. "Whoa. Who was that?"

It was taking me a second to smooth my bunched nerves. "That was Eula Hansford. Formidable matriarch of Hansford Meats."

Roxy fluffed the curls visible under her pink hat. "I think she likes you. Only I'm not sure that's a good thing."

I took a second to replay the weird exchange when a high-pitched woman's voice, way too cheerful with a mousy squeak, rose from the log fence behind me.

Sandi radiated morning sunshine into the reception area. "Jefferson!

Oh, hi!"

While not as decked out as Roxy, she had her own unique style. Her blond hair was curled and flouncy as it puffed out from what we Foxes called a dumb-shit hat. That would be a bent and fake-worn straw cowboy hat that no self-respecting rancher would even wear to the hayfield. Her jeans were skin-tight and tucked into knee-high cowboy boots that had probably never stepped in mud, let alone manure. No tiara, so I guessed that made Roxy the winner.

A fluffy white scarf with silver sparkles, more stripper boa than winter wear, was pulled tight around her neck but left a wide swath of cleavage exposed. She clapped her hands on her heart, barely padded by a white puffy coat that didn't quite reach her waist and featured a fur collar I figured the animal rights folks would love to deface. She made direct eye contact with Jefferson and waved with the exuberance of those on the *Titanic*'s deck in bon voyage.

He separated himself from the cluster of officials and met her at a space between two sections of log fencing.

She beamed at him. "You look good today."

And out came charming Jefferson, almost shy and embarrassed from the attention.

She widened her shrewd green eyes. "You were white as a ghost last time I saw you. I mean, I couldn't sleep all night, worrying about you."

Roxy folded her arms over her chest, coincidently pushing up her impressive assets. She wore a pouty expression as she watched Sandi work Jefferson. She elbowed me while shooting acid at Sandi with her eyes. "Look at that two-bit parasite. I can't believe Jefferson would fall for that song and dance."

That was a lot of cliché even for Roxy. I bet it bruised her ego for the men in her radius to focus on a younger, arguably cuter, and more vivacious vixen.

I hadn't realized Aria had joined us until she muttered, "Jefferson isn't very discerning, I'm afraid."

Aria was usually so upbeat and positive, the bitterness in her voice surprised me. "I thought we were meeting at the pens," I said.

She scowled at Sandi. "I wanted to drop in on the meet-and-greet to see if Aunt Eula needed help, since I assumed Jefferson would be at his hotel resting." She glared at him and then turned to me with a look that clearly said I should have kept him there. She narrowed her eyes at Sandi. "Looks like someone's going fishing this morning."

Roxy did a tiny stomp of her boot. "That's exactly what I was saying to Kate. Do you want me to go over there and distract Jefferson? Kate can be my wingman."

Aria hadn't taken her eyes off Sandi. "I think I can handle this." She inhaled and straightened her shoulders. Today she wore jeans and hiking boots, a long-sleeved Henley under a heavy down vest. Understated makeup and her hair loose, she looked like she'd stepped from an Eddie Bauer catalogue. My guess was that she rolled out of bed looking like that. No wonder Baxter loved her.

Aria shrugged into an airhead persona and bopped to Jefferson and Sandi. She grabbed Sandi's arm. "Oh my God! I'm so *glad* you came back. The stock show is so big, I was *terrified* we'd never see each other again. And I so wanted to get to know you."

Sandi's mouth dropped open, and she stepped back as if Aria might be contagious.

Jefferson lowered his eyebrows and shot Aria a warning look.

Aria took hold of Sandi's arm. "I just *know* we're going to be friends. Let me buy you a coffee and we can talk."

"But, I..." Sandi started.

Aria flipped her head, sending her hair flying. "Oh, *come on*. I vet all of Jefferson's friends. You can't be too careful." Her giggle hit me like biting into a raisin cookie when you thought it was chocolate chip.

Sandi turned questioning eyes to Jefferson.

He conceded. "She's right."

Aria dragged Sandi away.

Roxy stared after them, her eyes sparkling with admiration. "She's good. You could learn a thing or two from her." Then she slapped her hand over her mouth. "Oh, I forgot. You're not sheriff anymore, so you don't need those kinds of undercover skills."

Thanks for the reminder. Even though that dull thud of failure hit my chest, it was good to remember why I was here at the stock show. I was managing a herd of cattle. Expensive, purebred cattle. Cute cattle with a pedigree.

And we were due to meet the breeder of the bull I wanted. But Aria was gone. Again.

Without warning, Roxy reached out and pulled me in for one of her smothering hugs. "I'm so glad you're not sheriff anymore. It was too hard to support my husband and my best friend at the same time." She let go. "I've got to get to work."

I blew air out my nose, trying to rid myself of her perfume, fearing it might kill brain cells. Which might explain a lot about Roxy.

Jefferson went back to working the crowd, and I didn't want to wait around for Aria to bond with Sandi, so I headed down to the pens to drop off Jeremy's hoodie. And maybe catch a glimpse of Brodgar.

Jeremy was taking a rare break when I found him, leaning against a panel with one foot crossed over his other, tipping back a giant can of Rockstar. "There she is," he said when he saw me. "You look a lot better not covered in mud and blood and shivering like a hairless cat in Siberia. Hey, I heard the twins got you kicked out of Casa Bonita last night."

Since I doubted he'd talked to Louise today, I assumed word spread somehow through Diane to Carly, Carly to Susan, Susan to Jeremy. As in: sister-niece-sister-brother. Or maybe from Diane to Douglas, Douglas to Michael, Michael to Jeremy. As in: sister-brother-twin-brother. It's possible there was some kind of Fox telepathy at play in our family. Which made my point that we knew way too much about the details of each others' lives.

Until we didn't.

Something Mom had proved.

"I hope Louise isn't too hard on—"

Jeremy's eyes riveted to something behind me like an eagle on a mouse. He straightened and slammed his can on a worktable. "Hey!"

I sprang around as Jeremy bounded past me.

"You!" Jeremy shouted on the run.

16

Slipping on some loose hay while he rounded a corner of pens, a guy wearing a ski cap and a puffy parka sprinted away.

I dropped the sweatshirt and took off after them.

The guy wouldn't have realized this, but Jeremy was the most persistent person I knew. He might seem laid-back. Growing up, he often disappeared when chores were handed out. He didn't do well in school and considered having fun a holy pursuit. But, like a good cuttin' horse, when he sighted a target, he wouldn't give up until he held it or he'd broken a bone in the process.

I had no idea why Jeremy was after this guy, but I wanted to be on hand when he brought him down in case Jeremy needed help with anything.

We all slipped out some open barn doors, scrambled through the food trucks and the gathering crowds, and through a maze of pickups with stock trailers. The smell of greasy carnival food, popcorn, and cotton candy curdled in my stomach that was still full from breakfast.

At least today I wore a barn coat against the winter weather that I was sure hadn't hit that twenty-five degree mark they'd promised. A few wispy clouds flawed the sapphire sky, but there was no wind and if you had a protected spot with a southern exposure, and if the temps rose another ten degrees, it'd be downright springlike. There was much to love about high-altitude winter.

This race seemed irritatingly familiar to chasing the thief yesterday, and I was getting danged tired of running after people. This time, though, if anyone had to make a dive into the mud, it could be Jeremy. But it turned out, no one was doomed for the dirt today.

The guy stopped suddenly, threw his arms in the air, and then doubled over, resting his palms on his knees. "I give. I'm not in shape for this."

Jeremy skidded in front of him, hands on his hips, breath puffing in gray clouds. "Who the hell are you?"

The guy hung his head and panted. He held up one hand in a wait-a-minute gesture.

By the time I reached them, the bottoms of my feet were tender from running all out in thin-soled cowboy boots. Next year, I'd train for a marathon and wear running shoes to prepare for the stock show. The heck with trying to look professional.

The guy slowly tilted his head up and peeked at me.

Dang. Recognizing him threw me for a loop. "Keith?"

He slowly straightened. His face glowed red, from running or embarrassment, I couldn't say. "Yeah. Hi."

What the heck? I flipped through a bunch of questions and finally blurted, "You were at Casa Bonita last night, weren't you?"

Keith looked away quickly. "Yeah. I hoped you didn't see me."

No longer even breathing hard, Jeremy gave me an accusing look. "You know this guy?"

Keith looked hopeful and guilty at the same time.

"Not really," I started. "He's—"

Keith interrupted. "We met yesterday. She took off after a thief, and I was...I was just so impressed."

Jeremy spared a testy look for Keith, then turned back to me. "He was sniffing around you yesterday and now today. Do I need to kick his ass?"

There'd been a time not long ago when Jeremy might have supplied any stalker with a tracker and darts to take me out. It felt darned good that he seemed concerned enough to notice Keith yesterday and then go after him today.

Jeremy was tough and fearless and could come out on top with men twice his size. Keith must have figured that out because he paled and looked shaken, and I didn't think it was because of the cold.

"I don't think he's dangerous." I crossed my arms. "But I would like to know why you're following me."

The building blocked the sun, and we felt the true temperature. Keith rubbed his hands together and looked like he'd like to run away. "You are really interesting, and I kind of wanted to know more about you."

This seemed sleazy. "And instead of asking me for a cup of coffee or even getting my phone number, it seemed better to stalk me?"

Keith looked at his feet. "It's dumb, I know. But I didn't mean any harm."

Jeremy slapped his shoulders. "You stand here in your coats and shoot the breeze out here all day if you want. But it's freakin' freezing, and I've got work to do."

My fingers had started to tingle, and my damp hair felt frozen. "Come on, Keith. You can tell me your sad story inside."

Keith backed up. "You know, I'm just going to go. I won't cause you any more trouble. I promise."

Jeremy hesitated. "You gonna be okay?"

I winked at him. "I can handle this. Thanks for being here."

Jeremy shook his head and trotted back to the cattle barn.

"For future reference, next time you want to get to know a woman better, don't be such a freak about it. You seem like a nice enough guy."

Keith suddenly locked eyes with me. "Look, I don't know how else to say this, but I'm not the creepy one here. It's the Hansfords. You really need to get as far away from them as you can."

Shy and weird Keith had seen me with Jefferson. Did that trigger something? "What do you mean?"

Keith turned and strode away, then twisted back around to leave me with one last thought. "I'm warning you."

Keith had been at Casa Bonita last night. I'd seen someone running away, but I couldn't tell if it'd been Keith or not. "Hey, wait."

He glanced over his shoulder, then started to run.

Running? From little ol' me? Though curious to know why, I wasn't feeling like another race through the icy back lots.

And Brodgar was waiting to meet me, so I hurried to the barn to join Aria by the Highland pens. Just inside the cattle barn, I took the opportunity to use the restroom.

A cluster of young women were changing from work clothes to crisp jeans and Western shirts suitable for the show ring. They chattered and laughed, creating a joyful chaos.

They clattered out while I washed my hands and leaned into the mirror to inspect my chin.

Someone appeared directly behind me and, startled, my heart hit high gear. Cigarette smoke clinging to her clothes tainted the air.

"Fancy meeting you here." It was the black-haired woman from Casa Bonita's bathroom.

Taken by surprise, I needed a second to recover. "Are you some kind of bathroom bandit? Who are you?"

She seemed to enjoy my shock and smiled, almost playfully. Today, she wore jeans with tatters in all the right places. No dramatic makeup, just a bit of quiet lipstick. A peacoat and beanie made her look as normal as rain. "Who doesn't love cows?"

I moved to leave, and she reached out to stop me. "Look, I don't mean to scare you or anything. And yeah, I am stalking you. But not to hurt you."

This was weird. Keith had already unsettled me enough. No one likes to think they're being watched. "What do you want?"

A middle-aged woman in a cowboy hat and tall rubber work boots entered the bathroom. She didn't give us any notice and went into a stall.

The black-haired woman considered the stall, as if not wanting to be overheard. "I'm here to warn you. Do you a service. Because no one was there to help me out."

Instead of taking off, as I'd have liked, I waited for her to go on.

She sighed, letting go of some of that tough-bird persona and looking a little sad. "I've seen you hanging around the Hansfords. They're bad news. Them and all the people they associate with."

"Okay, thanks." I scooted out the door before she could stop me.

She followed me and raised her voice. "They're users. They take what they want and then toss away what's left. I don't want to see that happen to a decent person."

The last two days had been too full of drama. And this was nuts. I faced her while a group of people parted around me. "I don't know your game. Maybe you wanted to hook up with Jefferson and he wasn't interested."

She laughed, again, a well of sadness pooling in her eyes. "You have no idea what you're messing with. Get out now, while you still can."

I gave her my back and continued into the cattle barn.

What a strange morning.

Aria stood in front of Craig McNeal's banner, poking at her phone in her palm while stealing glances up the aisle away from me. Everything about her screamed impatience. No furry red cattle were in Craig's pen and no sign of his white hair and dancing gray eyes.

I strode up to Aria and tapped her on the shoulder.

She let out a squeal and jumped. "You scared me!"

We spoke at the same time, some version of "Wait'll you hear this."

I tipped my head to her. "You go first."

She sounded breathless and flushed. "You're not going to believe this. But I got Sandi's real name, and it's not Sandi Peters."

"Back up. How did you get her real name?"

Aria beamed with pride. "I dragged her to a coffee kiosk, all the time telling her how I just knew she and Jefferson would be good together. I laid it on so thick it gave me a canker sore."

"Ew."

She agreed. "When we got to the window and ordered, I made a big deal out of forgetting my wallet in the car."

"She bought that?"

Aria puffed through her nose. "She has an IQ six points higher than pudding. Anyway, she pulled out her card and—you'd have been so proud of me—I knocked into her, and she dropped it. The wallet flapped open."

"And?"

"And I'd already had my phone ready. I leaned over and shoved into her to knock her off balance so she couldn't reach for it."

That almost made me laugh. "You're so devious."

She bounced a little in excitement. "I got a pic of her license, and she had no idea." She shoved her phone at me.

I really was impressed. "Have you thought about applying to the CIA?"

Or maybe talking to Diane and Carly to get in on whatever they had going. *If* they had something going. I tried not to think about it. But it worried me anyway.

I held the phone to my face and read the slightly blurry image. "Janelle Shepherd. California. Huh." The picture showed a plain-looking woman with straggly hair the color of a rotten potato. If I squinted and used my imagination, the photo sort of looked like Sandi.

Aria took back the phone and studied it. "Glenn knows an investigator from when he was looking for your niece. Maybe he can get her to check out this Janelle Shepherd."

I pulled out my own phone and pressed a number. "I can do you one better."

She watched as I waited for the phone to pick up. Then smiled when she heard the greeting through the phone.

"Sheriff." Zoe Cantrel's confident voice made me glad. She'd been appointed sheriff after my recall, the youngest person to ever hold that office. In her mid-twenties and a woman to boot, she'd raised eyebrows and concerns. But it didn't seem like she let any of that daunt her.

After we greeted each other and reported on the cold temperatures in both Nebraska and in Denver, I got down to business. "Do you have time to run a license for me?"

Her throaty laugh came through the line. "You mean between reffing the ongoing battle between Ethel and Betty and hanging out at the junior high basketball game in my uniform to assure the good citizens of Grand County I'm on the job?" Betty and Ethel being Grand County's treasurer and assessor/clerk involved in a forty-year feud.

Yeah, most of the time being sheriff in the Sandhills was a snore. At least, when it didn't mean crime, danger, and murder. "It'll come from Aria Fontaine's phone."

I heard Zoe's grin. "Hanging with the rich and famous, I see."

If I told her about the fundraiser I hadn't yet agreed to attend, she'd get a big laugh. I signed off and sent Sandi's driver's license picture on Aria's phone.

When I handed Aria's phone back, I said, "Where's Craig?"

"I had to postpone until tomorrow." She fiddled with her phone, tapping a rapid message, then looking up at me. She must have read the frustration on my face. "I'm sorry. I still don't have a project manager, and I need to deal with the attorneys."

I understood her busy schedule. Maybe not the level of working on a national and international scale, but obligations are obligations. And I believed my obligation right now was being the best ranch manager I could. That meant building her herd. I quashed my frustration. "I'm available to see Brodgar. It's why I came here."

She frowned at her phone and started typing. "I really want to be there." Then she huffed, swiped a couple of times, held the phone to her face, and started speaking into it. "It's just easier to talk. Can we meet with the environmental minister and see if..." She turned away and walked down the aisle, her head down, seemingly unaware of the cattle, the noise, or our mission.

My phone buzzed with Zoe's message.

This was interesting.

17

While Aria conducted her international business, I followed up on the information Zoe sent.

Several minutes later, Aria finished her call and rushed to me. "I've got to go." She took a few steps, then turned. "Oh. There'll be three dresses delivered to Diane's house this afternoon. Keep the one you want, and someone will pick up the others tomorrow."

Pulled into her orbit, I followed. "I'm not—" I started to speak, but she kept going.

Breathless, she shot out, "I know you didn't say you'd go, but I really need you."

How could I say no?

She walked backward. "Jefferson will need to be at the Brown Palace way early, so it'd be best if you come with Diane. Your name is added to the list, so there won't be a problem getting in." She spun around as if ready to rocket away.

I shouted to stop her. "You'll want to hear this."

She looked over her shoulder, momentarily annoyed, then turned and retraced her steps.

"Janelle Shepherd. She's got a rap sheet. A lot of small stuff. Bad checks, shoplifting, outstanding parking tickets."

Aria narrowed her eyes. "I knew she was sketchy."

"There's more. There's a restraining order against her, filed by Jennings Moore."

Aria frowned. "Is that the rapper?"

I laughed. Not because I knew better, since I'd had to look him up while I waited for Aria to get off the phone, but because, apparently, she was no more a country music fan than I was. "He's an up-and-coming country singer. Got a reputation as a tough guy, womanizer type."

I held up my phone. "Here's a picture of Sandi when she was Reena Starr." Maybe Sandi was trying for something to make people think of Reba. If so, it didn't work, since there was no hint of red hair, which seemed like a missed opportunity.

Aria took my phone. Her eyes widened and her mouth opened in the same astonishment I'd felt. "Holy mother. Is she even the same person? She doesn't look anything like Sandi. Or Janelle Shepherd."

I took the phone back and studied the woman with piles of curly hair and stage makeup so thick she'd look odd even on TV news. She was shielding her face in a photo of her emerging from a courthouse where she'd just been convicted of assault. "I scanned through some articles. Given they were celebrity gossip mostly, the general gist is that Reena Starr drugged Jennings Moore with ketamine, but it wasn't enough to knock him out. She claimed he came after her and she hit him with a baseball bat in self-defense. Apparently, he was convincing, because they issued the restraining order."

Her glance skidded over the light-colored Highlands in the next pen, but I doubt she noticed them. "Sandi was at Casa Bonita last night, wasn't she? Do you think she had something to do with the attack?"

I'd seen her in the bathroom, but then she'd disappeared. She'd have time to follow Jefferson into the back room. But was she strong enough to smack him with a gun and send him into the pool?

Aria's forehead crinkled, and I thought of Grandma Ardith cautioning us to not do that or we'd encourage wrinkles. "Can you hang out with Jefferson? When I left Sandi, she said she was heading back to her hotel, but I don't trust she didn't go back to the reception."

That's not what I'd come to the stock show to do, but... "Sure. But what do you think she'd do to him? Even if she is a bloodsucker, she's not going to kill him before she gets his money."

Aria tensed at me mentioning murder, then seemed to understand my exaggeration and relaxed a little. "You're right."

Aria thought for a moment, and her phone buzzed in her hand. She glanced at the screen and frowned. Seeming somewhat distracted, she said, "Anyone could have attacked Jefferson last night. Maybe those deranged animal rights people. Maybe Nanette or someone she hired."

"The whole incident is so strange and couldn't have been plotted for long. It seems like it would be a lone wolf kind of thing." Then I remembered who else was at Casa Bonita. "I need to tell you something else."

Her face looked tight with stress, and I didn't know if it was the desalination plant, the fundraiser she was organizing as a favor to Jefferson, or the attack on him. "Keith was at Casa Bonita last night, too."

She didn't seem to register that and went on with her own thought. "I wonder if Blaine has something to do with it."

"Do you really think Blaine would go after his own brother?" Not that I hadn't caught hostility when Blaine was around Jefferson. And though I couldn't imagine wanting to hurt any of my siblings—well, not much, anyway—I understood sibling rivalry went back as far as Cain and Abel, probably farther.

Tension rolled off her like heat waves on the desert. It was unusual for Aria, who seemed to deal with crises as easily as sipping tea. "I don't know. All I can tell you is that when we were growing up, Blaine was always the one who bailed us out of trouble. We wrecked Uncle Wendel's speedboat when we took it joyriding. We must have been about twelve. Blaine bought a replacement and had it delivered, and Uncle Wendel never knew. He bailed Jefferson out of jail for Minor in Possession and hired a lawyer. Don't ask me how that all got solved without going to court or notifying Aunt Eula. I imagine Blaine paid off someone. He used to take us for ice cream and movies and the water park. I adored him."

"Then what happened?"

"When Jefferson came back from Stanford, it all fell apart between them. I'm not saying Jefferson didn't have some blame, but Blaine always gets way too offended." She tsked. "He's always been his mother's son."

She paused to read another message on her phone, clearly unhappy with it. It took a second for her to pick up the thread. "I think he's always been jealous because he thinks Jefferson is Aunt Eula's favorite. Which he is, but it doesn't matter, because she's a cold, hard bitch who doesn't love anyone very much."

Her phone buzzed. Before she could read it, the buzz sounded again. And again. She read a text. "No," she mumbled, and her thumbs started flying.

"I'll check on Jefferson."

She nodded, focused on her phone. "Thanks. I've got to talk to my attorney before he signs some documents. Damn, I need to find someone. And then I need to see what's happening with the fundraiser."

Aria bustled away.

Brodgar now only a dream, I trudged back upstairs to the Expo Hall. But as I reached for the doors, I snatched my hand back.

18

What would it hurt to take a peek at Brodgar? I mean, Jefferson was safe at the reception, surrounded by a ton of people. Sure, maybe Arlo and Gwen would show up again. We already knew Sandi was out and about, but I wasn't too concerned about her. And Blaine or Keith wouldn't attack Jefferson in plain sight.

The loudspeakers blasted country music, and the roar of generators and fans from the food vendors filled the air, along with all the usual festival smells.

I jostled a few people who'd closed in behind me and hopped back down the metal stairs. The smell of savory brats hit my stomach and brought an immediate shout of hunger. Since breakfast had been hours ago and who knew when I'd get dinner... Dang. That reminded me I'd be attending the fundraiser. Drat and double drat.

Ritzy and gourmet or not, the banquet would be a long time away. I got into the brats line, hoping it moved quickly so I could hurry down to see Brodgar and get back to check on Jefferson. If all went well, maybe I'd have time to visit with a few other Highland breeders before I needed to be at Diane's to prepare for tonight's shindig.

Making plans while my mouth watered anticipating the warm brats with lots of mustard, my gaze wandered the crowd, not taking note of much. Until suddenly, I rocked to full attention.

Thinking I might not be seeing what I thought I was, I narrowed my eyes and leaned around the people in front of me. Nope, I wasn't mistaken.

Keith stood almost hidden by a cotton-candy truck. Mostly his back was to me, but from the side of his face, I recognized his neat appearance and ski coat. What surprised me was who stood in front of him, her face only partially visible from behind a group waiting for cotton candy.

Sandi Peters. Or Janelle Shepherd. Or, if you will, Reena Starr. And she looked steamed. In her white coat, her red face glowed as she spewed words fast and forceful.

Keith frowned and shook his head.

"What'll it be?" A man's voice shot out at me.

Startled, I realized I'd made it to the food truck window. "One spicy brat with cheese." I handed over my card and glanced back at the cotton candy truck to check on Keith and Sandi.

Sandi strode across the food court, flipping her hair over her shoulder.

Keith followed her with his eyes, a worried look on his face.

The guy in the brats truck thrust my food and card at me, and I fumbled to get hold of both without dropping either to the freezing concrete. When I succeeded in the juggling act, I looked up to see both Sandi and Keith had disappeared.

Maybe Keith had come out for a bite and run into her. She'd asked about Jefferson, and he'd told her to back off. Or something like that. Maybe I'd circle by the SharpCo booth and see if Keith was still helping out. But first, Brodgar.

I had a pretty good idea where the Highlands were located in the stock-yards on the other side of the railroad tracks. I pocketed my food and was lucky enough to grab a gold cart headed in that direction. It took us through an underpass to the outer limits of the show.

New construction marked this section of the complex. Lots of new roads and multistory buildings. The stockyards covered several acres with row after row of steel-paneled pens lined in straw. Some pens contained basic structures with three sides and a narrow roof to offer a bit of shade or shelter from storms. Only serious livestock people ventured to this area that was like walking through a feedlot, except with purebred, pampered animals.

I hoofed it between the rows of pens, grateful for the strong sun, even if the air stayed cold. My plan was to have lunch with Brodgar. A little bubble of excitement filtered through me.

I congratulated myself on my stock show knowledge as I maneuvered right to the Highland section, all those furry, horned animals in their element in the cold. It didn't take much wandering until I found the pens labeled with Craig McNeal's logo.

I stopped, my heart taking a little leap. Not the rollercoaster drop you get when you see your true love, I wasn't a complete lunatic. But that feeling when you meet someone and you know you're going to be friends. Like I'd felt when I met Aria.

Brodgar's pen wasn't marked with his name. But I knew him from the glint in his eye when he swung his massive head around and studied me.

"Nice to finally meet you, big fella," I said.

He watched me as I pulled my brat from my pocket and unwrapped it. The meat hadn't cooled all the way, and the first bite exploded with spice and creamy cheese. My stomach let out a cheer of ecstasy. No zillion-dollar-a-plate dinner would rival this satisfaction.

I spoke around the bite. "I think you're gonna love the Sandhills. And wait'll you meet Fiona and the girls."

"Ey, lass, you best be careful or you'll be gettin' 'im all worked up." Craig's brogue was unmistakable.

I hadn't heard him come up behind me. Sheepish at being caught talking to a bull, I turned slowly, still chewing an oversized bite. I nearly choked when I saw the last thing I'd expected.

Craig's gray eyes twinkled, making his white hair seem like clouds. Behind him, a face wiped as clean of emotion as if someone had erased it, stood Baxter, eyes on me.

"*Omph.*" That was my response as I tried to swallow the lump of charcoal my delicious brat had somehow turned into.

Craig seemed amused as he peered from me to Baxter. He leaned on the steel-paneled fence and clicked his tongue to Brodgar. "Get over here, ya beastie. Say hiya to the lass."

With lumbering steps on thick, if short, legs, Brodgar made his way over to Craig.

I wadded up the wrapper around the remainder of my brat and shoved it in my pocket.

Baxter, dressed in jeans, a thick down coat, and a knit cap, looked outdoorsy and comfortable, not at all the rich executive he'd been last night dressed for dinner with Aria.

I tried to sound casual, but to say I was shocked would be like calling a whale a guppy. "What are you doing here?"

Baxter made a point of looking at the pocket where I'd stashed my brat. "Unlike you, I didn't have a lunch date, but I wanted to see this bull you're so keen on." Then he added, "You and Aria."

He came here on his own because he was interested in what fascinated Aria. That twisted a knife a little deeper.

"You didn't wait for Aria? You know it's going to bug her we met Brodgar without her." I'd thought about not mentioning I'd been here, but now that Baxter saw me, it wouldn't be right for us to keep a secret from her.

As far as I could tell, Baxter hadn't even glanced at the bull. His face relaxed, and he smiled at me, an expression I missed. Every. Single. Day. "I've got to get back to Chicago tomorrow, so I thought I'd better get here while I can."

By now, Brodgar stood at the fence, and Craig spoke to him with an accent so thick I couldn't understand him.

I stepped close to Craig and reached between the bars to scratch that place between the long horns. Brodgar closed his eyes and leaned into my hand.

"Would ya look at tha'? He likes ya."

Baxter moved close but didn't reach over the fence. "He's got good taste."

Craig winked at Baxter. "He does at tha'." He backed away. "I gotta git back to the barn. Enjoy yer young selves, now." He hurried down the path between pens.

I continued to rub Brodgar's head. "He's a beauty. I hope Aria gets a chance to see him so we can make an offer before Craig sells him to someone else."

With my attention on Brodgar, I didn't see Baxter's face, but he sounded annoyed. "She's got this desalination plant she's working on, and I'm kind of worried about it. She's got superpowers to multitask, but I'm concerned she's lost perspective about this one."

I wondered if I could help Aria somehow. "What's so different about this?"

He let out a breath, and I glanced up to see him scowl. "She's trying to work with some environmental restrictions that don't make sense. But laws are laws. If she can't get around them legally, she won't be able to go forward, and she's already invested a lot."

"It raises my blood pressure to even think about it. I'd rather worry about blizzards and drought." I couldn't help but admire Brodgar's shag of hair over his eyes that made him look as rogue as the Beatles must have seemed way back when. His forehead barely made it as high as Baxter's chest, but his horns swooped up and ended in sharp points that would make an attacking coyote take notice.

Baxter ventured a hand over the fence to rub Brodgar. "He *is* a hand-some fellow."

We stood like that, petting the bull, who seemed more like an oversized teddy bear than breeding stock. It went on for long enough to be awkward, but I didn't want to be the first to stop. With Brodgar there, I had an excuse to be close to Baxter, to imagine the heat of his body, smell his mix of cologne and skin.

"Aria said you're teaching her to rope." It sounded like he was trying to bring Aria into the conversation.

I laughed. "As you'd expect, she's a natural. All I've done is help her to be patient."

He spoke to Brodgar's head, sounding tolerant. "Patience and Aria don't mix. She tells me that while she's swinging the rope, you're some kind of Roping Whisperer." He spoke in falsetto in a bad imitation of me. "Wait. Don't rush. Let the world slow. Focus on the foot."

I couldn't help my belly laugh. "I don't sound like that."

I heard the grin in his voice. "She also says she's teaching you to tie knots."

"Yeah. That's my weakness."

And then our hands touched on Brodgar's forehead. We both jerked back as if burned.

Blood pulsed into my brain and my ears roared for a second, as if a bomb had exploded. I spun around. "I've got to go. I promised Aria I'd check up on Jefferson."

"Kate," Baxter said. Something heavy hung in that one word, and I couldn't stand to hear it. I struggled to maintain dignity as I forced myself to walk away. Maybe I didn't run, but it wasn't because I didn't want to.

19

Aria was my friend. For me, that was as good as family. That meant I'd do anything to protect or help her. And that meant I should not, could not, would not remain in love with Baxter. Starting immediately.

Even I knew it wouldn't be that easy. But all I could do for now was hide and deny and shove any thought of Baxter far back into the recesses of my brain. Then I'd pray any clinging tendrils around my heart would dry up like tomato vines in October and fall away.

Not really knowing how I got from the cattle pens to the Expo Hall, I found myself heading to the reception area where Jefferson had handed out the cool duffels. While the attendance had doubled since I'd been there earlier, I saw no sign of Jefferson. I recognized a few stock show officials from earlier. Most of them were engaged with who I assumed were big donors or potential donors. I zeroed in on a woman who'd seemed particularly attentive to Jefferson earlier.

Probably in her forties, she wore a tailored black blazer over a silky shirt and jeans that fit snug over her slender frame. Her dark hair was secured in a Montana Silversmith clip in a low ponytail. She looked up from her conversation when I approached and offered a polite, if curious, smile. She didn't recognize me, of course, but probably didn't want to be rude if I ended up having a bucket of money I wanted to donate to the stock show.

There didn't seem to be any reason to explain myself, so I simply said, "I'm looking for Jefferson Hansford. He said to meet him here, but I don't see him."

All the welcome slid off her face. "This is not a pickup bar."

Oh. Wow. That came at me hard and fast. My sheriff tough came out blazing. "If you know where he is, I'd appreciate your cooperation. This is a serious matter." At least, it was serious to Aria. And that made it serious to me.

She considered me for a second and then accepted what I said. She rolled her eyes. "Excuse me if I thought you were another hustler. Doesn't matter if you are. He's already been taken."

"Taken?" The word alarmed me.

She huffed in disgust. "He left with some pip-squeak blonde."

Whoa. That's how I'd describe Sandi. Aria wouldn't be happy about this. "How long ago?"

She shrugged. "I don't know. Maybe an hour."

I'd seen her at the food court not long before that. "Did he say where they were going?"

A knowing chuckle was followed with, "I'll give you three guesses, and you're a fool if you don't think all three involve a bed."

This didn't sound good. I thanked the woman and, in just short of a gallop, headed back into the bright but freezing afternoon to Diane's Mercedes and its heated seats and steering wheel. Since Jefferson would call a driver to pick them up at the stock show and take them to The Four Seasons, they'd get a sizable jump on me. I'd need to head out to the north forty parking lot. I couldn't wait for a shuttle, so additional running along cold pavement in cowboy boots for me. I definitely needed more appropriate footwear next year.

Since I didn't have Aria or Jefferson to sync up my phone with Diane's car, I navigated to The Four Seasons parking lot the old-fashioned way, hearing Ms. GPS speak from my phone in the cupholder. I parked in the second row from the building and shot from the car, my focus on those big glass doors and the heat I knew was on the other side.

A massive, shiny black limousine glided into the lot, stopping between me and the front door as if I didn't exist. Good thing my brakes worked better than that monstrosity's seemed to.

Before the precious cargo could exit the wheeled yacht, the front doors of the hotel slid open. I couldn't believe who I saw running from the lobby into the parking lot.

Clutching her white puffy coat to her chest, Sandi raced outside. Either her mascara had smeared, or she was sporting a bruised eye, or maybe both. Her mouth was open, eyes wild, blond hair in a tangle. She looked around in a panic.

"Sandi!" I called her.

She didn't seem to hear me or maybe wasn't used to that name.

The people in the limo started to tumble into the parking lot. There seemed too many for the vehicle, and they were too drunk or high for this early in the day.

"Hey, Sandi!" Some of them picked up the call, laughing and waving their hands.

A small white car roared into the lot behind the limo. It was one of those nondescript vehicles that looked like a billion others. Toyota, Hyundai, Chevy, whatever. A dirty, beat-up compact with tires the circumference of a large pizza, it slid to a halt, and Sandi, Reena, or Janelle ran to it, jumping inside. It took off before she'd even closed the door.

The party folks thought it was hysterical. They laughed and shouted, and one of them shot a hand out and banged on the roof of the white car as it sped away.

Sun glared on the windshield and driver's window, and I was too far away to see the driver.

At least two of the partiers weren't interested in hooting it up in the cold. They hurried into the open doors of the lobby.

I skirted the limo and dashed after the smart ones, hoping they had a key card to get me into the elevator.

Sure, I could stop at the desk and try to explain my fears. Describe Sandi and her alarming exit. Beg for a card to access Jefferson's room. But they had rules and protocols for the protection of their guests, and I—or more importantly, Jefferson—didn't have time for that.

I slipped into the elevator with two partiers from the limo before the doors closed.

The couple, probably in their mid-thirties, dressed in Western clothes, seemed uninterested in me. They kept up their conversation. "I'm so over that bull crap," she said.

The man answered, "I told you we should have taken our own car."

The woman turned to me. "What floor?"

I glanced at the panel and chose their floor. "Eleven." That settled, they turned back to their own business and ignored me. I had to agree with them that their choice of companions wasn't the best.

When the doors opened, I jumped out, eliciting an annoyed grunt from the woman. I located the emergency sign and entered the stairwell. Taking two stairs at a time, I lunged up the next three floors, my boots echoing against the walls. I didn't know how I'd get from the stairwell to the sixteenth floor, but maybe it'd be like the door at Casa Bonita and mistakenly left unlocked.

But I was even luckier. Someone from housekeeping was taking a break. A young Latina sagged on the steps, looking wrung out. Her folded arms rested on her knees, and she'd laid her head down. I apparently woke her up as I clattered up to her. She was startled and looked frightened to see me there. I hated to use that against her, but I thought maybe she was taking an unauthorized break and wouldn't want to get caught.

"I lost my key card," I said. "Can you let me onto the sixteenth floor?"

She concentrated on my words. Then in a thick accent said, "Floor *dieciséis*?"

I tried not to show my anxiety. I didn't want to scare her, just get her to think helping me onto the floor might be better for her than making me get a new card downstairs.

Luckily, I must have had that authentic air that Aria laughed at, because the woman offered a tired smile and led me the one flight to the penthouse floor. She slid her card, and the door clicked.

I banged the bar, pushing the door open, thanked her, and walked slowly down the hall until the door clanked closed behind me, then I shifted to turbo mode and raced to Jefferson's room, my heart pounding.

I caught another break at Jefferson's door. Sandi had obviously left in a hurry, because that fluffy scarf was wedged in the door just enough it hadn't shut all the way. Shoving the door open, I barreled into the suite. The afternoon sun blaring through the windows nearly blinded me. "Jefferson," I shouted, lunging into the living room.

Squinting against the blasting sunshine, I searched the living room. Jefferson wasn't there, and I bounded down the short hall to the bedroom.

"Jefferson!"

He lay on his back on the floor, no shirt or pants, just navy blue briefs that looked skimpy compared to his legs that shot from his torso like runways. A smattering of dark hair sprouted on his muscular chest. His eyes closed, his face nearly as white as the bandage on his forehead.

20

Rapid and light breath told me he wasn't dead. I knelt by him and patted his face. "Jefferson. Can you hear me?"

He didn't move, made no signs of waking up. I grabbed the bedside phone and jabbed the 0 for the front desk. "Call 9-1-1. We have a medical emergency in room 1602."

I kept up steady reassurances to Jefferson, even though there was no indication he heard me. There was no blood that I could see and no visible injuries.

In a few minutes, hotel security crowded the room, making sure no one removed evidence and basically trying to cover their butts and being official before the real cops arrived.

While I sat with Jefferson, I studied the room. The white comforter had been shucked from the bed and the sheets were mussed, pillows strewn everywhere. It could have been a struggle or sex, or maybe housekeeping hadn't made it to the penthouse yet and Jefferson was a restless sleeper.

It seemed like forever before the emergency team arrived, though my phone told me it was less than ten minutes.

The EMT asking me for details, though I had few, said he thought it was some kind of drug overdose. Aside from Aria mentioning Jefferson's minor drug charge as a young man, she hadn't said anything about drugs. I'd ask her later. But from Sandi's panicked exit, I figured she had a few answers.

When I found out the hospital they were taking him to, I called Aria. Even though I assured her Jefferson seemed stable and we wouldn't be able to see him until he was examined by the ER doctors, I could tell Aria was already on her way out the door.

After giving the security team my contact information and all I knew, I left for the hospital. I hadn't known Jefferson for much more than twenty-four hours, and he'd already visited the ER twice.

Aria arrived about the same time I did, and we ran from the parking lot. I stood with Aria as she filled out patient information and answered all the intake questions needed, then we were pointed to the waiting room and left on our own for over an hour.

Aria paced, worry creating lines on her face I'd never seen before.

When I asked if we should call Eula or try to track down Nanette, I was met with a death stare that said I'd better not even think about it.

I felt like I'd grown barnacles and aged a decade before a uniformed cop walked in. She carried a phone and came over when she spotted us.

After we'd identified ourselves, she said she was with the Denver PD. "They called us as routine. They do that when someone's been drugged."

Aria drew in a breath, her eyes registering confusion. "Like a date-rape drug? A roofie or ketamine? Why would someone do that?"

The cop, a pretty young woman with thick black hair pulled into a tight ponytail, typed into her phone and said, "That's what I'm asking you."

Aria's phone buzzed, and she ignored it. "There's a woman going by the name of Sandi Peters. She was with him. She was named Reena Starr before that. But her real name is Janelle Shepherd. From California."

The cop typed quickly. "Can you slow down?"

I added, "She'll send you the driver's license. But I'm not sure Sandi is the one who drugged Jefferson. She looked like someone had attacked her, too. And she was scared."

The cop studied me. "You're the one who found him, right? Did you see this Janelle person?"

I told the cop everything while Aria AirDropped the license photo to her.

"Do you think you can find Sandi Peters? Even if she wasn't the one who drugged him, she should know something," Aria asked.

The cop shoved her phone into her breast pocket. "Honestly, this isn't much to go on. These cases are hard to solve. We'll do our best."

A nurse passed the cop in the doorway. "He's in his room now. But he probably won't wake up for six to ten hours."

"Are you kidding me?" Aria barked at the nurse. "Can't you give him something to bring him out of it?"

I put a hand on Aria's arm to calm her down, and she flicked her gaze to me. A glint of rage in her green eyes dulled, and she covered my hand with her cool one. She turned to the nurse. "I'm sorry. It's not your fault."

The nurse didn't acknowledge the apology, but then, she hadn't ruffled up at Aria's attack. I admired her steady attitude. "He'll sleep this off and probably be pretty out of it for a couple of days. Maybe depressed. If there aren't any complications, he'll be released tomorrow." She gave us the room number and left, probably a thousand things to attend to.

Aria's phone buzzed again. She scowled, pulled it out of her coat pocket, and held it to her ear. Although her cheeks blazed with what I assumed was impatience, she sounded firm and calm. "Look, you're going to have to do your best. Jefferson isn't going to make it tonight, so I've got to work up some remarks. Whatever you decide, I'm sure it'll be fine."

After she'd stuffed her phone back in her pocket, she grabbed my hand. She squeezed it tightly as we walked from the waiting room to the elevator.

Aside from a boyfriend or two in my teens, or when I was very young, I couldn't remember another time someone walked with my hand in theirs. Ted and I hadn't held hands much, and seeing how he and Roxy were often attached in public, maybe that was another reason he preferred her over me. Taking Aria's hand felt strange but not entirely wrong, as if we were refueling each other.

Aria went to Jefferson's bedside and leaned into him on the mattress. "I know you don't like charity events, but this is an extreme way to get out of making your damned speech."

When he showed no response, her eyes teared up.

"I can stay with him," I said, hoping that would make her feel better.

She dabbed at her eyes. "Oh, no. He'll be safe here in the hospital. It's not like this is one of those thriller movies where people sneak in and suffocate victims." She sniffed.

This wouldn't have been my choice of how to get out of the gala, but I wasn't against seizing the opportunity. "I don't mind. And it would stop you from worrying."

She seemed to gather herself, her beauty replacing her tension like someone had used an invisible eraser to eliminate stress on her face. Roxy would be desperate to know how Aria accomplished that. "I really need you there. Especially now that someone has attacked Jefferson again."

She sounded like she had more in mind than me enjoying a free cocktail. That made me more nervous than a parakeet at a cat convention.

She seemed to warm to her idea. "Ask questions. People love you and will open up. See if you can figure out who did this."

I held up my hand to stop her. "Nuh-uh. No way. Whoever is after Jefferson isn't going to suddenly confess at a party."

She focused her intelligent eyes on me. "Someone is targeting Jefferson. Maybe trying to kill him. And my guess is that it's all about money."

Maybe. There were other reasons to kill someone. Love, for instance. Or a sense of justice. "Maybe it's Gwen and Arlo who want to stop him from destroying the Earth."

She drew back in disbelief. "Why would they do that?"

I was reaching here. "Like anti-abortion protesters murdering doctors."

She scoffed at that. "I think I saw Nanette yesterday. Blaine is like a bomb whose fuse has been lit, and we know Sandi is after Jefferson's money. Maybe we can smoke someone out tonight and they'll make a mistake."

It wasn't going to work. "No one is going to tell me anything revealing. I'm not one of them, and they'll know it."

This made her laugh. "You need to stop selling yourself short, my friend. And when you see your transformation tonight, I want you to radiate confidence. They'll all believe you're a queen."

I stumbled on something she said. "Transformation?"

That mischievous glint in her eyes told me I was in for trouble. "I've hired a makeup and hair person for you and Diane." She pulled out her phone. "And you'd better hurry, because they're going to be there in an hour and you need to be showered and ready for them."

I wondered if whoever drugged Jefferson had a spare dose for me.

21

Diane was already home when I arrived, and I was grateful for her input. Aria had sent a black dress with long sleeves and a plunging back, an off-the-shoulder champagne-colored gown that bubbled with elegance if you didn't count the exposed side-boob, and a red strappy number with so little fabric it screamed hypothermia. While Diane urged me to go with the red, I think she approved when I chose the black. It was the most conservative, but even then, it revealed more than I thought it needed to.

Diane wore a silver chemise with layers of fringe that shimmered when she moved.

Ensconced in Diane's luxurious master suite, every bit as impressive as The Four Seasons, with thick cream-colored carpet and a sitting room with the most comfortable arm chairs near a fireplace. Her walk-in closet featured a three-sided mirror and a collection of smaller built-in closets the installer probably displayed in their brochures. Hard to believe all of that Dianeness began in our crowded upstairs bedroom with a sink and toilet with no door.

Marta, Diane's live-in nanny, supervised Kimmy and Karl completing their homework in the study. I mean, a study? No one in the Sandhills had a study.

We were both happy with the hair and makeup people who arrived in time to give us both "manis and pedis," as Diane said.

While being pampered and coiffed could have felt luxurious and been a whole lot of girl fun, I couldn't lean into it. Which seemed okay with Diane, since she kept up a constant text exchange. She didn't comment on her messaging, but from the concentrated look on her face, I figured it was serious.

I stewed about Jefferson and who might be out to get him. If Diane had been less distracted, I would have run it past her. But I knew better than to interrupt. From the time we were little, Diane hatched plans and schemes. She'd let Glenda and Louise battle over clothes or who used the car they all shared, and when they weren't looking, she swooped in and took the best of everything.

While black sheep were familiar in most families, Diane was the golden fleece in ours. She never wanted to stay in Nebraska and had set herself on a path for success from the first. She didn't run for student body president or want to date the most popular guy. She started investing in the stock market as a teen, first with money from summers in the hayfield and county fair premiums she'd saved forever. As her earnings compounded, she'd made better investments. Her financial worth now was anyone's guess.

Never one to fritter away her hard-earned money, she'd nevertheless surprise us with generosity when we needed it. If one of our brothers or sisters wanted a short-term loan, or a bump to buy some frivolous thing, they'd usually ask me, knowing I had a hard time saying no, and that Diane would need a business plan and spreadsheets before she coughed up a dime. More than any of us, Diane had an iron shell around her. I'd seen her vulnerable only once, and it had ripped us apart. I'm not sure we'd have ever found our way back if we hadn't been forced to come together over Mom's troubles.

Diane strapped on silver sandals with spiked heels and gave herself an inspection in the full-length mirror of her bedroom. She dabbed at the makeup in the corner of her left eye and smoothed a strand of her updo.

"You look gorgeous," I said, pulling the back strap of my sandal over my heel, grateful the shopper had opted for kitten heels. Aria probably considered my inexperience with heels. I might not look as elegant as my sister, who seemed to glide along as if skating on smooth ice instead of balancing on stilts, but I'd be a lot more comfortable.

I stood beside her, my hair piled in a complicated weave of braids with tiny hints of rhinestones here and there. I fingered the diamond pendant Diane had loaned me and smiled in wonder. It sounded childish when I said, "I feel kind of pretty."

Diane slapped my shoulder. "What the hell is wrong with you? You're a stone-cold fox. Damn it, Kate. Embrace your inner diva for once."

I stared at myself, the skillful makeup that made my eyes look bigger, my cheekbones more pronounced, any hint of fatigue erased. "It's not the real me. Like a kid playing dress-up."

Diane skimmed across the plush carpet to her closet that was bigger than my living room. "We're all playing dress-up every day. I've got corporate outfits. You've got cowboy clothes. It's fun to switch up the costumes and play new games."

I watched myself swish to the right and then the left, the dress clinging to all my curves in a way I admired. "Feels kind of artificial."

She yanked out a drawer and sorted through evening bags, selecting a black velvet pouch for me and a silver clutch for herself. "Not artificial. Enhanced."

Before the car arrived—to my surprise, a regular Lyft and not a limousine—Diane gave the nanny and Kimmy and Karl their evening directives. Kids kissed good night, doors locked, seated comfortably in the back of a Subaru Outback, Diane pulled out her phone and resumed the rapid texting while I stared at block after block of commerce that seemed to repeat itself every couple of miles, another Home Depot, Target, convenience store, King Sooper. Every fast-food franchise on repeat as we made our way from her tony suburb to downtown and the legendary Brown Palace.

The history of the hotel is long and storied. Taking a place of prominence in downtown Denver, it was built in the late 1800s by entrepreneur Henry Cordes Brown, and not named for the Unsinkable Molly Brown, as my ex, Ted, always claimed. I knew it as the swanky place where the big-deal cattlemen met. Diane had taken Mom and the sisters for high tea in the atrium after she'd got her first big promotion. That's where I'd read the history of the hotel that had a triangular structure—it'd be called a flatiron building if it were in New York. Built of red granite blocks, it had been a true palace when Denver was a wild frontier threshold.

I'd been in high school when we'd enjoyed the high tea and remembered feeling awkward in a borrowed dress and shoes—kind of like now— and yet being excited to sit in that posh, fancy place, eating delicate sandwiches and pastries and drinking tea.

As our driver approached the elegant entryway at the Brown Palace, my stomach sank. I glanced at Diane's white fox coat. "You might want to turn that inside out."

Diane pulled her nose from her phone and scowled out the window at the small band of protesters waving their animal rights signs. Although a charity event for a children's disease shouldn't attract them, I was sure they zeroed in on this place because the stock show elite would be here this time of year. "The hell I will," Diane growled.

Since I'd opted to borrow a black wool coat, I jumped out first so I could run interference. When Diane unfurled from the back of the Subaru, her attitude and sophistication seemed to rivet the protesters' attention. Two women, well bundled so only their eyes showed, came at us.

I scanned the rest of the crowd for Gwen and Arlo and didn't see them.

"Shame!" the women shouted. Maybe it was too cold for spray paint and tar, because they only had one poster between them, showing a dead coyote tangled in barbed wire.

I'd sure like to bottle the fierce glower Diane shot at them. It wasn't so much a look that could kill as it was one that promised their complete annihilation, along with their children and grandchildren. It wasn't enough to blow the women out of their mukluks, but it did give them pause, as their protests died in their throats.

It gave me a second to consider their fuzzy boots. I doubted they were real leather and animal fur, but why would you even pretend if you were so dedicated?

We had time to enter the door the hotel worker held open for us before they started chanting again. Diane hadn't been in a hurry, other than to escape the cold before our toes developed frostbite.

The energy changed the moment we entered the lobby that glowed with golden light. The center of a vast atrium held a sunken dining area with intimate tables arranged on a carpeted space, soft lanterns letting off warm light. Around that, shining floors created a boundary with two-story arched openings hiding the hotel front desk and gift shops. Wide stairs led to another circular corridor and an open second floor lined with cast iron railings featuring intricately fashioned grillwork. Rising up from the ground were eight floors of rooms with more balconies adorned with more fancy railings.

It was a massive, exquisite Renaissance structure in the middle of a cow town.

Among the many banquet and event rooms, Diane knew where the Brown Palace Ballroom was located, and she led us there with her usual confidence. If I held back a half step, I could mimic everything she did, including shucking my coat and handing it to a cloakroom attendant.

My hands were sweaty as I clenched my velvet bag. It might have been because Aria expected me to conduct a secret investigation. It might have been because I was so far out of my element I may as well have been shot into space. But the real reason was because I knew I'd soon come face-to-face with Baxter. Again.

While I'd seen many photos of him dressed in a tux at formal events, he'd never seen me dolled up. Heck, *I'd* never seen me dressed up like this. Would he like it?

For the ten millionth time, I reminded myself it didn't matter. He didn't care. He had the most beautiful and accomplished woman on the planet, and I'd no doubt she'd far surpassed any charms I might have had for him.

And, for tonight, I needed to concentrate on the job Aria wanted me to do.

Diane and I stepped into the room swarming with glitz and glamour. My natural habitat was an open prairie, dealing with whatever conditions Mother Nature sent my way. From the danger of an unexpected January blizzard to the frequent north wind, a gray day of showers, the blistering heat of an August hayfield, to the rare golden days of September and the fresh promise of an April rainbow.

While there was plenty to consider with the three or four hundred preening peacocks prancing around this ballroom, I couldn't spot the threats from the finery, the people from the costumes.

Thank the forces of good in the universe that I had my sister with me. Nothing daunted Diane.

A silver-haired man in a crisp black tux and a comfortably plump woman wearing a long-sleeved cream-colored dress without all the spangles and sparkles approached Diane. The woman, who bore the heavy wrinkles of someone who eschews facelifts, gave Diane a hearty hug, and much to my shock, Diane's face cracked open in sheer delight.

"Mavis! I didn't know you and John were back." Diane held out a hand to the man, and he gave it a squeeze.

Mavis pounded a heavy palm on Diane's back, making all the fringe on Diane's dress hop and jiggle. "The cruise was a bore. The food was lousy, the service worse. I'd rather freeze my ass off at home, thank you very much. But tell me, how did that little thing end up?"

John's eyes darted to me when Mavis asked Diane. But Diane gave a tilt to her head as if to say, *She's cool.* "About how we expected."

Mavis chuckled and said in dismissal, "What are you going to do?" She turned intensely intelligent eyes to me. "And you must be one of the famous Fox sisters Diane talks so much about."

Shocked that Diane thought about us at all, let alone chatted about us with friends, I was at a loss.

Mavis said, "Don't tell me. You're Kate. The sheriff." She winked at Diane. "I see it."

Diane looked smug, and I wanted to slap them both for this insider conversation, and yet, it felt nice that Diane had actually mentioned me.

Mavis gave Diane one last pound on her back. "Keep up the good work. I understand it's heating up." With that, she and John walked away.

Diane watched their backs with a deep frown of concentration, as if working out a complicated puzzle. I waited, and suddenly her face cleared, and I knew she had an answer. She accepted a glass of white wine from the tray of a passing server and handed it to me.

I took a sip of the cool, crisp wine, not surprised it tasted far better than the twist-off-top Chardonnay I was used to.

She scanned the room and without looking at me, said, "Sorry about this, but I've got to go."

The sip of wine gurgled down my throat. "Go? Now? Why?"

An armor seemed to shroud her, like Iron Man getting ready for a mission, but invisible and a lot more subtle. She showed no emotion when she said, "Something's come up."

I spun around to see Mavis and John exiting the ballroom. Then back to Diane, a million questions on my face, I was sure.

She lit up in a genuine smile. "You really are smart. Smart enough not to ask." With that, she headed out of the room, apparently confident I'd get myself home.

All the fish clichés hit me. Fish out of water. Tiny fish in a huge pond. Well, fish sticks to that. I sipped my wine while couples milled around me connecting with friends, being introduced, hugs, air kisses.

Since it was a big room and I couldn't see everyone, it was possible there might be other single people, but I didn't spot any. The beautiful people of Denver being beautiful, and me wondering if any of these people would feel out of place at a Sandhills wedding reception where all the decorations were constructed with silk flowers and barbed wire by the bride's cousin, the sheet cakes decorated in the bride's colors were made by the groom's aunt, and people wore their best Wranglers and stood around with sweating Coors Light cans in their hands.

I was a bigot. Rich people couldn't be any different than not rich people. They just wore better clothes. And I was darned sure wearing a mint tonight, so I might as well act like it.

A whisper of air on the back of my neck and soft words, "Our table is this way," made my knees go weak. With relief, sure, but with so much more.

I gulped in a breath before turning around to see Baxter standing behind me. He looked exactly like I'd imagined. Not a burly or tall man, he looked immaculate in his tux and black tie. And I struggled and failed not to notice how completely sexy he was. Hair neat, as usual, fresh shave, lion eyes taking me in with a familiar look, reminding me of one magical night in a Wyoming cabin...

I coughed and drew up an image of Aria grabbing my hand for

support. In an even voice and with a bland expression, he spoke with about the same tone as if he were accepting a cup of coffee at a café. "You look nice."

Totally appropriate. Not the reaction I'd somehow dreamed of, despite refusing to think about him. In that one, he caught sight of me across the crowded ballroom. The world stopped turning for both of us as people stepped out of our way and we approached each other in slow motion, Baxter's eyes riveted on me, not able to look away. Unable to deny his love after seeing me in all my "enhanced" glory.

"Thanks. So do you. Is Aria here?" How 'bout that? My voice sounded believably casual.

Baxter greeted a foursome of distinguished people. The attendees were all starting to look the same to me, like a car lot full of Mercedes, all the same general feel, just different models and colors. "She slipped out to go over her speech one more time." He led me to the VIP table right up front. "I thought you and Diane were coming together."

As far as I knew, Baxter knew vague bits and pieces about Diane's activities as I did. It was possible he was more clued in, but when international intrigue was involved, secrets abounded. It wasn't a world I wanted anything to do with. "Something came up at the last minute."

My stomach dropped when I saw Eula pulling out a chair at our table. She wore a pants suit similar to the one she'd worn at the stock show, but this one was black. Along with a shiny polyester blouse with lapels popular in the seventies, she'd gussied up the whole outfit with a triple string of tiny pearls.

She assessed Baxter and me when we approached. "Aria said you'd offered to stay with Jefferson tonight but she wouldn't allow it. I think that's a mistake. Someone should be with him."

Baxter gave her a stony look and paused a moment, as if considering a retort. Instead, he said, "Isn't Blaine supposed to be here?"

Eula blinked in obvious disgust. "Yes. He is supposed to be here. But he refused to attend. Says he doesn't like to get dressed up and hobnob. It is not my favorite thing, I can assure you. And yet, here I am. Duty."

I wondered if any of these glittering people would mind if dour Eula had stayed home, or better yet, sat with her hospitalized son.

Baxter looked at the table, set for eight. "Without Jefferson, Blaine, and Diane, that makes the table look empty."

Eula lowered herself into her chair and raised her water glass steeped in condensation. "Can't be helped, I suppose. I can only hope Aria's remarks will be appropriate."

Why wouldn't they be? But I assumed Eula hadn't had a chance to approve them beforehand. She struck me as a woman who liked to have her hand on the controls. All of them.

Aria appeared from a door behind the stage, looking so much like a swan I was caught off guard. She floated toward us in a snowy gown, with bare arms and back, wide ruched fabric ribbons wrapped around her breasts and tucked into a broad garland of satin circling her tiny waist. From there, the skirt flowed to the floor, ending in a hem of feathers. Radiant, with her dark hair in exquisite waves down her back, she was easily the most beautiful woman in the room.

She beamed at me. "Oh my God. Glenn, did you see this?" She grabbed both of my hands in her warm ones. "You are a total babe. I knew you'd be amazing."

Baxter fidgeted. "Very nice."

Aria let out a pshaw and waved him off. "Don't listen to him. You're stunning." She had enough luminance to shed some on Eula. "So good to see you. I love that you wore Grandmother's pearls."

Eula humphed and continued to glower at the room at large.

Aria took my hand and tugged me away from the table toward a group of younger people. Meaning, they were in their forties as opposed to the boomer generation who made up the majority of attendees. She whispered to me, "These are Blaine's contemporaries. Maybe he's confided in one of them. See if you can find out anything."

Baxter followed us, pausing to talk to a man who stopped him.

"Everyone," Aria announced. "This is Katharine. Katharine, this is Tom and Edie Cushing."

I shook hands with the pretty couple.

"Maude and Ethan Smithson."

Again, I offered my hand.

"And finally, Megan and Rosen Hall."

My face felt as "enhanced" as the rest of me as I tried to look enthusiastic and involved.

"She's Jefferson's new...friend."

Wait. The way she said it implied Jefferson and I had a thing going. This was not our plan. "I'm really not—"

She winked at me and giggled like a schoolgirl. "So you all need to give her intel on all things Hansford. Just so she can be prepared."

Aria was much like a cheerleader at homecoming. She seemed a master at personalities, from the bestie having coffee with Sandi, to the sorority sister with her insider friends. With me, she'd been a completely different person. Maybe it was like Diane said about getting dressed up. It was fun to play different games. She eyed the room as if scouting for disaster. "Excuse me, I've got to go mingle."

I was immediately fallen upon by all six of them, eyes glittering with interest. The women more so than the men. Maude, or maybe it was Megan—I was pretty sure it wasn't Edie—began, "Has anyone filled you in about Eula?"

Maude/Megan—the other one—had a wicked twist to her mouth. "The dragon who only loves two things in this world."

Both Maude and Megan swept their highlighted hair in similar updos and wore black sheath dresses that announced their complete lack of body fat. With flawless skin and hazel eyes, they looked like sisters, maybe twins. I had no interest in trying to figure out who was who.

Edie had sly eyes, the same sort of tight black dress, but her blond hair wreathed her face and looked soft enough even I wanted to run my hands through it. "Eula only has eyes for Hansford Meats and Jefferson."

It occurred to me I actually might fit in thanks to the slinky black dress I wore.

Megan/Maude—the first one—said, "What about Nanette?"

The second M woman said, "That was doomed to fail. She wasn't ever going to fit in."

Edie raised an eyebrow. "I don't know, Eula seemed to like her."

"Probably because neither one of them has a sense of fashion or taste," one of the others quipped.

I kind of felt sorry for Nanette, having to navigate these vipers. I was sure without Aria dressing me, I'd fall into the same vicious pit. Actually, they were probably waiting for me to walk away to start feasting on my shortcomings.

Behind the women, Baxter stood a few feet away, hands dropped to his sides. He stared at me, and I couldn't read his expression, somewhere between my-dog-just-died and I'm-going-to-beat-bumps-all-over-you.

I kept my eyes on him and suddenly lost the sound of the people around me. The movement of the crowd stilled, the colors faded. And there was Baxter, his eyes drilling into me, his face riddled with disapproval. And that made me want to backpedal on everything I'd said, if only to see a welcoming glint in his eyes.

Edie's voice broke through. "Katharine, how did you and Jefferson meet?"

"Oh. Uh. Aria introduced us." Succinct and true. The perfect answer.

Both Maude/Megan clamored for details, and one said, "He told me Nanette was the love of his life and he was destroyed when they started having problems."

Edie snorted. "As if that grubby opportunist could be anyone's true love."

I hadn't met Nanette, but that seemed cruel.

The other one cackled. "He told me the same thing, but he was looking for sympathy." She glanced at the men to see if they were listening, and when she determined they were in their own conversation, lowered her voice and waggled her eyebrows. "I figured he was trying to get *a lot* of sympathy, if you know what I mean."

The first one faked shock, then laughed. "That was my take, too."

Edie gave them a chastising look. "Stop it, or Katharine will get the wrong idea."

The Maude/Megans didn't seem cowed. One said, "She ought to know so she can be prepared."

It looked like Edie grimaced, but her forehead didn't wrinkle; probably fillers prevented that. She acted as if I wasn't standing right there. "Katharine is an adult. She seems like she knows how the real world works, and if she wants to be with Jefferson, I'm sure she has her reasons." I was certain she meant I was after his money.

There were many reasons I didn't want Jefferson, but having to endure this pack of jackals might be the biggest deterrent. Since they were so willing to dish, I wanted to ask what they meant about Jefferson wanting sympathy. According to Aria, he was a clueless, generous, loving and loyal guy. These gossips gave me a whole different view.

Aria swept past us. "Seems dinner is about to be served. Excuse me while I try to get some order." With such nonchalance, she sailed to Baxter, and they shared a quick peck on the lips before she whooshed away, the hem of her dress swirling and flirting as she made her way to the platform.

The three fabulous couples gathered together and surged away. The women's heads were together, and they covered their mouths with their hands. No doubt sharing a few opinions about me. That went a long way toward making me feel like an imposter.

Baxter was standing at our table by the time I'd maneuvered through the milling crowd. The look of rage he cast at me made me want to run the other way. I hesitated, and he jerked a chair from the table, holding out his hand to show me where to sit.

Eula's empty water glass sat next to a half-full one she'd pilfered from another place setting. She took note of me and Baxter. Seeing a crystal glass of amber liquid on the table in front of Eula surprised me, but I kind of liked the idea of this strict matriarch sipping a bourbon on a night out.

I chose a chair on the opposite side of the table from Baxter and seated myself. He was treating me like a child who needed to be scolded, and I chafed at his attitude, my cheeks burning.

He shoved the chair to the table and in a smooth motion, chose a seat next to me and planted himself.

I kept my eyes on the platform, posed as straight as possible, clutching my velvet bag in my hands to keep them still. Temper simmered in my chest.

Eula didn't exactly smile, but she seemed amused.

Baxter angled toward me, speaking to the side of my head. "What the hell are you thinking?"

I didn't turn to him, though I swore I felt the heat of his anger billowing at me. "Not your business."

I didn't need to see his eyes to know they were shooting flames. "I know what Aria said isn't true. So, what's going on?"

My fury was too big for the situation, and I at least had the awareness to know I was channeling other emotions into it. Any time I was with Baxter, I felt unnerved. "You don't know diddly about me and what interests me." Why did I suddenly sound like Louise?

Eula sipped her bourbon, observing us as if watching a play. One she enjoyed. It embarrassed me, but I couldn't do much about it without making a bigger scene.

Baxter's temper matched mine. "The hell I don't. You love your family and the sunshine on Wild Horse Hill in June when the spiderwort is blooming. A good burger suits you better than a complicated meal at a Michelin-starred restaurant. You'd rather work cattle on horseback and eat a peanut butter sandwich than dress in an evening gown and sip champagne."

I still wouldn't look at him. Because if I did, I might disintegrate like mud pies in a Sandhills rainstorm. "See? You don't know squat." I guess I was still going to talk like Louise. "I love lobster and champagne. And I'm having a pretty amazing time wearing this dress and hanging out at the Brown Palace." All of which was true, not counting that I wasn't loving the people in the Brown Palace Ballroom.

His fingers closed on my chin, and with gentle pressure, he forced me to look at him.

It was as if he'd zapped me with a cattle prod, and it burned all the way to my toes.

"Stop it. Tell me what's going on." His voice was tight and low, his face steely.

A tapping on a mic made us whip our attention to the platform.

Baxter's hand dropped from my face.

Aria sailed onto the stage holding a mic and smiling into the room. She sounded assured and cheerful. "Everyone, if you can take your seats, we're about to start serving. We're lucky to be having the finest grass-fed Angus filets donated by Wesley Angus in Tynedale, Nebraska. And you don't want to let them get cold."

Grass-fed. Sounded good and healthy, but give me a corn-fed with all that flavorful marbling and I was in.

While the room seemed to bustle with the energy of a koi pond at feeding time, I resumed staring straight ahead. In a matter of seconds, Aria appeared and Baxter jumped to his feet, pulling out a chair on his other side.

She smiled and replied to someone at the next table and turned to us, her face stern. She whispered, "What is going on with you? I could see you from the stage."

Aria wore the expectant look of a parent waiting for an explanation.

Eula lowered her bourbon with a pleasant face, as if enjoying the entire evening. "There seems to be some disagreement about how well Glenn knows Kate."

Not knowing what to say, I let my gaze slide to Baxter. His mouth was set in an angry slash as he glared back at me.

Aria placed a hand on his arm. She sounded like a second-grade teacher coaxing a confession from a kid. "Glenn? Why would you treat Kate like that?"

It worked on him, and he turned to her, irritation evident. "I want to know what scheme you two have cooked up."

That glint of devilry rose in her eyes. "We haven't done anything."

Eula talked out of the side of her mouth, as if giving me an aside. "Exactly what she said a thousand times after dragging Jefferson into some shenanigans."

Baxter spared one disdainful look for me before he turned to Aria, and I got the back of his head. "That's BS, and I know it."

She broke into a grin and kissed him quickly. "Keep it down, will you? We're trying to smoke out the bad guy. Or girl. Woman. Whatever."

Baxter leaned back and tipped his head to the ceiling in exasperation. "I knew it. This has something to do with Jefferson getting drugged?"

Eula perked up. "What have you discovered?"

Aria glanced at her aunt. "Jefferson told you about being attacked at Casa Bonita, and I told you about him getting drugged. You know about the protesters at the stock show. But did he tell you his house was broken into?"

Eula's face looked like a volcano about to erupt. "I'll send him out of the country for a time until we get to the bottom of this. Let our security team handle it."

Baxter glared at me. "You've got no business playing spy."

I pretty much agreed with him but took offense to the way he said it. "I'm a trained law enforcement officer. I can handle myself."

He scoffed. "Twelve weeks of training."

"And three years of experience."

"In a sleepy county in Nebraska with a population under five thousand."

"With more than its share of crime lately."

Eula again seemed fascinated with our argument.

Aria had watched the two of us like a ping-pong match. She held up her hand. "Will you two keep it down?"

Baxter clamped his mouth shut. His dark gaze rested on me, then shifted to Aria. "I don't know who's being more stupid and stubborn. But I'm not going to accept this."

Ready to attack his arrogance, I opened my mouth to fight back.

Aria beat me to it with a combative look on her face, the smooth olive skin on her cheeks flaring crimson. "Accept it? I don't remember asking your permission."

I'd rarely seen Baxter more frustrated. He shoved his chair back. "Do what you want."

We both watched him stride from the room. I didn't know what Aria was thinking, but I wanted to run after him. Not to acquiesce to his agenda, but to fight it out with him until we were both pulling the same wagon. But it was probably better for everyone if we stayed on the outs.

Aria lifted her chin and seemed to struggle for equilibrium. I looked at my hands clutching my bag and tried hard not to agree with Baxter's opinion that our scheme was a dumb idea.

Before Aria could say anything more, the banquet manager in the black suit approached and whispered to Aria.

Aria nodded and thanked the woman, who bustled away. With a heavy sigh that seemed to return everything to normal in her world, Aria's face settled into a pleasant passivity. She tilted her head to me. "And now I've got to make a speech. Remind me that if someone else doesn't get to Jefferson first, I'm going to kill him." She sailed away.

I slumped back in my chair and reached for my half-empty wineglass. Maybe I should drain it and find a server to bring me more.

Eula cleared her throat. "I like you."

How should I react to that? I raised my glass to toast her.

She measured me unselfconsciously. "You're the type of woman Jefferson should have married."

Not feeling at all amiable, I grumbled, "Marriage doesn't have to be forever. Maybe he'll have better luck next time."

"Hansfords do not divorce. We understand commitment." She paused and drove the point home. "Or else they aren't real Hansfords."

Where was that server?

Eula didn't seem to need me to answer. "You're someone who can stand up to threats and protect those who need protecting. I see myself in you."

I balked at her presumption. "I'm an ex-sheriff and now Aria's ranch manager. I don't see much similarity between us."

Eula gave me a cagey smile, the first I'd seen from her. It revealed a set of crooked teeth, making me wonder about a woman with such deep pockets who wouldn't spend money to get her teeth fixed. "It's too late for Jefferson." She held up a hand as if warding off an argument from me. "Don't mention divorce again. I don't believe in it. Any more than I believe in drinking alcohol to excess." She looked pointedly at my glass as if knowing I craved a refill.

Keeping eye contact with her, I took a sip.

Instead of irritating her, as I intended, it seemed to amuse her. "But Blaine is single."

I nearly choked on the wine. "You want to set me up with Blaine?"

She puffed out a breath. "I know he seems cold and humorless."

You think? Not to mention mean and perhaps dangerous.

"But he's got a soft side. It's the sensitive ones who always act so tough. Like Jefferson, he needs a woman with some backbone who can guide him."

"How does Blaine feel about you matchmaking for him?"

She glanced away as if thinking about her answer. "He's never been as naïve and sensitive as Jefferson, and I might not have protected and provided for him as much. But I've come to believe he needs my guidance. At least, if I'm ever going to get an heir. I pride myself on being a good judge of character."

She seemed to value straightforwardness, so I said, "I'm not interested in dating either of your sons."

She pushed her chair back and stood. "You might reconsider. It won't do you any good going after Aria's fiancé."

It felt like a bucket of ice water down my neck.

She sniffed. "If you'll excuse me. I need the little girls' room. I drank too much water waiting for Aria to get this show rolling." She left the room with a stride like a bull rider leaving the arena.

Relieved to be at the table alone, I downed the rest of my wine.

Aria walked out onto the stage, all poise and beauty. She scanned the room with her winning smile and finally brought her gaze to my table. All the color drained from Aria's face before I heard a woman's voice and smelled cigarette smoke.

"I didn't think that old battle-ax would ever leave. Mind if I sit down?"

22

I was more than startled to see the black-haired woman with the violet eyes. The bathroom bandit, here at my table. Tonight, her short hair was gelled to her skull like it was paint. Her makeup was dramatic and dark, with several rhinestones that looked embedded in her left temple and cheeks. She wore a skimpy and filmy dress that matched the color of her eyes, along with patent leather Docs.

Without waiting for an answer, she pulled out a chair and slumped down, setting a glass with amber liquid just like Eula's in front of her. She leaned back, draped one leg over the other to let a heavy boot drag her foot down, and rested her elbow on the back of the chair. She smirked at me.

I flicked my gaze to Aria, who seemed to be fighting with herself whether to start her address or fly from the stage at the black-haired woman she so clearly detested.

The woman seemed arrogant and confident beyond even Diane levels. She uncrossed her legs, leaned forward with her hand extended to me. "We haven't been formally introduced."

I didn't take her hand, and she flicked her eyebrows up in amusement and lifted her glass. "I'm Nanette Hansford."

Aria spun around and started for the stairs at the side of the stage. A dowager-type woman with hair more blue than gray and a shapeless gown nearly the same color met her before she could descend. The woman obviously didn't want Aria to abandon the stage.

Nanette leaned back, clearly enjoying herself.

I tried for death eyes. "Looks like you're not welcome here. I think it'd be best if you left."

Nanette reached down to her boot and slid a creamy envelope from her ankle. She held it up. "I've got this invitation right here."

I flipped open the flap on the heavy stock and pulled out an embossed card bearing the initials *JH*. Her name was printed, and a hand signature authenticated it. "Jefferson invited you?"

Nanette slouched back. "Of course he did. Jefferson loves me. At least, that's what he wants darling Eula to think." Her scathing look rested on me. "I warned you away from this mess, and yet here you are, falling for all their manipulations."

Why would someone put so much effort into being off-putting and offensive? "You need to leave," I said.

Nanette raised her eyebrows, and an arrogant sneer wrinkled her nose. "I'm a guest of the host. Even if he's not here. You can try to throw me out, but I won't be leaving without a scene. And we all know how perfectly perfect Aria Fontaine hates a scene. Especially when she's the one running the show."

Aria had returned to center stage, and she focused on Nanette, her smile forced and her eyes lasered on Nanette like a blue heeler on a coyote.

At least with Nanette here, we could assume Jefferson wasn't in any danger from her. She swung her booted foot and gave me a challenging stare.

Aria spoke with a smooth tone, as if she weren't boiling inside. "Good evening, everyone. While the servers bring out your dinner, I'd like to take this opportunity to welcome you."

Like an invading army, lines of servers infiltrated from the outskirts of the room carrying silver-covered plates that they distributed to the seated guests.

Nanette lifted her drink and sipped while a plate was set before her and the cover whisked off to reveal a filet the size of a fist, two glazed carrots and a spear of asparagus, and a smattering of tiny roasted potatoes. The same happened for me.

Aria's voice floated over the clinks of silverware on plates and the murmur of conversation, though I doubted many listened with any more attention than I did. "As you know, pediatric heart disease is a tragedy that strikes too many children. Your participation here tonight will ensure..."

Nanette pushed away her plate. "You're not very good at playing Aria's game, you know."

Baxter leaving and Nanette arriving might have dampened my appetite, but I wasn't going to let her know that. With as much disinterest in her as possible, I wielded my steak knife and cut into the filet that was so tender I could have sliced it with a teaspoon. Before I set it on my tongue, I said, "Looks like a better meal than the enchiladas at Casa Bonita."

Where had Eula disappeared to?

Aria went on to speak about the promising research going on at National Jewish Health in Denver.

My first bite was so succulent and juicy, and so delicately seasoned, the true beef flavor shone. I doubted the line about it being grass-fed. I was lost in such ecstasy I nearly missed Nanette's snarkiness.

She set her glass down. "Jefferson and I were supposed to meet at his hotel last night, but he tracked down that little blond number before he left the stock show. So, I followed him to Casa Bonita." She shrugged. "Classy place."

I ate another bite of steak because it was delicious, and I refused to let Nanette ruin it for me. She waited while I took my time and finally swallowed. After a sip of water, I said, "Did that make you mad? Him being with another woman? Mad enough to try to kill him?"

She shook her head quickly in an exaggerated way, as if I'd spoken too fast and confused her. Then she tilted her head back like a wolf and let out a howl of laughter. "I couldn't care less who Jefferson sleeps with. Except for that blond munchkin. I'm trying to get as far away from him as I can. But I'm not going without what I'm owed."

I tested one of the roasted carrots, and it nearly rivaled the deliciousness of the steak. "I heard your prenup is generous."

Her lips curled. "For someone like you, maybe. But I've developed expensive tastes."

I looked her up and down. "And yet, this is the best you can do?"

I chewed a bite, letting the flavor fill me while she did her best to murder me with her eyes. I set my fork down. "Why not take the prenup, get on with your life, and let Jefferson move on with his?"

She laughed, a sound as inviting as nails on a chalkboard. "Why should I settle for the paltry prenup amount when I deserve so much more?"

I held a bite of steak on my fork. "I'd guess you already got more than you're entitled to."

The nasty mirth bled from her face, and her eyes glinted with malice. "You have no idea what I've had to endure. I can guarantee he'll give me what I'm asking for or tomorrow's board meeting will be *very* interesting."

Aria's lilting voice carried over the room. "Please, enjoy your meal. Wait until you see the dessert our chef has in store for you. We've got some amazing entertainment lined up and—"

A loud clang at the back of the ballroom interrupted her. That was followed by a shout of alarm and then sounds of dishes crashing. A herd of stampeding cattle might make the same kind of disruption.

I jumped to my feet to see what was happening, but most of the other people also stood, and being so short and so far from the disturbance, I wasn't able to get any idea what approached. I glanced over my shoulder at Aria. She looked furious, not frightened.

It only took a moment before I heard that maddening chanting: "Shame, shame, shame."

Maybe a dozen protesters, most bundled up against a cold January night, surged between the tables, swiping plates to the floor, shouting and chanting. Several wore lifelike animal masks with signs pinned to their chests that coincided with the likeness of the animal. They said, "This is the face of alpaca, or wool, or cashmere." They looked terrifying, though I didn't see guns, just a few placards. But Gwen proved she could wield one as a weapon.

The tables around us cleared as people scurried from the protesters, some pulling out phones, some yelling for security.

Then I saw them.

23

Gwen and Arlo made their way straight for our table as if they'd planned their attack. Exactly the way my brothers ran for Space Mountain the moment we'd entered Disney World. I didn't have time to worry how Arlo and Gwen had ambushed hotel security.

They wore similar homespun and scraps as at the stock show, and their wiry hair still in the same ponytail and braids. This was probably what Mom looked like now, hanging out with her one true love somewhere in the Canadian wilds. Maybe it wasn't entirely Gwen and Arlo's fault that I disliked them so much. But they gave me enough reason. They closed in on us, holding posters that read, *Animals Are People, Too!* and *Animals Are Not Clothing.* Gwen shoved a tuxedoed man out of her path, keeping a straight course for our table.

The fight with Baxter, the weird parrying with Nanette, and now these yahoos, all contrived to steal enjoyment of eating the filet, the one thing that had actually brought me joy tonight. I'd had enough.

While most guests seemed paralyzed, one older man stepped in front of Arlo and ripped the sign from his grip. They wrestled, and I left them to duke it out.

I braced myself on my kitten heels, halfway hoping I'd be forced to throw a punch as Gwen rushed the table.

"Where is he? Where is the coward who puts immigrants through a living hell so he can line his pockets?" She swung her placard at me like a club, and I jumped out of the way. Instead of using my fist, as I'd anticipated, I reached for my plate with half a filet sitting in a pool of beef juice. I hated to make the sacrifice, but I lobbed the plate at Gwen before she could swing the placard again.

She shrieked like the Wicked Witch when Dorothy tossed the bucket of water. She didn't fall back, as I'd hoped. With lightning speed, she cast away her poster, grabbed a steak knife off the table, and came at me. The look in her eyes told me she intended to skewer me. She wasn't much taller than me, with the slight build of a vegan, and she was older, if her wrinkles and white braids told the truth. But I was wearing heels and trussed into an evening gown. Still, I thought I stood a fair chance of taking her down without getting gutted.

She looked about ready to charge when she glanced up and slammed on her brakes, her eyes full of alarm.

Still braced for attack, I flicked my gaze beside me.

Eula stood straight and tall, her arm extended, a small pistol in her relaxed grip. Her voice was as hard as a hammer. "Are you sure you want to do that?"

Gwen backed up, then spun around in a smart move to flee. Except she smacked into a wall of white.

Aria had been on the run toward us when Gwen plowed into her. They tottered back and forth, wrestling and grunting.

In a languid movement, Eula stashed her gun behind her back, probably in a cute pancake holster. She seemed irritated that Aria had interrupted her Wild West shoot-out situation. "What did you do that for? I had it under control."

Aria stumbled to the right and grabbed her ankle in pain. She turned frantic eyes to me and said, "Go after her. She's on the run."

It took me a moment to realize she was talking about Nanette. I caught sight of her slinking through a side door I'd only seen staff use.

For my part, I didn't see the point in chasing down Nanette. She'd been at Casa Bonita and had opportunity, and maybe motive, to attack Jefferson, but she hadn't done anything tonight besides irritate me and ruffle Aria. But Aria wanted her contained, so that's what I'd do.

Slipping a bit in my sandals on the carpet, I took off for the service entrance. I dodged hotel security on their way to corral the protesters. A little too late, by my reckoning. Attendees huddled at the edges of the ballroom, but the dining tables were deserted, half-eaten steaks starting to congeal on the plates.

The industrial simplicity of the service hallway was in direct contrast to the opulence of the Brown Palace Ballroom. My thin soles clacked on the bare tile as I trotted down an empty hallway that must lead to the kitchen. Trolleys filled with water pitchers, stacks of metal plate covers, used napkins, and other service items lined the walls of the dimly lit space.

I might have caught the shimmer of violet netting swish around the corner ahead in a well-lit area. When I got there, I swung into a bustling kitchen with an array of stations and what felt like an army of cooks. A few glanced up at me in irritation but bent back to their work.

With only a few options of where Nanette might have run, I chose the most obvious choice, straight down the main aisle and out another door into a wider but still bare hallway. I thought I heard the thud of boots and a door open and clang closed.

When I made it to the end of the hallway, I had a choice of a service elevator or a metal door. I hit the bar on the door and emptied out to a carpeted hallway and soft music. A cluster of well-dressed people waited for elevators, and they glanced at me without much interest.

Sounding like a movie cliché, I asked, "Did you see a woman in a purple dress run from here?"

While two elderly couples looked at me like I'd scuttled from under the fridge with antennae swinging, a younger woman in a pink cocktail dress grinned like she was helping me on a scavenger hunt. She pointed down a corridor that led to another meeting space. "She went that way."

I mumbled my thanks and took off. Down the carpeted hallway, around a bend, through a maze of conference rooms, and back to the elevators. No sign of Nanette. With a sinking spirit, I tromped back to the Brown Palace Ballroom, not taking the kitchen route but using the boring path the guests used. The doors were closed, and I eased one open to see the stage lit with laser lights and a man in a black felt cowboy hat playing a guitar and singing a Hank Williams song into a standing mic. What a mix of old and new. Was this Aria's first entertainment choice or one further down the line?

I caught my breath while I surveyed the room. About half of the seats were filled. The head table was empty, so I assumed Eula had ridden off into the sunset. I'd guessed the protesters had put a damper on the festivities for the others. I had no interest in going back in, and I hoped Aria would forgive me for bailing on her.

I doubted we'd get anything more accomplished here tonight. The lights in the wide corridor cast a low glow, like a theater lobby during showtime, and it was quiet, with the constant orchestra music piping from speakers, everything muted because it was after eight.

I hadn't gone too far back toward the atrium when a looming shadow up ahead caught my eye. He appeared out of one hallway, crossed into the main corridor, and faded into the edge, looking away from me, toward the atrium. Though I'd only met him twice, he looked familiar enough that I suspected this shadow was Blaine. Eula said he'd begged off attending the fundraiser, so what was he doing here? I almost called out to him, but decided to follow him.

Not needing to muffle my footsteps on the plush carpet, I stuck close to the wall and peeked around the corner down the hall where he'd disappeared.

Maybe I should have suspected it, but it shocked me to see Nanette pop out of an adjoining hallway and clasp Blaine by the arm. He was startled but didn't seem to be completely surprised, as he quickly followed her around another corner.

I hurried to the hallway as yet another metal door clanged closed. Maybe Nanette had worked here, or planned events at the Brown Palace, or cased the joint earlier, but she seemed to know all the hidden accesses.

By the time I eased open the door and slipped inside a stairwell, Blaine and Nanette had vanished. This was the second stairwell I'd found myself in today, and I wasn't any happier here than I'd been earlier this afternoon. With eight floors and services from housekeeping to food, and a dozen conference rooms they could have escaped to, I gave up the chase and plopped down on the stairs.

What a stupid idea. What a stupid night. What a stupid bunch of people, living stupid lives, trying to latch on to as much money as they could. Stupid.

I slid the straps off my heels and removed my sandals. Also stupid to wear sandals in Denver in January. And though I was happy for the long sleeves, my back was downright frigid in the cold stairwell. What was I doing here, anyway?

I hated that Baxter was right when he said he knew me. I wanted to be home in the Sandhills, curled up with Poupon at my feet—except he'd be lying on the couch with me pretending he wasn't. Even if a blizzard raged outside, I'd much rather be battling the elements than trying to outmaneuver greedy criminals and radicalized activists.

The door pushed open, and I braced myself, ready to spring at Nanette, Blaine, Gwen, Sandi, or maybe some other threat.

A head with neat salt-and-pepper hair poked in, lion eyes scanning the stairwell and finally resting on me. Baxter inhaled with what looked like relief and stepped onto the landing, letting the door bang behind him. "I thought maybe that was you going down the hallway. Then I wondered if you'd escaped in here. Hiding?"

I rested my elbow on my knee and propped my face in my hand. "I was chasing Nanette, and this is where she lost me."

He frowned and moved toward me. "Nanette? Why would Jefferson's ex be here?"

For someone who pushed all my buttons and whom I'd wanted to pummel not long ago, I was happy to see him. Whatever had gone on between us, I knew I could trust him. "Not an ex yet. She appeared after you left. We had an interesting exchange right before the protesters burst in."

"I'm sorry I wasn't there for that. If I'd known there was a threat, I'd never have left."

I knew that. "Is Aria okay?"

He nodded. "Mad enough to chew nails, and she twisted her ankle, but it's fine."

"If she hadn't hurt her ankle, she'd probably have caught Nanette."

Baxter nodded. "Aria doesn't like her, I know. But she'll be out of Jefferson's life soon, won't she?"

"Eula might have something to say about that. She doesn't believe in divorce."

"A person ought to make their choices based on more than inheritance." He lowered himself to the step, and I scooted closer to the wall to make room for him.

Though his thigh didn't actually touch mine, I felt the heat of his skin through the thin fabric of my dress. "I think the answer you're looking for is money. There's the possibility Eula will cut Jefferson off if he commits that sin."

He rested both forearms on his knees and leaned over his clasped hands, looking so casual and sexy that I nearly couldn't breathe. "I'm sorry I jumped all over you and Aria earlier."

I elbowed him. "You were an ass."

He chuckled. "Aria is one of those people...what did you say once? She's the kind who shoots first and aims later."

I wouldn't stand for him to disparage her. "Aria is a phenomenal person. You're damned lucky to have her."

He was quick to respond. "Absolutely. I didn't mean to insult her. Just being honest. She's great, really. Nearly perfect."

"Just so we're clear about that." What a washing machine full of bleeding colors agitated inside me. I loved Aria. I was trying hard not to love Baxter. I didn't wish either of them pain. But I hated that these two people who meant so much to me were shredding my heart by being together. We sat in silence for a moment, then we both started speaking.

Though not in exact synchronicity, we both spouted variations of, "Aria is wonderful, but this scheme is ridiculous."

"Why did you go along with it?" Baxter asked me.

I thought about it for a moment, debating whether to tell him the whole truth. "It's clear someone has it out for Jefferson. I agree with Aria that he seems oblivious or unwilling to take precautions. But I didn't know she was going to say we were seeing each other."

Baxter's eyes clouded. "I think you both underestimate Jefferson."

"Because you got bad vibes from one dinner? He might have had a bad night."

He shrugged. "He sheds personalities like a snake sheds skin."

I laughed. "Not that you have an opinion about him." I added, "Aria said he learned to present an image to Eula. I can see why."

He didn't argue. "I don't know him very well. Aria thinks he's gullible."

I accepted that. "He bought whatever Sandi was selling and trusted her enough to invite her to his hotel. And she drugged him, for whatever reason."

Baxter paused. "But Aria said Sandi ran out of the hotel with a black eye, so how do you explain that?"

"Don't know." I hated that dead end.

He looked at me with concentration, totally absorbed with the mystery. "Aria thought that Nanette was behind the break-in at Jefferson's house. Suppose she somehow drugged him?"

"She may not want to be married to him, but she didn't seem happy he was with Sandi." I dropped my arm straight and rested my chin on my bicep. "Nanette's got something going with Blaine, I'm guessing, since I just saw them together."

Baxter's forehead furrowed as he thought. "Nanette and Blaine? Together?" I loved the way Baxter always paid attention to me, listened to the situation, whether it was my family, or problems as sheriff, or what to do about aphids in my garden, and then tried to work with me on a solution. "What would he and Nanette be cooking up?"

"Nanette wants more money than the prenup provides. Maybe she's trying to convince Blaine the company should pay her off." My bare feet and back were not loving the stairwell, and I shivered.

Baxter shrugged out of his tux jacket and draped it on my back. "That seems pretty dramatic."

The warm Baxter aroma emanated from his jacket, and I struggled not to choke up with longing. "And where does Sandi fit into this?"

He fidgeted as if uncomfortable. But his voice rolled out wrinkle-free. "Maybe she's an outlier?"

He focused on the wall of the stairwell, as if trying to ignore I sat so close beside him. He spoke with logic, and I went on. "Jefferson says he hates working for the company but he feels obligated to his mother. It's sad he's letting love for his mother make him settle for a loveless marriage and a stifling career." I wondered if Baxter's heart was thudding against his ribs the same as mine.

Baxter said, "Aria said Eula would cut off Jefferson if he left the company or got divorced. Basically, if he did anything she doesn't approve of. And I take it she doesn't approve of a lot. I'd say Jefferson is tied to the company for life if he wants to get his hands on the Hansford fortune."

When I caught myself itching to touch the gray hair at his temples, I put force into my words. "Or he could get a job like the rest of us and earn a living."

Baxter laughed. "Real people understand that. But these are people born into wealth. They can't conceive of a life where they scrub their own toilets, make their own peanut butter and jelly sandwiches, and can't jet off to the Maldives for the weekend."

I tried to understand that way of thinking. "It would be different from how he grew up, but we're talking about adults. I'm sure Jefferson has contacts and investments that he could call on and make a fresh start. He'd still live a comfortable life."

"Comfortable for you isn't the same as it is for him."

"What about you? You've had deep pockets for decades. You don't cook, clean, shop, or even plan any of that. Could you go back to living like you grew up?"

His crisp white shirt and black tie, shiny shoes, and relaxed posture were irresistible. But I resisted anyway.

"I only have those luxuries because I'm too busy to worry about them. I delegate so I can focus on what I do best. I like nice things, expensive things like good wine and exclusive vacations. But I like to work, so I'm not desperate to hang on to what I have."

"This," I indicated my dress, "this is fun for a change. But I don't think it's really me. I feel fake."

He let his gaze travel from my bare feet to the crown of my head. "Aria was right. You look fantastic. But you look like a million bucks when you're riding the range and the wind's tugged your ponytail in every direction. Or when you're wearing shorts and grilling in your backyard. None of this is fake. It's Kate, through and through. Just different facets of the diamond."

That embarrassed and thrilled me in a tidal wave of confusion. I reached up to scratch my hair, forgetting the complicated coiffe. My fingers tangled with one of the rhinestone clips, and I ended up pulling a straggle of hair free to dangle on my neck. "Dang it."

Baxter turned away to gaze at the door, but not before I noticed the gold in his eyes had darkened. It was a look I knew, and my heart thudded against my ribs.

As if he fought against an invisible force, Baxter's head swiveled slowly toward me.

I knew I should jump up. Turn my head away. Say something. Do something to stop this.

His hands rose to my hair, and with deft fingers he plucked a few more rhinestone clips out and dropped them to tink on the concrete steps. A couple of braids spilled onto my shoulders.

I couldn't take my eyes from his. The golden eyes with brown flecks drilled into mine, and I felt powerless to change the course we'd taken, even though I was sure both of us knew it was wrong.

I leaned into him at the same time he put gentle pressure on the back of my head.

Our lips met in an explosion of passion that forced my eyes closed to take in the flood of emotions running from him and through me and back again. My ears roared, and I was wrapped in the heat that burned with a welcome fire.

It lasted forever and for less than a millisecond. The Big Bang and a frozen void almost simultaneously as he abruptly pulled back and leapt to his feet.

"Shit." He stepped to the door, his hand to his forehead, the other on his hip. He stared at the door, spun back to me, and looked at me with crushing misery. He closed his eyes, taking in a deep breath as if to clear everything out.

I was nothing more than a helpless puddle on the steps. Unable to move or think or function. Frozen, not from the chill of the stairwell and my evening wear, but from the ravaged wasteland within. The raw and terrible knowledge that I'd never get over Baxter. I was doomed to love a man who loved someone else.

"I'm. I'm...sorry, Kate."

I found the will to nod and pull myself to stand, my fingers like ice on the stair railing. "Yeah."

His jacket slid from my shoulders and tumbled to the ground with a tender whisper. I couldn't pick it up. My sandals dangling from my fingers, I somehow managed to stumble from the stairwell into the heated corridor and the mellow orchestra music playing on as if my world hadn't collapsed. Again.

24

Sounds of Diane's household stirring rousted me from restless sleep. I'd done valiant battle with my sheets all night and finally dropped off toward dawn. I couldn't keep my thoughts from Baxter and the exhilaration of our kiss. And then the plummet to Death Valley's dusty floor when I thought of Aria. How would I navigate working for Aria and my irrepressible attraction to Baxter? The only way to manage my desire would be to never see him. Could I make that work?

Diane's guest suite faced east, and the blinds couldn't contain the bright sunshine as it infiltrated the tiny spaces between the slats. I'd bet Colorado boasted the brightest skies on the planet. I squinted into the morning as I twisted the rod to open the blinds. Sunday serenity cloaked the neighborhood of wide lawns, immaculate landscaping, and homes with more square footage than the Grand County Consolidated High School gym. The gated community, not more than a decade old, featured massive lots with sweeping drives and thick carpets of brown grass that would look like acres of a fairway come spring.

I gave my black evening gown a once-over on my way to the shower, running my hands across the shimmering fabric. "Not likely I'll wear you again." It surprised me that the thought made me sad. Although, sad was a state above the despair I'd wrestled with all night and only barely contained.

I'd been without Baxter for two years and had somehow limped through those many days and nights, but I'd survived. I'd go on without him again. Maybe I'd spark a little with someone else. Maybe someone like Jefferson? Diane would encourage me, and I ought to force myself to fill the gaping cavern created by Baxter's absence. Even if I feared it would remain empty.

I dressed in soft jeans and a cuddly flannel shirt, even though I hoped Aria and I could meet with Craig McNeal and finally negotiate to bring Brodgar home. After last night and the sting of loss, I wanted comfort, and short of diving headfirst into a bowl of gooey macaroni and cheese, my outfit would have to do.

When I made it to the kitchen, Kimmy and Karl were bargaining over a box of donuts on the counter.

Karl, his blond hair a tangle and his pajama pants bunched and wrinkled, was wearing a combative pout. "You got the chocolate sprinkles last week. You said I could have it this time."

Kimmy and Karl looked so much alike there was no mistaking them as siblings. She was two years older and, this morning, wore a clean pink sweatsuit, her hair in a neat French braid down her back. She was her mother's daughter, through and through. "I told you that to make you feel better. I didn't want to hurt your feelings by telling you that chocolate makes you fart and gives you zits. And if you get zits, Kasia won't like you. Mom won't let us get donuts at all if we don't eat them, so if I eat the chocolate one, you won't have to, and Mom will keep getting them on Sundays."

He wasn't buying it entirely. "Why won't chocolate give *you* zits?"

She gave him a "duh" eye roll. "Because. My genetics. It's science."

In that exaggerated way all kids indicate disbelief, he said, "Oh, huh." He probably wasn't aware he and Kimmy had similar genetics, and hit with his standard comeback. He obviously didn't trust Kimmy but didn't know how to argue her point.

He hesitated a second too long and Kimmy snatched the donut, eliciting a yelp while he lunged for her. She licked the top, then held it out to him. "Fine, here. Get zits."

He wailed, "You licked it."

Since I had eight brothers and sisters and a dozen nieces and nephews, I'd seen versions of this show and wasn't inclined to see more. "Where's your mom?"

Kimmy took a bite of her donut and let Karl answer. "She had to go on a business trip last night. Left Marta a note to get us donuts."

I was sure it was business that made her bail on the fundraiser, but I doubted it was bank business. "Did she say where?"

Karl chose a bear claw, the biggest offering in the box.

Kimmy spoke around her bite. "Nope. Marta is going to take us to my dance recital this afternoon. Do you want to come?"

I tamped down my curiosity about Carly's and Diane's secret doings. Nothing good could come of me knowing. I surveyed the box of donuts and picked a maple log. "Sorry, but I want to get my stuff done and head back to Hodgekiss today. We're supposed to get a storm, and I want to get out of town before it gets too bad."

Kimmy considered that. "Snow? Wonder if Mom will get back before then. How do you know it's supposed to snow?"

One generation had removed that daily routine of checking the weather. Everyone in the Sandhills kept a constant eye on the weather forecast. I tugged her braid. "We're gonna have to school you on the ways of the West. Where's Marta?"

"Starting the laundry," Kimmy said. "Want some milk?"

I took her up on the offer, and the three of us enjoyed our Sunday treat, with Marta joining us. Sharing family time with Kimmy and Karl soothed some of the raw parts from last night. But I felt heavy, and forced myself to make an effort to keep moving.

After I'd loaded my bag in Elvis, my 1973 Ranchero, and hugged the kids and invited them to come see me anytime, I headed toward the hospital to check on Jefferson.

Nothing felt right this morning when all I could think of was Baxter's lips on mine, kindling a fire that had felt so right but now smoldered like piles of tires, toxic and doomed to never extinguish.

Well, look at me, all poetic and stuff.

Jefferson was dressed and sitting on the edge of the one chair when I entered. That's when I realized I should have brought flowers or some kind of gift.

Aria was already there, looking more fatigued than I'd ever seen her. Dark circles underneath her eyes didn't make her unattractive, just less perfect. She stood on one side of Jefferson's chair, arms folded in a standoff with Eula, who stood on the other side.

Jefferson had that wide-eyed look of a third grader asked to recite the times tables. "Please, stop. There isn't anything to these attacks. I'm sure it's coincidence."

Eula wore men's jeans cinched with a wide leather belt, along with a plain blue blouse and down vest. Her hair still looked like it was hard enough to knock on. "Don't try to make light of it so I won't worry."

"Good morning," I said, both to let them know I'd arrived and to, hopefully, defuse the tension.

Aria nodded at me, then said, "It's Nanette. And I think it's serious. If you're dead, she gets your money."

Eula scoffed. "That's ridiculous. She's not a polished diamond, like you. But that girl has grit. She didn't have the advantages you kids did. She grew up rough, but she's a quality person."

Baxter and Eula both had nice things to say about Nanette. Aria even said she liked her in the beginning. Nanette had tried to warn me off the Hansfords, and I'd taken it as aggression. But maybe she really meant it sincerely.

Aria's mouth opened in disbelief. "Since when have you been a Nanette fan?"

Eula looked down on the top of Jefferson's head. "She wouldn't have been my choice for Jefferson, but she has potential. And I think she could help him find focus and ambition. At any rate, she's his wife, and that's that."

Jefferson seemed like a toy boat in a turbulent pond, tossed by crosswinds. He kept silent. And that was a wise plan for me, as well.

Exasperated, Aria unfolded her arms and smacked them down her sides. "Whatever is going on, Jefferson needs to get away. Can't you see he's a wreck?"

I didn't notice he was so much of a mess. But then, I didn't know him well.

Eula glanced at him briefly, then back to Aria. "Maybe he and Nanette should take a vacation. Go to your grandparents' place on the Cape for two weeks. It could help."

Aria thrust her hands on her hips in frustration. "No. Not two weeks. I know you don't want to hear this, but I don't think Hansford Meats is the place for him."

Eula looked more confused than angry. "Not the place? It's his legacy. As it was mine. He just needs to grow into it."

Aria moved a half inch in front of Jefferson. "You and Blaine love it. And you run it so well. You don't need Jefferson. Let him go after his own dreams."

Eula gave Jefferson a puzzled glance, then spoke to Aria. "He doesn't have any dreams. And I can't let him float. If he doesn't work, how will he ever have self-respect?"

I'd certainly listened without comment when my family argued about how I should live my life. But this felt like Jefferson was allowing Aria to fight his battle. Feeling eight shades of awkward, I wondered if anyone would notice if I backed out of the room.

Aria folded her arms again, as if she couldn't release all of her agitation. "Think of it this way, he could take a leave of absence until he figures out what to do with his life, and by then, whoever is after him will either quit or get caught."

Eula wrinkled her forehead as if deciphering a math theorem. "If he's not working at Hansford Meats, how will he make a living and support himself and Nanette?"

Aria was struggling to stay calm, I could tell by the tightness around her eyes. "Jefferson and Nanette are on the verge of divorce."

That was putting it mildly.

Eula's face hardened. "That will not happen."

Aria pressed her advantage. "Part of the problem is that Jefferson is working so hard to please you at a job he hates. It's putting strain on the marriage. Maybe give him two years. You don't have to give him a big stipend, just enough to take the pressure off so he and Nanette can work on their marriage. Maybe give you a grandbaby?"

She was so convincing, I was rooting for Jefferson and Nanette to reconcile.

Eula turned to Jefferson. "Is this true?"

Those blue eyes held such a depth of pain, I couldn't see how Eula could deny him anything. And I doubted she had, despite her reputation as a dragon. "I'm sorry, Mother. I hate the thought of disappointing you. But Aria is right. I'm not happy in my position as spokesman. Maybe I would be better in a management role. But right now, my main priority is fixing my marriage. And taking some time away is the only way I can do that."

Eula kept her eyes on him as if trying to read his heart. "If you were suited for management, I would have placed you in a position before now. With all your people skills, I thought you'd love the job I created for you. Honestly, Jefferson, you're a grown man and should be able to deal with a wife and a job at the same time."

Aria doubled down. "I know he's going to kill me because he doesn't want you to know this, but a couple of months ago, Jefferson told me he was thinking of taking off. Running away and not telling anyone where he was going. He's that far gone. Aunt Eula, look at him. He needs a break."

Jefferson didn't answer. The baleful look in his eyes held apology and hope, shame and a hint of groveling.

I got the feeling this wasn't the first time a similar scene had played out.

Eula lifted her face and gazed at me with those remarkable blue eyes, but she didn't really see me.

There was no actual clock in the room, but I swore I heard it ticking as the silence lingered for too long.

Finally, Eula blinked and inhaled enough to fill three sets of lungs. "I'll give it some thought. If I decide to make some changes, I'll announce it this afternoon at the board meeting. I trust you'll be there with your report on the charitable activities for the coming year." She glared at him and pointed her finger. "But there will be no divorce. Not being a part of the company is something I may have to accept, but divorce is a sin against God."

With head high and shoulders straight, she marched toward the door, on a collision course with me. I jumped back, and it seemed to surprise her

I was in the room. She quickly continued her route out of the room and down the hall, heavy footsteps receding.

Jefferson and Aria both let out a whoosh of air and deflated with relief.

Aria placed a palm on her forehead. "That went so much better than I'd thought. We should have done this ages ago."

Jefferson flopped back in his chair. "Thank you, thank you, thank you. I could never stand up to Mother like that. You're my savior."

Aria looked peaked, as Grandma Ardith would say. "You know I'm always on your side. Between Eula and Blaine, you've been bullied too long. But next time, you need to fight back, too."

Jefferson frowned. "But what if Mother contacts Nanette?"

Aria tipped her head back. "If you offer her money, she'll tell Eula whatever it takes."

Jefferson looked doubtful. "You bought me a year, maybe two. But I don't have the kind of money Nanette will demand."

She rolled her eyes. "You have a fat trust fund."

A hint of anger lit his eyes. "It's not even a fraction of the family money. And not enough to give it away."

She let out a huff of annoyance. "Stop worrying. We'll figure something out."

He reached up and grabbed her hand. "Thanks for saving me. Again."

"You're not out of the woods yet. She didn't agree. Just be pathetic at the board meeting, and she'll cave." Aria acted as though manipulating Eula was an old game. It made me squirm.

Aria turned to me. "Sorry you had to see all of that."

Me, too. But I didn't want anyone to feel worse. "I've got family, too. There's always some drama." That felt a little dismissive for the sea shift I'd just witnessed.

"I feel like I can actually breathe for the first time in my life." For a guy who'd been drugged, Jefferson looked surprisingly alert.

I tried for a light tone. "You recovered fast."

Aria collapsed on the bed, probably exhausted by the emotional joust. "Right? The doctor said it's probably because Jefferson is in such good shape and the dose might have been for a smaller person."

I acknowledged that, then added, "You probably ought to lie low today.

First to rest up, and second because you still don't know who or why you were attacked."

"See?" Aria poked him. "That's what I said."

He gave us a mocking pout while his ocean-blue eyes danced. "The dynamic duo at it again. I'll tell you what I told Aria. I've got to get ready for the board meeting this afternoon."

Aria sat up on the bed. "Your life has been threatened, pea-brain. You shouldn't go anywhere until we figure out who and why, or you're on a plane out of the country."

Jefferson considered her for a second. "Ask Blaine where he was on Friday night. Or Saturday afternoon."

I knew where he was on Saturday night. "You think Blaine is behind this?"

He and Aria exchanged looks before she said, "He's been threatening Jefferson for a couple of years."

"Threatening? With what?"

Jefferson winced and let out a breath before he started. "A few years ago, I borrowed some money from the company."

Aria tilted her head in a way that urged him to correct himself.

"Okay. I embezzled a few hundred thousand dollars. Nanette had gone nuts on remodeling a house, and we needed the money. Blaine found out and fixed it. He fired a guy, Bradley Heimlich, who worked in finance. Blaine convinced the board that pressing charges would draw unwanted attention to the company, so the guy never had to get outed."

"He wouldn't get outed, since he hadn't actually done anything." I wanted to point out they'd fired an innocent person.

Aria shook her head. "That was his name? Like Heimlich maneuver?"

Jefferson shrugged. "Yeah, I guess. But the point is, Mother doesn't know it was me. Nanette knew about it, of course. And she threatened me and Blaine that she'd tell Mother about it if we didn't do whatever she wanted."

A messy situation was getting messier.

Aria rubbed her forehead and closed her eyes. Fatigue from the whole last few days might be rolling over her. "It's not Nanette divorcing you that scares you. It's that she'll tell Aunt Eula about the money, isn't it?"

Jefferson continued. "It wouldn't only be bad for me, it would ruin Blaine, too. I don't want to be responsible for taking him down. Nanette says she's going to the board if I don't give her a million dollars."

"But going to the board won't help Nanette, since Eula won't pay her off after that," I said.

Aria agreed. "If Tiger doesn't pay her off, she won't be rich but she'll get her revenge."

"A million dollars is a lot of money." I stated the obvious.

"Blaine said he'd take care of it. But he wants me out of the company. Out of the will." He paused. "Maybe out of his life completely."

A tap on the door made us turn. The cop from yesterday entered and introduced herself. "Officer Estes. Just want to ask a couple of questions before they turn you loose." She pulled out her phone to take notes.

Jefferson looked resigned. "Okay. But I don't remember much."

The cop, a woman in her mid-thirties with a figure more suited to watching football on the couch than running marathons, had a round face that looked prone to smiling. She wore her hair pulled back in a tight pony-tail. In her blue uniform, complete with Kevlar vest and a well-appointed tool belt, she carried herself like a real professional. "Do your best. Your cousin said you'd gone to your room with a woman named Sandi Peters. That's an alias for—"

Jefferson interrupted. "Yes. Aria told me. But she wouldn't have hurt me."

Estes kept her eyes on her phone. "Why did you take her to your suite?"

That didn't seem to give him a problem. "I got hit on the head the night before, and I started to get a headache. Sandi offered to help me back to the hotel and rub my shoulders and then stay while I slept because of the head injury."

Estes's smirk told me she doubted they'd gone to the suite for some-thing so innocent. "What happened when you got to the room?"

He stared at the floor for a moment while he thought, then he seemed to remember something. "You know, those animal rights people were at the hotel when we got there."

Aria flared up. "What? You didn't tell me that."

He looked contrite. "I forgot. They were shouting at us when the car dropped us off, and we ran inside."

It all seemed weird. "How did they know you were staying there or that you'd be there in the middle of the day?"

Estes typed on her phone. "These protesters, you know who they are?"

Jefferson shook his head, so I supplied what I knew. "They called each other Gwen and Arlo."

Good humor snuck onto Estes's face. "Makes sense."

Now we were getting somewhere. "You know them?"

She raised one eyebrow. "Oh, yeah. Gwen and Arlo Smithburg. They've made a career out of protesting. I don't even think they care so much about the cause, as long as it's against The Man. I swear their house must be packed with protest posters for everything. Arlo likes to harass people so they'll take a swing at him. But Gwen, she's likely to be the one who escalates things."

Aria jumped at that. "Do you think they're dangerous?"

Estes considered it. "Well...Gwen did spend some time in prison. I heard it was manslaughter." She clicked her tongue. "But I'm not sure."

I pulled out my own phone and texted Zoe. She might be in town after church and could run up to the courthouse to use the computer.

Estes turned back to Jefferson. "Did they come upstairs with you?"

Jefferson concentrated, then said, "No. Not right away. But not long after we got there, they started shouting outside the door and banging on it. I don't know how they would have gotten up there because you need to swipe your card."

I knew how they might have gotten around that, but I wasn't going to say anything.

"Then what happened?"

He wrinkled his forehead, and we waited. "Sandi and I poured a drink, and then I don't remember after that."

Estes typed. "You went up there because you had a headache, but you drank alcohol?"

He chuckled. "Yeah. I guess that sounds bad, especially that time of day. But I thought maybe I was tense, because there was a fundraiser later I needed to speak at, and I hadn't started writing my speech. So, I thought, if I have a shot, then I'll relax enough to get some sleep."

"And Sandi Peters was there when you drank. That's all you know?"

He clenched his fists in his lap. "I know Sandi didn't do it. Maybe that Gwen and Arlo did something."

The cop gave him a deadpan look. "I can't see how they would have worked the logistics on that one. We've got a warrant out for Janelle Shepherd. But honestly, I wouldn't hold my breath we'll find her."

Aria was indignant. "Someone can just drug someone and get away with it?"

Estes pocketed her phone. "Yeah. Usually, it happens to naïve young women, and a lot of bad things go on." She turned an amused look on Jefferson. "Rare to happen to a middle-aged white guy with lots of money."

The struggle traveled across Aria's face. Anger that Estes didn't seem to care about Jefferson, awareness of the truth of what the cop said. Injustice and outrage and fatigue were taking a toll on her still stunning face.

Like me, Aria wanted the people she loved to be safe. But the world can be a dangerous place.

25

I was surprised when Aria told Jefferson she'd ordered him a car to take him to The Four Seasons. I'd assumed she'd want to tuck him in herself. Maybe this meant we were a go to visit Brodgar. Finally.

But as we parted ways with Jefferson in the parking lot and we climbed into Elvis, she had different plans. "We need to find out where this Gwen and Arlo live. I think it's time we pay them a visit."

Despite my hopes to visit my dream bull, I figured Aria would have an alternative plan. I pulled up my phone and showed her the text with the Smithburgs' address that I'd received in response from Zoe. "Got it. But I'm pretty sure Gwen and Arlo will take exception to that leather jacket."

Aria threw her head back and laughed. "I love you so much, Kate Fox."

That sent a wave of warmth through me. Not everyone in my life showed me such genuine appreciation. We drove east to Commerce City, a suburb that had seen better days. As we wound through the downtrodden neighborhood of homes clad in dented aluminum siding, some of it bent and torn from the frames, the yards became barer with an increasing amount of junk decaying into the dirty snow. A few chain link fences protected the precious crap from passersby or maybe kept dogs and small children from escaping into the street.

"Do you think Eula is going to let Jefferson take off for two years?" I asked, wondering what it would be like to have income you didn't need to work for.

Aria hesitated. "Aunt Eula was always so strict while we were growing up that it was a game to trick her into letting Jefferson do things or to get him out of trouble after the fact. But it's not fun anymore. She has some legit concerns."

"You think Jefferson is manipulating her?" Which would mean he was doing the same to Aria, and she'd be smart enough to see it.

She hesitated. "Oh, no. Not really. I mean, someone has attacked him. Put him in the hospital twice. Maybe he needs to do some growing up, but getting out of here is probably for the best."

Sights of the majestic mountains rising into the clear sky provided the luxury of an insurmountable view, even if some of these people couldn't afford a neighborhood like Diane's.

Aria tapped a fingernail on her thigh. "What was Nanette doing at the fundraiser last night?"

"She had an invitation from Jefferson." I told her about seeing Nanette at Casa Bonita and that she said she deserved more than the prenup provided, and ended with their supposed date to meet at the hotel Friday night.

"Bullshit," she said, surprising me with her rare cursing. "If she can't get him to pay her off, she plans to kill him and inherit his estate."

I followed Ms. GPS, making another turn down an equally run-down street. "Then why are we chasing Arlo and Gwen?"

She slapped her thigh and gave me a helpless look. "Because I don't know where Nanette is. I swear, Jefferson has the worst picker for women."

"What do you mean?"

She grimaced. "He hooked up with this chick at Stanford. I kind of liked her. Cute and smart. I thought maybe it was serious. But then she shows up with bruises and claims Jefferson beat her up."

I wanted to ask if he had, but figured that would be a stupid question. "What happened?"

She growled. "I paid her a few thousand dollars. I mean, it's what she wanted. And was willing to have someone hit her to stage it. But Jefferson didn't learn his lesson."

"It happened again?"

She looked out the window. "He never asked me to cover it, if it did."

Which didn't sound like a rousing no.

We pulled up in front of a square house not much bigger than my Stryker Lake cottage. This one had blue siding that had faded to gray. The front door opened onto a block of concrete porch. Gwen and Arlo had embraced the whole xeriscape design ideal but without a plan, as if they let nature take over. Dried grasses and weeds with dead thistle heads didn't give off a welcoming vibe.

Aria straightened her jacket when we stepped out of the car and winked at me. We managed to make our way up a cracked sidewalk to the front door without a machete. I didn't fight Aria for the lead and let her rap with authority on the metal door.

A dog yapped and Arlo shouted, his voice clear through the thin walls. "No soliciting. Can't you read?"

Aria's voice came out two octaves lower than normal. "Mr. Smithburg. We'd like to discuss a march for women's rights coming up in March." She raised an eyebrow and gave me a *how-about-that?* look.

It must have plucked a heartstring, because the click and slide of locks started. His instant excitement felt pathetic. As the door opened, he started, "I have a line on where we can get pussy hats. It's China, but I feel like in this instance we can make an except—"

He swung open the door, and all his excitement vanished. Before he could slam it closed, I stuck a foot in the jamb and the door bounced against my boot.

Aria rushed inside, pushing him backward. Maybe she was channeling every cop on every TV series from the eighties. Whatever the inspiration, she sounded tough. "Okay, dirtbag. Start talking."

A three-toned mixed-breed dog about the size of a beagle with scruffy hair and a body too long for its short legs stood in the doorway between the kitchen and the living room where we entered. He put up a racket and bounced on his front legs with each bark.

I shut the front door to keep him from escaping and to hold in some of the heat from a wood-burning stove on a brick platform taking up most of the living room.

Arlo wore faded flannel pajama pants, and his hair hung long on his shoulders. Scuffed leather slippers (or maybe faux leather because of his sensibilities—who could tell?) and an oversized sweatshirt completed his casual attire. "What are you doing here? This is harassment. Or intimidation. I'll sue."

Aria had skills from managing a financial empire, to training as a first responder, to being a knowledgeable ranch hand. But hard-nosed investigator might be one of her most proficient. She had the expression of someone not about to tolerate a kid's temper tantrum. When he stopped sputtering, she said, "Okay, Arlo. You call your attorney, and I'll call mine. My colleague and I are merely visiting you. I'm not the only witness to your wife, Gwen, pulling a knife on someone after bursting into a ticketed event for which you were not invited. I think that's, at the very least, assault with a deadly weapon."

Arlo glared at us for a second while the pooch kept up its manic barking. Poupon didn't often conjure up the energy it took to bark with that much zeal, and I suddenly missed my apathetic sidekick.

Arlo's nose curled up as if he smelled something bad. Honestly, it would have to be real bad to be worse than the cooked cabbage odor in the house. "How can you wear dead skin on your body. That's disgusting."

Aria preened. "And comfortable and stylish."

Arlo snapped at the dog, "Shut up, Al."

Al growled but quit barking. His eyes said he'd love to take a bite out of us to see how we tasted.

Arlo leaned against the door jamb into the kitchen. "Fucking Gwen. Man. She's a problem."

Aria folded her arms. "That would be Gwen, your wife?"

He raised his tone in sneering imitation. "Yes, that's Gwen, my wife." He shook his head. "She's always been a loose cannon. One step forward in our fight for justice, and she takes us two steps back. Every. Fucking. Time."

I looked around at the small room crowded with worn furniture. Newspapers and magazines covered every surface, along with books about climate change, world banking, corporate greed, and probably more of the world's ills, but I quit reading titles. "Where is your lovely bride?"

He gave me a disdainful ugh. "Long gone. At least I hope."

Aria stepped closer to him. "What do you mean by that?"

He tilted his head up to the ceiling. "She came into some money, she said." He gave *some money* air quotes. "Said she was tired of living like a pauper. Pauper. She actually said that. Like all of a sudden she's English royalty."

"And she's moved out?" Aria said.

"Left me goddamn Al Gore, a dog she *had* to rescue because society threw him away. Even though, mind you, I said I didn't want a dog."

I looked at poor Al Gore, who seemed to understand the state of his abandonment and dropped to the gold-and-green linoleum kitchen floor, chin on his paws. I agreed with Arlo's description of Gwen. Who could leave behind a soul you've rescued?

Undaunted by Al Gore's status, Aria stayed focused. "How did Gwen come into a sum of money so large she can skip town?"

His bitter laugh filled the small house. "You tell me. Gwen and I, we were supposed to be a team. We met in Berkeley. And you know how crazy that time was. People were passionate about saving the world. Getting rid of LBJ. Stopping the killing fields, the slaughter in Vietnam."

A wave of PTSD rolled toward me, too close for me to duck. Mom had embraced that world of passion and protest. She'd hidden from her deeds for forty years, marrying Dad, raising nine children in the isolated Nebraska Sandhills. It was a weird upbringing, as all my brothers and sisters would admit, but nothing had prepared us for the crimes Mom had committed in her past. When it caught up to her, it steamrolled over our family, nearly destroying us. I'd never understand the weight of betrayal Dad would carry for the rest of his life.

Apparently, Aria wasn't suffering from the trauma Arlo and I were. Her voice held no compassion. "So, you and Gwen, together since the Earth was young. Where the hell did she get the money to leave you after a millennium?"

I bent down and scratched Al Gore's ears. He rolled over to his back and presented me a belly I couldn't resist rubbing.

Arlo dropped his head, not ready to answer Aria. "We agreed to sacrifice our lives to the betterment of this country." He flipped his chin up. "It may surprise you to know how much we love the United States. We only want to make it better. More sustainable. A home that welcomes all."

Aria rolled her eyes. "Focus, Arlo. Gwen. Money."

He pushed himself from where he leaned and glowered down at Aria. "She sold her soul. She had a weak streak, always loved when things got violent." He locked eyes with Aria as if he sought sympathy. "In the last few years, she changed. Maybe it was aging. You know, things start to hurt, to break down. We don't have insurance, and Medicare only goes so far."

Aria sighed with impatience, but she didn't interrupt.

"She found an easy way. Said someone offered to pay us to threaten Jefferson Hansford."

I left off rubbing Al Gore. We were hitting pay dirt.

"Who?" Aria sounded breathless.

"First it was the Casa Bonita thing."

"Who?" Aria insisted.

"Then it was at his hotel."

"Did they hire you to be at the Brown Palace?" I asked.

He seemed to suddenly remember I was there and blinked at me. "No. That was on me. All those greedy elite assholes eating steaks and pretending to care about someone else. At first, Gwen didn't want to go, but she was hyped up and decided to do it. I should have known she was out of control."

Aria grabbed the front of Arlo's sweatshirt. "Who paid Gwen to go after Jefferson?"

He flicked her off. "How should I know?"

26

On our way to The Four Seasons, Aria simmered. It was still sunny, but a few clouds were sauntering in, the first to start the party.

Aria frowned. "Someone hired Gwen to mess with Jefferson. Not kill him. Why?"

"We have a few suspects. Sandi, who wants his money. Nanette, who also wants his money. And Blaine, who resents him because he's Eula's favorite."

She stared out the windshield in deep concentration. "My money is on Nanette."

"But what could injuring him do to help her?" I maneuvered through midday traffic, as we'd jumped on and off I-70, all four lanes busy despite it being a Sunday.

We rode in silence for a bit, and my heart sank to see Aria slump back in Elvis's bucket seat. I wanted to support her, even as guilt stuck in my throat for that damned kiss. "That display at the Brown Palace was a real mess. You'd put so much into planning that to have it go so sour. How are you doing?"

She pinched her nose between her eyes. "I appreciate you not saying I look like hell."

"You could never look bad."

She laughed. "You're a pretty good liar. But, yeah, I didn't sleep much last night. It wasn't the fundraiser, though. I mean, we'd already collected for attendance, and most people had bid on the silent auction before dinner."

"Worrying about Jefferson?" I wanted to ease her mind. "I think you convinced Eula to let him quit, and maybe he'll get out of the country for a while."

"No, not Jefferson." She closed her eyes and winced, as if a wave of pain hit her. Then she looked out the windshield again, her face as bleak as a prairie after a flood. "Something's up with Glenn. But he won't talk about it. I shouldn't have pushed him to tell me, but he looked so upset I thought it would help him to open up."

Damn it. I was the last person that should hear this.

"He didn't fight with me or anything like that. But he shut down. It was like having a sandbag in bed with me. I swear he didn't move, or even breathe all night. And I'm certain he didn't sleep, because I didn't, either. He left at sunrise, saying he needed to get back to Chicago early. But I think he just wanted to get away from me."

I searched for something to say that might help. I had nothing. "I'm sure it's a work thing and he'll get over it quickly."

She laughed again. "That's about as convincing as you saying I look good."

We parked at The Four Seasons and entered the tasteful lobby with a cozy fire. Aria used the key card she'd insisted Jefferson give her, and we rose to the penthouse.

She knocked as she opened the door. "He's probably sleeping," she said when he didn't answer and wasn't in the living room or kitchen. She tiptoed back to the bedroom, and I was drawn to the windows overlooking the mountains. The approaching clouds hadn't made it as far as the mountains and the sun highlighted the rugged peaks, gleaming white as they thrust into the blue sky, the color of Hansford eyes.

Just seeing them made me draw in a lung-filling breath. My shoulders started to unkink, and it occurred to me I might survive Baxter. I had a new business venture and couldn't wait for Aria to meet Brodgar and seal that deal. I had my family, including my best friend, Sarah, and the two little nieces in their home. If I got myself unstuck from Baxter, maybe I could even date again. Thirty-six was hardly in the grave.

"Damn it, Jefferson!" Aria shouted with frustration.

I spun around as she crashed into the living room, phone in hand. She jabbed at it and held it to her face, barking into it. "Where the hell are you? What about *rest* don't you understand?"

A bit of a tinny voice filtered to me before she swiped at her phone and shoved it into the pocket of her leather jacket. "That dimwit is at the stock show. There's a presentation for the winner of the Junior Angus steer show, and he thinks he owes Eula to be there."

I understood not wanting to let your family down. I couldn't fault him for feeling like he needed to finish a job he'd started. I'd helped Zoe out after she'd been appointed sheriff, not that she was actual family but she felt like it sometimes. "It must have been a small dose if he's feeling ener-gized enough to get around. That's good news, at least."

Aria gave me an irritated humph and started for the door. "He's an idiot. Someone might be trying to take him out, and we don't know how far they'll go and what they really want, and he's going to be around thousands of people. Anyone could get to him there."

I agreed and followed her out. I did my best to steer Elvis through Denver's streets, awash in sunshine but with the white plumes of smoke from every tailpipe. I enjoyed my periodic forays to Denver, but staying more than three days tended to make me antsy, like a tiger in a zoo. Too many people, too many stoplights, too many smells of exhaust and commerce.

I dropped Aria off at the entrance and swung back to the overflow parking lot. Feeling too impatient to wait for the shuttle, I took off at a sprightly pace to the Expo Hall and made it there within fifteen minutes.

Glad to avoid the hustle of the Expo Hall, I hurried to the cattle barn and joined the cluster of people making their way to the arena. Angus were a popular breed, and the Junior show usually brought out proud families to watch their teens show an animal they'd worked with for months. The checks for winners were nice, sometimes going a long way with college expenses.

Since I wasn't there to look at cattle, I bypassed the main arena, descended stairs, and beelined to the prep arena. This was a smaller arena adjacent to the show ring where contestants gathered before entering the competition. I assumed I'd find Jefferson and Aria there, where Jefferson would be waiting to make the presentation of the oversized check to the winner.

Several nervous teens made last-minute adjustments to cowboy hats, tucked in shirts, primped their shiny black steers, and generally fidgeted and looked ready to barf. I didn't spot Jefferson or Aria, but caught sight of Blaine, his face so pursed it resembled a cat's back end with its tail raised. He stood beside the official woman I'd talked to yesterday at the reception upstairs. Professional in a plaid blazer and a different clip holding back her dark hair, she didn't look a whole lot happier than Blaine.

He caught a glimpse of me and stormed my way.

With no bomb shelter in sight, I held my ground and waited for the explosion.

It hit while he was still several yards away. "Where the hell is he?"

I didn't answer until I could see the whites of his eyes. Eyes only slightly less vibrant than his brother's. "I assumed he was here. With Aria."

He threw his head back in consternation. "Of course they'd be together. Screwing off and not attending to business."

I wondered where they'd gone. "Aria was meeting him here. Maybe they're getting coffee or something. I'm sure they'll be here soon."

Blaine growled, and I wondered about his blood pressure levels with all that anger roiling inside him. "Don't count on it. He's lucky I showed up." He glanced around in irritation. "And Mother didn't."

That made me wonder. "Why are you here?"

The woman he'd been talking to glanced over but turned back to the show ring. I figured she was eavesdropping and could probably catch the tone of the conversation, if not every word.

His eyes jumped to mine, and he scrutinized me as if weighing my worth. He finally made a dismissive face, as if telling me wouldn't matter. "You were at the hospital this morning for Aria's impassioned speech about poor Jefferson, so you already know Mother is probably going to allow him to go away for a year or two to work on his marriage." He probably couldn't resist the air quotes on that. "But he won't come back. And she'll keep paying him. And eventually he'll get half the estate."

Man, I guess when Eula decided to act, she didn't hesitate. Aria would be glad to hear of it. "That doesn't explain why you're here."

His brows were so furrowed they nearly covered his eyes. "We have some outstanding business, and I've taken care of it."

I tried for a thoughtful look. "Hmm. It wouldn't have anything to do with Nanette, would it?"

His startled look gratified me. I'd hit bone.

"Why would you say that?"

I pinned him with my gaze. "Because I saw you together at the Brown Palace last night. When you were supposed to be sitting that one out."

He shifted his eyes to the right and left, and I guessed he was searching for an excuse.

I got tired of waiting and pushed him. "It's okay. I know she planned on telling Eula you'd lied about Jefferson embezzling money and blamed it on some other poor schmuck."

He blew air from both nostrils, and it seemed wrong there was no steam involved. An old-fashioned telephone ring distracted him, and he yanked his phone from his shirt pocket. Of course he'd have an unoriginal and loud ringer. He was the most important person in the room, right?

He turned an alarming shade of red, contrasting with his Hansford eyes. He gave me his back and looked down, lowering his voice as he spoke into the phone. Because he wanted privacy, I leaned in to hear.

All I caught was, "Write it down this time. Maven 315."

He spun back to me with a suspicious glare. "Fine. Right. I was making a deal with her. She gets a payout big enough to enjoy the rest of her life without needing to worry about money ever again."

"Good for her, since it was her overspending that started the whole thing?"

He looked puzzled. "What are you talking about?"

What had Jefferson said? "He stole the money to pay for her house remodel."

Blaine laughed. "Oh, he got you, too. With what Mom pays him, Jefferson could afford remodeling. He needed that money to pay for a gambling debt. Good news is that he seemed to learn the lesson and, as far as I know, hasn't done a boneheaded thing like that again."

Huh. Jefferson wouldn't be the first guy to blame a mistake on someone else. "And the Heimlich guy? His life just gets crushed under the Hansford tires?"

Blaine looked at the ground as if dropping his guilt in the dirt. "There's a long line of destruction in Jefferson's wake. And most of it caused by me fixing it for him. For Eula, so she never has to know what he is."

This guy carried a forty-ton brick on his shoulder. "It should be easier on you if Jefferson goes somewhere else." Maybe easier on Blaine if Jefferson disappeared permanently.

Bitterness infused his voice. "Jefferson gets his portion of the company and can lie around on the beach till he rots. And me? Well, I get to keep busting my ass for Eula as long as she lives." He paused, and those remarkable eyes drilled into me. "And she'll probably live forever and never, ever, acknowledge all I do for her."

"Jefferson thinks you want to get rid of him and rob him of his inheritance."

His jaw dropped in exaggerated disbelief. "That's ridiculous. What I want is for him to shoulder some of the family responsibilities. He's entitled to his half, but he should have to work for it, same as me."

Wow. It was as if I'd stuck a pin into a balloon and everything whooshed out. On the one hand, I sympathized with him working so hard for his family and always feeling underappreciated. But the whole poor-me saga seemed too pathetic. It's not like there wasn't enough money to go around for everyone to live a happy life. Even if it meant confronting a cantankerous and controlling old lady.

I was still trying to figure out how to respond when he lifted a palm as if dismissing me. "I've made my choices. I'll see them through. But you." He pointed at me. "If I were you, I'd get as far away from Jefferson and Aria as possible. Those two will bring you down. I promise it."

I started to defend Aria, but the dark-haired woman appeared behind Blaine and tapped him on the shoulder. "You need to make the presentation."

Blaine paused long enough to shoot an extra portion of venom at me with his stare. Then he stomped past the stock show official. She immediately moved toward me.

We watched him, and when he'd passed into the show ring, the woman grimaced. "That's one messed-up family." She held out her hand to me. "I'm Grace. I saw you at the reception yesterday. Sorry I thought you were trying to pick up Jefferson Hansford."

I shook her hand and gave her my name. "Why do you say they're messed up?"

She guffawed. "If that old lady has a heart beating in that chest, I'd be shocked. Blaine hasn't smiled in all the years I've been working for the stock show, and Jefferson." She stopped to laugh. "Who knows what's up with that guy. Sometimes he's the best spokesman for their company and the stock show, and sometimes, like today, well, you don't know what you're going to get. But here's the deal. Whatever crap he pulls, Jefferson always gets you to forgive him."

That was my impression of Jefferson, too. "Have you seen him today?"

She shook her head, her face twisted in annoyance. "I haven't seen Jefferson, and I've been here for the whole Junior show." She checked her phone. "That's two hours."

"What about his cousin, Aria? She's not much taller than me, pretty, with brown hair?"

Grace nodded. "Oh, I know Aria. Gorgeous. Yeah, she was here. But not for long. She took off in a hurry."

"Do you know where she was going?"

"No." Grace checked her phone again and frowned. "I've got to take this."

I scanned the area, hoping to see Jefferson or Aria but not expecting it. A new group of young people had taken the place of those who'd filed into the show ring earlier. Still Angus, but these were heifers. The whole process would continue for days. Most people preferred the horse shows, which were held in a different barn across the stock show complex. And though I loved the horses, cows had a special place in my heart.

My phone buzzed, and I pulled it out of my back pocket. I'd missed a call from Louise and one from Aria. Maybe my butt had gone numb from the cold walk from the parking lot. But the current text was from Jeremy.

COME C ME

There wasn't much to do at the arena since Jefferson hadn't shown and I had no idea where Aria was, so I started for the pens on the other side of the arena, punching in Aria's number on the way. She didn't answer, and I'd nearly made it to the entryway that would either lead up to the trade show or down another corridor to the cattle pens.

"Kate! Oh my gosh! There you are!" There was only one person who spoke in so many exclamation points. Roxy. Great.

Since she had me in her sights, I stepped toward the wall and out of the flow of traffic.

She, of course, hugged me as if we hadn't seen each other in years. Today, she wore a red leather skirt with fringe, white cowboy boots, an intricately embroidered Western shirt with pearl buttons—that one I actually liked—and a black cowboy hat. She didn't look too outrageous, except for the ruby lipstick and thick false eyelashes. "So, how did it go at the Brown Palace thing? We weren't that busy here, but it was good I stayed to keep Marla company. We really needed to catch up. She's got the worst husband, cheating on her all the time. Makes me so grateful to have Ted."

So weird the Ted she talked about not only cheated on his first wife— me—with Roxy, but I knew of at least one other woman he'd been with after their nuptials. Why shatter someone's illusions? "It was fine."

She raised her eyebrows and opened her mouth in disbelief, taking a swipe at my arm. "Really? Because I heard those PETA people showed up and made a real mess of things."

So many routes the news could have taken to get to her. The only surprise was that she'd got the big picture correct. "Typical evening out with the Foxes."

She giggled. "Oh, you."

She plumped her hair and smiled one of her flirtiest. I glanced behind me to see a burly cowboy in a long barn coat give her a once-over and walk the other direction. She sounded irritated, and I didn't know if it was with me or because Mr. Stetson didn't fawn all over her. "Ted called and said it's already started snowing at home."

I'd love to get out of Denver to make it home before it got too bad. Fiona and her friends would be okay in the worst weather, but I didn't want to get stuck here any longer. That meant I needed to finally arrange for Aria to meet Brodgar and talk to Craig.

My phone vibrated, and I looked to see it was Aria. "Gotta take this. Have a good day." Not waiting for her to respond, I answered the phone and hurried toward Jeremy's pen.

Aria sounded out of breath. "Sandi is at the stock show somewhere, but I lost her. I can't find Jefferson, and he's not answering his phone. I'm really worried."

27

I hated that she was so rattled. "Jefferson is fine. Sandi can't get to him with all these people around."

Aria panted, sounding like she was rushing through the trade show. "I don't trust her. I know she's got something to do with all of this."

"I thought you suspected Nanette."

"Both of them," she barked back. "Or one of them. Bad news either way."

Whether Sandi had anything to do with drugging Jefferson or not, the idea of her being around wasn't comforting. "I was just in the arena, and Jefferson isn't there, so maybe he's not even at the stock show."

"He could be anywhere, and he's not answering. I swear when I find him, I'm putting a tracker on his phone."

"Jeremy texted me and needs something, so I'll meet you at Craig's pens after I talk to him." I hotfooted it through the maze of pens and varying cattle breeds.

The wide butts of two Hereford bulls greeted me when I made it to Bill Hardy's pen. They were chained to a bar at the pen's back wall, waiting to be combed, fluffed, trimmed, and doused with hairspray. Jeremy faced the corner of the pen, his back to me, his legs wide apart as if blocking the escape of someone tucked into the corner.

"What's all this about?" I edged behind him and pulled up short.

Keith stood wedged in the corner, his eyes glistening with worry and snapping from me to Jeremy, as if unsure what would happen.

I didn't say anything to Jeremy, just shot him a look inviting him to explain.

He lifted one shoulder and let it drop in a sort of half shrug, a gesture reminding me of when Mom had been called to the principal's office when Jeremy was in second grade. That day Mom's eyes had that glassy look, and she hadn't been wearing as much as her silk kimono when I'd taken the phone downstairs to her. So, I'd gone to get the story and learn Jeremy's fate.

When I found him seated in front of a stern Principal Barkley and asked him why he'd decked Justin Minor, he'd done that shoulder thing and said, "He pushed Tuff down and stepped on him, and Tuff is smaller than Justin."

"You are, too," I pointed out, not missing Mr. Barkley fighting a grin.

"Yeah, but I'm a Fox, and if Justin came after me, Michael and Douglas would be out for recess soon and take care of that nonsense." I'm sure Principal Barkley had as much trouble as I did not laughing at the turn of phrase my little brother must have picked up from a TV tough guy. Jeremy's unselfconscious charm saved him so many times. That time he got off with a warning.

This time, I hoped he wouldn't get charged with assault. "This doo-wah was lurking around down here where he doesn't belong."

Keith cleared his throat and sounded uncertain. "I...I wasn't lurking. I wanted to talk to you. And your...your brother attacked me."

I pinned Jeremy with a serious look. "Is that true?"

Jeremy sniffed in disgust. "I don't like this guy's looks, and if he wants to talk to you, he can darn sure do it where I can keep an eye on you."

"Thanks, I guess. You know I'm trained as a law officer. I'm certified to take care of myself."

That had never impressed Jeremy. "I'm your brother. It's my job to look out for you."

His words covered me and sank softly under my skin. I waved him away and motioned for Keith to join me in the aisle in front of the pen.

While Keith pushed himself from the hay-strewn ground, Jeremy hovered.

I gave him a little shove. "I know you don't have time to mess around like this. Bill's gonna want those bulls groomed or he's going to chew a hole in your pants."

Jeremy pointed at Keith and swaggered as he picked up a brush. "You stay where I can see you. Or I'll knock you into next week. You hear me?"

It took an effort not to laugh at my brother sounding so threatening, when I was sure the only reason he'd got the better in most brawls was because Jeremy had learned to hit first and run fast. On the other hand, I didn't mind someone keeping an eye on me as I talked to Keith.

We stood at the edge of the pen, letting the blast from the dryers, the rumble of the overhead heaters, and the garbled voice of the announcer build around us.

Keith wrinkled his nose and wiped it with the back of his hand. He tried for a friendly smile. "It stinks down here."

Roxy's perfume stank. Boiled cabbage stank. An oil refinery stank. The earthy aromas of stock show cattle barn did not stink. But I answered as every rural person learns in childhood. "Smells like money." That done, I turned to business. "You wanted to talk to me?"

He twisted his head to the right and left as if making sure no one was listening. Jeremy glanced up, tried for a mean look, then went back to grooming the bull. Keith said, "You need to watch out for Jefferson."

Ah. That was nice he cared. "You told me that before. Either tell me why or leave me alone."

Keith's innocent face went through a series of emotions. Frustration, consideration, confusion, and finally he huffed in resignation. "Can't you just trust me?"

Huh. "I'm supposed to trust the man who skulks around for days watching me and Jefferson." I paused as he seemed to be at a loss. "I saw you at the trade show before the animal rights dopes blew things up. You've followed me down here, to Casa Bonita. I don't know if you're after me or you're threatening Jefferson. What are you up to?"

He certainly wasn't a seasoned liar. A film of sweat made his face glisten. "It wasn't Jefferson. I s-s-saw you and thought you looked nice, and I ww-wanted to ask you out. But I'm n-n-not good at that kind of thing. I swear I'm not some creep."

My laugh sounded harsh. "That's a load of crap. There's more going on here, and I'm not convinced you aren't after Jefferson. I just don't know why."

Keith shook his head, looking like he'd like to run away. "No. I wouldn't hurt him. Or anyone. And, it's true, you seem like someone who would be fun to get to know."

Nothing he said sounded true. "But now you're warning me about Jefferson? Because you've gotten to know him so well?"

He shifted from foot to foot and couldn't look me in the eyes. "O-k-kay. I used to work at Hansford Meats. And, well, I know some things, and I just want to warn you to stay away from all of them. They aren't nice people, and you seem like a good person, and I probably should mind my own business but I don't want to see you get hurt." He'd hesitated to start, but once on a roll, he sped along.

I clamped onto him, squishing through the pile of his down coat to a thin arm. Despite his slinking around and general weirdness, I didn't get the feeling he was dangerous. I doubted this meek man could be behind the attacks on Jefferson. But I didn't want him around here. "How would I get hurt?"

Keith came along with me easily enough. He swallowed, but I'd bet his mouth was too dry it didn't give him reason to. "I c-c-can't say. But stay away from them, okay? Far away."

I kept my hand on his arm, urging him toward the exit as we crowded aside to let a few black bulls pass. "I think it's time for you to go home and stop worrying about me."

He pulled back. "No. Wait. I promised Ray I'd help him out today."

I'd had enough of his baloney. I tugged him to keep walking. "Right. That's a good excuse to hang out here and maybe try for another attack. Ray's your alibi."

He resisted my pull. "It's true. Ray needs help."

Still dragging him along, I said, "If you're so innocent, what were you talking to Sandi about yesterday?"

He drew in a breath and quit tugging against me. "I-I-I don't know what you're talking about."

Funny he didn't ask who Sandi was. "At the food court. You must remember."

That shut him up. I was about to chew on that a bit more, but decided I'd had enough of Keith and his antics.

We popped from the barn doors close to the front of the Expo Hall where a few taxis waited, hoping to get a jump on the Ubers and Lyfts people might call for. A bank of clouds had lumbered in, and a few flakes glistened in the sunshine. Since the temperatures hadn't climbed above twenty again, the flakes stayed dry and shimmered like diamonds.

I hustled Keith to the nearest taxi and yanked open the door. He'd quit fighting me and seemed a puddle of stress and worry.

I shoved him into the back seat. "Don't come back here."

He leaned out, seeming near tears. "Please, listen to me. Take the next taxi and get out of Denver."

He'd trounced on a few too many of my nerves, and I clenched my teeth to keep from telling him to shut up.

28

I watched the taxi drive away, white exhaust billowing into the milky sky as a few more snowflakes fell. I hated that I might be trying to outrun a snowstorm and drive back to Nebraska today. Keith's words felt like cold metal in my chest. It wasn't what he said, it was the urgency with which he said it. Maybe it was his paranoia about Jefferson. Or it could be a threat of violence from him.

A chill started at the crown of my head and stuttered down my spine. With the January freeze, that seemed appropriate. But the shiver wasn't from the weather. I spun around and took off for the Expo Hall, about fifty yards from the main entrance.

Sunday brought bigger crowds, and we swarmed at the double doors on the metal platform, all anxious to get out of the cold. My hope was to find Aria at the cattle show ring, where Jefferson would have miraculously appeared. Then Aria and I would high-step back to Craig McNeal's pen.

But as I waited to squeeze into the hall, my phone buzzed, and I pulled it from my pocket to see Aria's ID. I could barely hear her when I answered. Sounded like she played tug-of-war with a bull, along with a woman's high-pitched protests, and overhead announcements, and general stock show hullabaloo.

"...here now."

"What?"

She grunted. "I've got Sandi. Hurry." Some rustling and then a strained, "Would you hold still?"

I backed out of the people surging at the door, getting a few nasty looks and a humph or two. "Where are you?"

More wrestling sounds. "Horses. Big ones."

Well, dang. That would be the direction I'd just come from. I spun around and ran toward the horse barn. A bank of doors opened to a light-filled lobby. Up a flight of wide stairs led to the arena, a popular venue because everyone loves horses. Down a narrower set of stairs took you to the staging arena and back to the stalls.

Mumbling, "Excuse me, excuse me, excuse me," I shoved through groups of people meandering like turtles down the stairs and along the walkway around the staging area. It didn't make me popular, but no one was armed, at least that I noticed.

I might have missed Aria and Sandi because they were outside open barn doors large enough to allow the biggest tractors, trucks, and the Clydesdale teams that everyone adores. I couldn't miss the group of high school FFA students in their blue jackets congregated at the opening, all focused like kids ringing a playground fight.

Yep. They watched as Aria had Sandi pinned to the cold metal of the horse barn. A few inches shorter than Sandi, Aria nevertheless had shoved her against the wall with both fists clutching Sandi's white puffy coat at the collar. She wedged herself at an angle, digging her heels into frozen dirt and leaning her full weight to keep Sandi secure.

I blasted through the crowd of students. "Okay, time to move on."

They looked disappointed but used to authority, so they trudged away, still glancing over their shoulders.

Sandi fought and shoved but didn't break free. I'd been right about the shiner. Today it was starting to turn the color of a rotten banana, all mottled black and yellow. It looked nasty despite the concealing layers of makeup. "Get the hell off me."

I stepped behind Aria and addressed Sandi with a pleasant tone. "What a surprise to see you here."

"Screw you." Her words spit at me. Guess she wasn't interested in being my friend anymore.

Aria jerked against her, maybe trying to pull her back and slam her into the wall but not able to. She fired off questions like holding the trigger on an automatic rifle. "Why are you here? Where is Jefferson? What did you do to him yesterday?"

Sandi quit fighting and flared her nose, which was red from the cold. "What did *I* do to *him*? Lady, you're delusional if you think I was anything but the victim there."

Sandi grabbed Aria's wrists and shoved back, freeing herself. When Aria and I both closed around her, she seemed to give up on her plan to run off.

Aria's fists clenched, and she bared her teeth in a prelude to throwing a punch.

I shoved closer to Sandi to block Aria's shot. "You were the last one with Jefferson before we found him drugged. Did you plan to roll him? I mean, drugging your lover is usually not the way to get him to shower you with money and gifts."

Sandi, who looked older with her hair scraped back in a straggly ponytail, scrunched up her face in a mask of disbelief. "You're kidding me, right? I don't need to drug men to make them interested in me. And besides," she pointed to her black eye and stuck her chin at me to emphasize it, "you think I gave myself this? You need to ask those lunatic old hippies, because it sure as hell wasn't me."

Aria barked back at her, "We know it wasn't them. You're running out of scapegoats."

Sandi rubbed her nose with a hand chapped and reddened with cold. "Can we get inside somewhere before I freeze to death?"

Aria's hand shot out and connected with Sandi's shoulder, driving her back against the wall. "Who?"

Sandi's eyes watered. "I'm so sick of you and your family. You think money makes you special, but you're all piles of shit."

"But you wouldn't mind getting your hands on some of that money, would you?"

Sandi sniffed, the cold making her nose runny. "No amount of money is worth getting hit."

Aria didn't seem sympathetic. "From what we hear, Janelle, you're usually on the other end of the violence."

Snow fell harder, flakes disappearing on Sandi's blond hair and white coat, but pocking the crown of Aria's head.

Sandi wasn't impressed. "You know my birth name, so what? I can get a little cranky when I'm drinking and taking pills. But I'm clean now. I don't do any of that stuff anymore."

Aria seethed. "Your expertise sure comes in handy when you want to drug someone, though. You were arrested with ketamine. A date-rape drug. Maybe the same one used on Jefferson."

Sandi's bunny nose twitched in fury. "Jefferson poured. I took an opportunity to switch glasses. Figure that out."

Aria's lips curled back. "That's a lie. What did you do?"

There was more to this story. "I saw you tearing out of the parking lot. Who picked you up, and how did they know to be there?"

Aria glared at Sandi. "Save your breath, Kate. She's not going to tell us anything. But the cops have the security footage, and they'll see the truth."

If that bothered Sandi, she didn't show it. "Like cops are smart enough to figure out anything."

Since I'd been a sheriff, that sounded like a direct insult. "Cops were smart enough to get you arrested for assault."

She rolled her eyes like a surly teen. "Whatever."

Aria stepped back a pace. "If I ever see you within sniffing distance of Jefferson again, I'll make sure you disappear off the face of the planet."

Sandi thrust forward, suddenly full of bravado. "Tough girl, huh?"

I'd seen a lot of different sides of Aria, but this one, kind of like a mafia capo, scared me. "Oh, believe me, sweetheart. I've got money and lawyers, and I can do about anything I damned well please."

Probably wise, Sandi took her for her word. She tried for more of that bluster but edged sideways along the wall, not turning her back on Aria. "You and your whole family can go to hell."

"Have a nice day," Aria called after her.

We stood in the cold, the snowflakes falling on us. Aria reached out and clasped my fingers, hers like icicles that trembled in my palm.

"Thank you for being with me. I was so scared she was going to deck me."

I couldn't have been more surprised if she'd shed her coat and danced a hula in the snow. "You didn't show it."

"That's because Jefferson needs me." She squeezed my fingers. "And I need you."

29

We stepped back into the horse barn, not feeling much relief from the cold.

Aria glanced at her phone. She tapped out a message, shoved it back in her pocket, and took off. "Come on."

Already in step beside her, I said, "Where to?"

Roses bloomed on her cheeks from the cold, and she had a grim set to her mouth. "Tiger's at the cattle show. I'm going to chain him up so I don't have to worry about him anymore."

"Then we can go see Brodgar?" I sounded like my nephews begging to go to Casa Bonita.

"Then," she said, trotting across the cold pavement to the cattle barn, "we find Nanette. How we're going to do that, I don't know."

I felt my destiny with Brodgar slipping away and the familiar ache of disappointment landing in my gut. "I think I know where she is."

Aria stopped and stared at me. "How?"

I told her about talking to Blaine earlier and that he'd said he'd fixed things with Nanette. "He got a call and seemed mad at someone. Sounded like maybe whoever it was had forgotten some information. Blaine said, 'Maven 315.' So, maybe it was his fixer who was dropping off Nanette's payoff."

Aria squeezed me in a spontaneous hug. "Damn, Kate. You're a marvel."

We retraced the now familiar route back to the cattle barn and wound through the crowds and down to the prep arena.

"It's got to be Nanette." Aria bit each word.

It was a struggle to keep up with her, as we sped through both the crowds and her theories about Jefferson. "So, now you don't think it was Sandi?"

She raked a hand through her hair. "I don't know. They're both pretty sketch. But now I'm thinking Nanette is the one. We have to find her."

"Why do we need to see her, though? If Blaine gave her money, she'll be on her way and no more of a threat to Jefferson."

Aria gave a mirthless chuckle. "You're so nice you don't consider people like Nanette might enjoy being mean. I wouldn't put it past her to go to the board meeting today and tell Eula and everyone else about the embezzlement. I can't let her destroy Jefferson's future. If Eula finds out, she'll never give Jefferson his inheritance."

Jefferson stood near the entry to the show ring, smiling after Grace as she walked away from him. She noticed us approaching and gave me a wry arch of her eyebrows as if to say, "See? I told you he could charm his way into forgiveness."

Aria broke away from me, raced to Jefferson. She slapped at his arms and chest, an intimate gesture I'd done myself when one of my siblings showed up in one piece after I'd been spooked into thinking they were in danger. "What are you doing? Why can't you stay at the hotel? Just stop scaring me."

He held his hands up over his face. "Quit! Calm down, will ya?"

She quit hitting him and threw her arms around his neck. "I swear I'm going to kill you if someone else doesn't get to you first."

He patted her gingerly until she stepped back, dragging him to the back wall of the arena away from everyone. I followed.

He looked adorably contrite for a man in his late thirties. Like Aria, he seemed to have a persona for different occasions—unlike Blaine and Eula, who seemed consistently firm or angry. "I accidently left my phone in the car, and the driver had to bring it to me, so I didn't see that you'd been calling."

Aria's momentary relief washed away quickly, and she swatted at him again.

He ducked. "What?"

With each word, she smacked his arm with her open palm. "You didn't tell us Nanette was in your suite."

His jaw dropped. "What are you talking about?"

"At The Four Seasons. She's the one who drugged your drink."

He rubbed where she'd swatted his arm. "That can't be right. She'd never harm me."

Aria was worked up. "What do you call harm?"

Jefferson took a step back against Aria's verbal assault. "You don't understand. I was trying to convince her not to file for divorce."

Aria's voice rose in disbelief. "Have you seen her since then?"

Jefferson's eyes looked exactly like Jeremy's at age seven when he'd accidently admitted to eating all the cookies. It looked like he battled whether to tell Aria and then decided he didn't have a choice. "At the hospital. She stopped in after the fundraiser to tell me how it went."

It took Aria two quick inhales to answer. "Hospital? Last night? Visiting hours were over before you even woke up."

A hint of a smile fought its way to his lips. "Nanette isn't much of a rule follower."

Aria twisted her head away from him and stared at the collection of Simental cattle ready to enter the ring. To me, she said, "She comes to his room to extort money, and he thinks she's there to chat. He's always been blind about her."

Jefferson frowned at her. "You and Blaine never liked her. You don't understand her. She's really sweet if you ever took the time to know her."

Strain showed in Aria's face. "Sweet enough to rack up a fortune in debt that you ended up stealing from the company to pay back."

Except Blaine said the debt had been Jefferson's. Somebody or somebodies in this family lied.

He rose to her defense. "She never asked me to steal. That was my stupid idea."

Aria looked like she wanted to swat him again. "Even before you were together, she was trouble. I swear she's set on bringing down the Hansfords."

That sounded like a loaded statement, and I jumped in. "What does that mean?"

Jefferson and Aria exchanged a look that I'd guess discussed whether to air their family laundry. They must have decided to go ahead. Aria answered. "It was Pokey. He was dating her first."

Jefferson had lost that sheepish expression and seemed defiant, as if they'd had this argument before. "I know I should feel bad about that. But their relationship was over before we met."

Aria's studied calm told me she thought otherwise.

"Blaine said he loved her and probably did at first. But then he got so wrapped up in the company and keeping Mother happy that he started taking her for granted," Jefferson explained. "She fought for him as long as she could stand it, then had to give up. It broke her heart."

Aria snorted. "You can't break something you don't have."

Jefferson gave a shrug of defeat. "I think Blaine resented me for Nanette falling for me. That's why he's so quick to point out how hard he works and how lazy he thinks I am."

Aria shook her head. "Oh, honey, Pokey resents you for a lot more than that."

Jefferson pursed his lips. "I never meant to hurt Blaine. If I thought he really loved her or that she still loved him, I wouldn't have even considered a relationship."

Aria filled me in on some background. "Me and Blaine and Jefferson were the Three Musketeers when we were growing up. Pokey was older but he never had many friends, so he liked to hang around us."

Jefferson gave a sad laugh. "I don't know that he liked it so much. I think he was trying to keep us alive. We spent every summer at our grandparents' summer home on the Cape. Turbo always had some scheme going. If it hadn't been for Blaine, we'd have drowned, or burned the house down, or at least ended up in juvie. One time, Aria made us stuff our beds to make it look like we were asleep, and we took the sailboat out at night."

She lightly punched my arm and told me about it. "That got us all grounded for two weeks. Even though Blaine was old enough to drive by then. But we figured out how to sneak from our balconies, and we played poker in the boathouse."

We were silent for a moment. I thought about last night. "Do Blaine and Nanette get along now?"

Aria curled her lip. "No one gets along with either of them."

"I feel like it's my fault," Jefferson said.

Aria snorted. "Not gonna lie to you, dude. It *is* your fault."

He looked stricken.

Aria nodded at me. "But Kate and I are going to fix this."

She didn't tell Jefferson about Blaine's involvement, so I didn't either. But I thought a visit to Nanette might be useful in assuring Aria that Jefferson would be safe.

He looked nervous. "How?"

Aria tapped his chest. "You go back to your suite and rest. That's all."

"But the board meeting."

She slashed the air. "Nope. The hotel. Promise."

"Promise."

30

It didn't take long to get to LoDo, the thriving lower downtown neighborhood that spoked out from Union Station. But it felt as though it took a decade to find a parking place. So many people, all looking fit and outdoorsy in their casual, but probably expensive, athletic gear. It seemed to me most of the folks making their way up and down the sidewalks despite the January chill were young, thin, and white. That made me think all the restaurants and bars might be pricy.

We eventually docked Elvis several blocks away and scurried through the falling flakes to The Maven Hotel. The uncharacteristically gray sky made me feel gloomy. The snow hadn't started to stick yet, giving the streets and sidewalks a glossy glow. The ground floor housed some kind of micro mall with a trendy bar and grill, gift shops, a drinks cart made from a one-horse stock trailer, and a crowded coffee shop. Smells of bacon and coffee gave the place a warm, Sunday brunch vibe. But not for us. We were on a mission, and Nanette better beware.

We located the elevators and tried to look innocent while we waited for someone with a key card to enter so we could poach our way to the third floor.

Two women in their sixties, obviously sisters, hit the button for the second floor. They gave us a pleasant smile, then picked up their conversation about someone named Gladys who should never have married Burt and one sister "had told her so to her face."

Aria fidgeted until they exited on the second floor, then said, "I'm glad Blaine paid her off. But I'm going to make sure she knows she's done with this family. If she ever threatens Jefferson again in any way, it will be the last thing she ever does."

We popped out of the elevator, took a second to orient and find the right direction, then Aria was off like a shot. Coming up on noon, we hurried past a loaded housekeeping cart in front of an open door next to Room 316. Country music, probably from a TV station, filtered out.

Aria didn't hesitate but pummeled her fist on Nanette's door, banging without a thought to disturbing the other guests. "Open up."

After a few more pounds and shouts, the woman cleaning the room next door poked her head out. Younger than me by a decade, she wore yoga pants and a baggy beige housekeeper uniform top. A black knit beanie stretched on her head with long brown hair hanging down her back. "Dude. What's the problem?"

Aria's face turned from fury to concern in a heartbeat, and she sounded frantic. "Our friend is staying here. She's been depressed, and I'm afraid she's done something. She won't answer."

The girl studied Aria, then the door. "Look, I can't open it up for you. You understand, right? I mean, you could be murderers or something."

Aria had a desperate scent to her, and I wondered how much was for show. "Sure. Yes. Can you maybe get a security person or a manager or someone up here?"

Was Nanette on the other side of that door enjoying this exchange? Full of rage at being hounded? What could we expect if we got into the room? Or had she already checked out? Maybe out causing all sorts of trouble.

The girl acknowledged that and slipped a phone from the side pocket of her yoga pants. She turned her back to us. "Yeah. There's two ladies up here on the third floor. They need a wellness check."

She waited. "Yeah, I know. But, you know, maybe you call them and then come up to check. They're pretty worried about their friend. Time can be a killer, you know? So, you don't want to wait if there's an emergency."

She hung up and turned. "The front desk is calling the cops."

Aria pressed, taking advantage of the girl's concern. "What if we don't have that kind of time?"

The girl eyed the door with a worried expression.

We both kept quiet while she debated, but watching her with all the distress we could summon.

Finally, she inhaled and let it out in a huff. "Okay. Let's have a look."

"Thank you." Aria embraced the distraught friend persona so much I almost believed it.

The girl pulled a key card from a lanyard around her neck and bent to the pad. The light turned green, the door clicked, and Aria was shoving inside before the girl straightened up.

"Nanette!"

I piled in right after her and was hit with a terrible smell of poop, only so much more sinister. Muted light from the overcast sky shone from the window, and flurries swirled in slow eddies, not in any hurry to hit the pavement below. The décor was all whites and grays with the hard tile that looked like fake wood. Everything was swanky and immaculate, and no doubt cutting edge. The one king-sized bed was a mess of fluffy comforter and sheets that spilled to the side, a herd of pillows tossed on the mattress and the ground. It was quiet, not a shuffle or bump.

"She's not here," Aria spit out in a rush of frustration.

The girl stayed in the hallway. A man's voice came from the doorway. "Damn it, Colleen, I told you not to let them in."

Colleen didn't back down. "It's on me, man, but if someone was ODing while we spun on our thumbs waiting for the cops, I don't want that on my conscience, you know?"

He burst into the room, a short man in a navy blue button-up and khakis, his stomach hanging over his belt, not much older than Colleen. He was only a few inches taller than me, but he spoke with a voice loud and deep enough to come from a man ten feet tall. "You can't be in here. This is an invasion of privacy and against The Maven's policies."

"Oh, shit!" Aria slammed back against the wall, a hand clasped over her mouth. Her glistening eyes stared at the floor between the bed and the window.

I beat Mr. Hotel Man to Aria's side, and my stomach flipped over and crashed to the wood-grained tile.

The guy crushed behind me and let out an anguished cry. "No. No. No. This is... No." He backed out and started yelling. "Out. Everyone out. Out."

Aria and I didn't move but kept staring at Nanette, those violet eyes bugged out and focused on the ceiling, but never seeing anything again.

A SharpCo Manhandler planted in her chest.

31

"Goddamn it!" Mr. Hotel Man yelled and slapped the wall in the hallway. "Not on my shift. How do we even handle this?"

Colleen sounded tentative. "Is she...?"

"Dead," he shouted. "Damn it. Damn it. I don't know..."

Colleen spoke calmly. "The cops are already on their way here. Call Ms. Torres. She'll need to be here to talk to them."

I pulled Aria from the room, and the manager slammed the door closed. He had his phone out and punched away with shaking hands.

Colleen's eyes sparked with tears. "I'm so sorry."

Aria's bloodless face turned to me. "She's dead. What does that mean? If someone killed her, have they also been after Jefferson all along? Are they after him now?"

Not that I was immune to murder and death, but I'd had some experience dealing with it. I addressed Colleen. "Have you been here all morning?"

Her eyes drifted to the closed door, and Mr. Hotel Man's voice vibrated on the edge of hysteria.

"Colleen?" I prompted.

She drew her attention back to me in the dimly lit hallway. "Oh. Um. Yeah. I like to get an early start so I can study in the afternoons." Her attention wandered back to the door.

"Colleen. Think. Can you remember if anyone visited this room? Did you see anyone on this floor?"

She drew herself together as if having something specific to focus on helped the shock. "Uh. Mostly I'm in the rooms, you know. I try to concentrate on memorizing things like anatomy. I'm pre-med. So, not really."

Aria had a decimated air to her. "She can't be dead. It's so horrible."

Jefferson had been targeted at the stock show by Gwen and Arlo, then attacked at Casa Bonita. Someone had paid Gwen to hurt Jefferson but not kill him.

Nanette had seemed like the obvious suspect for all of Jefferson's mishaps. She'd had motive: to get a big payout, and maybe extract some revenge, since she'd hinted Jefferson hadn't treated her fairly. She'd had opportunity being at the stock show, at Casa Bonita, and at Jefferson's hotel. But here she was, no longer a suspect.

Logic pointed to one person.

Aria and I looked at each other and said together, "Blaine."

Colleen watched us both with curiosity and alarm.

I hated to scare her, but I needed her to concentrate. "Did you happen to see a man?" I struggled to find some remarkable feature and remembered. "With really blue eyes. Kind of serious or tense?"

She studied my face as if replaying her morning. "Yeah. Like midmorning, maybe? I ran out of body lotion. We always run low because it's so dry in Colorado and people swipe them off the cart. So, now that you mention it, a guy like that jumped for the elevator when I was on my way up. I got off on the second floor, but he stayed on."

It wasn't a hard trick to figure out. The manager was still on the phone, his back to us.

"Come on," Aria said, not telling me where we were headed.

Colleen's mouth opened in shock. "Don't you, like, need to wait for the cops? You were here and saw the body and stuff."

We wouldn't be able to add much to their investigation, and staying would keep us from doing what we needed to protect Jefferson. "We'll call them to give a statement."

Aria was already to the stairwell, probably to avoid running into the cops in the elevator and being detained. I lunged after her, and we clattered down the stairs, spilling out on the sidewalk to a whirl of flakes.

My heart was kicking wildly in my chest, and I couldn't quite feel my feet hitting the pavement. The world spun, and I struggled to keep everything in focus.

Aria had a hint of panic in her eyes, like a horse when a rattlesnake shakes.

"Where are we going?" I asked her.

"That damned cousin of mine." She stopped and looked directly at me. "Do you have a gun?"

I sputtered. "Gun? No. Why would I have a gun?"

She started off at a fast clip toward Elvis. "Blaine scares me. I'd like you to be armed when you confront him."

I blinked back the flakes in my eyes. "You think he killed Nanette? And now he's after Jefferson? We should tell the cops. Let's go back."

"No. They might or might not believe us, but even if they do, it'll take too long, and Jefferson could be in danger right now." She pulled out her phone, and we kept walking. She listened for too long, then shouted, "Damn it! He's not answering. Take me to his hotel, and you go to the board meeting."

"What if he's not there?"

She ran a hand through her hair in a frazzled way I'd never seen her do. "Then I'll figure something out and order a car."

Keeping up with her as the cold air burned my cheeks, I huffed into a cloud of white breath, "We're not the cavalry. We really need to let the cops handle this."

She was close to running now. "Jefferson is like my brother. How would you feel if one of your brothers was in danger? The cops aren't going to believe us, and they aren't going to help Jefferson. You know Jefferson well enough to realize he's gullible. If Blaine makes some kind of apology or acts pathetic, Jefferson will forgive him and follow him anywhere. I just want to be with him."

"And you want me to go to the board meeting?"

We made it to Elvis, and Aria waited at her door while I trotted to the driver's side and unlocked the car. She said, "Don't let Blaine know you're there. As soon as you find him, call the cops. But keep an eye on him so if it takes them forever, he won't be able to get to Jefferson without us knowing."

Baxter didn't think Jefferson was such a big pushover. I wasn't sure I did, either. But that didn't help Aria.

She programmed the location of the board meeting into my phone. "It's at the corporate offices in the Tech Center."

"That place is a maze."

She handed the phone back. "I have faith in you."

I eased Elvis into the traffic and the whoosh of tires on wet pavement.

Midafternoon on a Sunday in a snowstorm and the traffic was still heavy. The clouds locked up the sunshine, and everything had a bluish tint.

I pulled up in front of The Four Seasons, and she opened her door.

"He's okay," I said to reassure her.

"You don't know that."

32

The sky hung low enough it made me want to duck as the snow now fell in quarter-sized flakes, starting to turn the ground white but still melting on the pavement. Compared to LoDo, the Tech Center on a Sunday afternoon was deserted. The building Aria had directed me to was one of the few with a smattering of cars in front, all parked close to the front doors.

I swung Elvis into an adjoining lot and eyed a shiny red Cadillac SUV. Would that be Blaine's? Or maybe it was the black BMW sedan. Possibly any of the other expensive cars parked there. The only way for me to know if Blaine was here would be to get a look at the attendees.

I locked Elvis and hurried across the wet parking lot, hoping none of the board was late to the meeting and would catch me slinking around. I made it without incident and pulled open the glass doors. I kept my footsteps light as I entered a wide lobby with polished floors, steel and glass with sharp angles everywhere. Clusters of geometrically cut mirrors were suspended on thin cables, maybe meant to look like birds, though they looked more like meteors cascading toward destruction. An abstract sculpture that rose several stories brought focus to the central atrium. With all the hard surfaces and nothing else to absorb noise, it was impossible to mask my footsteps.

Aria had said Hansford's executive offices were on the fourth floor. I didn't want to take the elevator because I didn't know if the doors would open to members of the board milling around, an empty lobby, or some other scenario.

I climbed a set of open stairs that ran alongside a wall of windows to a balcony two stories up. A wide walkway circled around each floor and overlooked the gleaming lobby. The windows showcased the Rockies, now hardly visible through the milky sky and snowfall, and the afternoon wearing on. I reached for my phone to text Aria and realized I'd left it on Elvis's dash when I'd used it for navigation. In the eerie quiet of the building, I stopped to scan for the stairs that would take me to the fourth floor.

I didn't know the front door had opened until I heard footfalls like a herd of elk on the polished floor and echoing in the empty lobby. It sounded like more than two people, but echoes cascaded around us.

"I hate being the last to arrive. It looks bad to the board." The cantankerous voice had to be Eula.

I recognized Blaine's voice answering her. "I'll explain about the traffic. Accidents happen in the snow. It's just lucky we got around it as fast as we did."

They clumped to a bank of elevators. In the silent building, the clank and whir of the car descending sounded like a rollercoaster. Blaine and Eula didn't speak as they waited. The ding was like a siren, doors slid open and closed, and the cables sang their songs again.

I debated following them upstairs against going to the car for my phone. I assumed I'd have an hour or two before the meeting would break up. Blaine would be contained until then.

I turned to the windows and the craggy gray of the mountains. A woman was dead. I hadn't known her, but my impression had been that she was a complicated person. Eula liked her, or at least respected her. Despite Eula saying she liked me, too, was she really a good judge of character? Nanette had seemed hard as obsidian, yet I'd observed a hint of tragedy in her. She might have schemes and the soul of an opportunist, but she didn't deserve to end up on a hotel room floor with a Manhandler shoved into her.

Still lost in thought, the clatter of a door bar and crash of slamming stairwell metal jarred me. Rapid whooshing of soft soles on the tile floor preceded the flushed and livid Blaine shooting from one of the hallways spoking from the atrium. He must have come from a stairway.

Aria was right. My gun could come in handy about now. All my senses flared as alarm sirens and adrenaline pumped through my veins, making me feel twitchy. The stairs to the lobby were too far for me to escape. I considered tearing down another hallway, but thought I stood a better chance out in the open, where someone might hear screams echoing in the atrium. Choice between flight or fight settled, I crouched, ready to defend myself.

He stopped about twenty feet from the stairway, arms hanging at his sides. "You didn't consider your reflection in the mirrors? Lucky for you Eula doesn't see as well as she used to, or she might have shot you on sight. She doesn't take lightly to corporate espionage."

I didn't doubt him. Eula did have that gun she carried even to the fundraiser. My only weapon was Elvis's key clutched between my fingers. "I'm not here for meat company secrets."

Blaine's hard blue eyes drilled me. "I didn't think so. Why are you here?"

There wasn't much I could say, but maybe Aria and Jefferson would have called the cops and they'd be on their way. "I don't know, Blaine, why would I be here? Can you think of anything?"

He sneered. "It's poor Jefferson again, isn't it? How he gets you all in league with him is beyond me."

"Jefferson didn't send me. I'm here about Nanette."

He leveled me with a murderous glare. "Nanette has a bad habit of sticking her nose where it doesn't belong."

"You were with her before she married Jefferson. What went wrong?" It would be great to have my phone so I could record his confession.

He looked downright venomous. "Jefferson is what went wrong. Like he always does. He couldn't stand that someone loved me more than they loved him. So he went after her. His looks and charm combined with his lies about me did the trick. And as soon as he had her, he...well, he didn't treat her right."

Devil's advocate here, I said, "And yet, he hasn't agreed to a divorce. If he didn't care about her, why wouldn't he let her go?"

Blaine's lip curled. "Because Mother doesn't allow divorce. And displeasing her might jeopardize all that money Jefferson depends on."

Maybe I could distract him and work my way to the stairs. "If Nanette was so unhappy, why did it take her so long to ask for a divorce?"

He made a *psht* noise to let me know it was a stupid question. "Same answer. Money. She never had more than two pennies growing up. And, from what she told me, she suffered plenty of abuse and neglect, so I'd guess she had a low bar for how she was treated. But, eventually, she'd had enough."

While he was busy enlightening me, I'd advanced a step and he'd absently backed up. "But she wanted more than the prenup, so she threatened to expose the embezzlement and your role in it at the board meeting if Jefferson didn't give her a trunk of cash?"

He furrowed his forehead in frustration. "I tried to get her to stay married. Ride it out as long as Eula was alive. She could have stayed out of Jefferson's way. Then I'd make sure she'd never want for anything again."

Another inch forward. "Why would you want her to stay?"

"Because," he raised his voice, then paused to get control. "Mother doesn't love many things in this world, but she loves Jefferson. For some reason, she and Father fell for all of Jefferson's lies over the years. He'd break something or get in trouble and somehow the blame would always land on me. To keep from getting in trouble, I kept an eye on him and fixed his screw-ups because I knew if I didn't, I'd get punished for it. Wrecked cars, sunk boats. Even if he had to admit to Mother and Father he'd done something, I'd catch hell for not keeping better track of him."

I knew my face must hold all the skepticism I felt as I stood with my arms folded. "So everything is Jefferson's fault? And Nanette was a victim of your narcissistic brother? And the poor girl finally came to her senses and wouldn't listen to your wise counsel not to divorce."

That sneering face reappeared. "But she's too stubborn. And Jefferson didn't have the money to pay her. So I guess she staged all these attacks and threats."

I tried not to focus on the stairs, especially when Blaine hadn't retreated at my last push forward. "What good would that do?"

"Nanette and Mother understand each other. Maybe not love, so much, but respect. And Nanette knows how much Mother protects Jefferson. If she can make Mother think poor Jefferson is being targeted and she can save him by giving him money, then Jefferson can afford to pay Nanette off to keep her quiet about his embezzlement. When that didn't work, she decided to throw a bomb into our family and tell Mother anyway. At the board meeting today."

I hadn't made it far enough to give myself any chance of escape, but I forged on with Blaine anyway. "But you couldn't let that happen because Eula would discover your role in it, by blaming the loss on someone else and firing him."

His jaw clenched as if fighting pain. "No. So I fixed it like I always do. I did what it took to make Nanette go away."

I couldn't believe he was laying it all out for me. "How did you fix it?"

He rubbed his eyes with a thumb and forefinger, like it hurt to say. "Cash. A bag of cash. Enough to set her up and keep her quiet. All untraceable, unless you count the Hansford Meats duffel bag it came in. I thought that would be a nice touch."

Here was his confession served up with a side of fries. "Come on, Blaine. We both know there was no need to hand over cash. Where you sent Nanette, she won't be spending it."

Something in my voice caught his attention. His eyes sharpened on me. "What? You're saying something. What is it?"

The first prick of doubt hit me. "Nanette is dead."

There was a moment of absolute silence. Neither of us moved. He grew pale, and a shadow seeped into his eyes as if he parsed the words, trying to deny what I said.

He sucked in a breath and fell back, landing on his butt, his eyes filling with instant tears. "Nanette? No. That's wrong. She's a force. She's strong. This can't be."

His grief seemed genuine, and it confused me. "You hated her. You just said so yourself." I waited a moment while he rolled his head back and forth.

He sniffed and wiped his nose on his sleeve. His voice broke when he spoke, pure pain and no anger. "I can't believe this. I said I hated her, but I didn't. I never hated her. I loved her so much." He sobbed. "I always dreamed we'd be together again. When she realized what Jefferson really was, I thought she'd come back to me."

He clamped both hands over his face and gave way to violent weeping.

I nudged him with my boot on his shoe. "Blaine. Listen to me. If you didn't kill Nanette, who did?"

He sniffled but didn't engage me.

"Are you sure you paid her and left? We didn't see any duffel bag of cash at her hotel room."

He swiped his fingers across his eyes in a way that looked painful. With an inflection as dead as canned peas, he said, "He wouldn't have needed to kill her if his plan was to steal the cash. Someone else got to her after the cash was delivered."

Such drama. "Who?"

"Jefferson."

"Oh, please. Quit blaming everything in your life on your brother. Someone has been targeting Jefferson." What a pain in the butt. No wonder no one liked him. "Help me out here. If you know someone who hated them both, tell me."

"You might start with that blond number who's been hanging around."

"Sandi?" I was getting whiplash with the on-again, off-again suspicion of that woman.

"If that's what she's calling herself these days. She and Nanette go way back."

"They knew each other?"

His laugh scraped my nerves. "Way back, like to the womb, or at least not long after."

I stared at him, trying to translate. "They're sisters?"

That seemed to set him off again, and he squeezed out a few words before he started crying. "They were. Now Nanette is dead."

33

I needed to find Sandi. I'd seen Keith arguing with her. He was the only lead I had. I crossed the cold parking lot under a sky that seemed gray as steel. I made it to Elvis, unlocked the door, and grabbed my phone off the dash.

Aria picked up on the second ring, sounding distracted. "I've got you on speaker. I'm helping Jefferson pack. I finally convinced him he'd be safer anywhere else, so he's flying to Italy tonight. Did you find Blaine? Are the cops on the way?"

I fired up Elvis. "He didn't kill Nanette. But he did pay her off."

Aria shot back, "You believe him?"

"Yeah. I think Sandi has something to do with this." I filled her in on what Blaine said, not adding that he'd accused Jefferson, since I was on speaker and didn't want to create more animosity between the brothers. I gave her my plans and said, "I'm going to look for a Hansford Meats duffel full of cash. I probably won't be that lucky, but if I am, it's the smoking gun."

She didn't answer. The phone went dead, and that was fine. She probably had to wrangle Jefferson, and I was done talking and needed to concentrate on driving.

I still wasn't convinced Sandi was responsible for the attacks on

Jefferson and was sure she didn't have anything to do with Nanette's murder, but she must know something.

The interstates and busier streets were slick and wet, but the side streets were starting to accumulate snow in the dimming late afternoon light. Temperatures had dipped and conditions deteriorated while I'd been at the Tech Center. I turned on the radio to get any weather updates and was bombarded with reports about accidents to avoid.

The crowds at the stock show had diminished substantially since I'd been there earlier. I'd like to be one of the lucky ones snuggled in at home, my biggest worry being whether I had enough popcorn to make it through chapter ten.

Ray sat in his woven lawn chair in the back of his booth, looking desolate and bored. A few people wandered the aisle in front of his booth, but he made no move to engage them. His face cracked open in a grin when he saw me. "Well, if it isn't Kate."

I wasn't raised to be rude, but I didn't have time for small talk. "Keith didn't happen to show up here this afternoon, did he?"

Ray waved his unwrapped wrist. "I'm back up to speed. So Keith was off the hook. He said he had plans for a few days but he'd rearrange them if I needed him. Good guy."

Yeah, weird-maybe-stalker guy. "Do you happen to have a contact number for him? Or maybe he said where he was going?"

Ray frowned. "I'd guess he was going home. Not that I thought it was a good idea, mind you."

Not only was he annoying, but now he was confusing, and I was running low on patience. "What are you talking about?"

"That little tart. She's been hanging around Keith the whole time he's been here. I think she's who he has plans with. At least, they seemed pretty chummy last time I saw Keith."

Whatever this meant, it wasn't good. "Sandi? Keith and Sandi are leaving town together?"

"That's what I said. I know how you feel. She's kind of like an alley cat. First, she's after Jefferson, and then Keith. Who is too nice by far for her."

I'd had my fill of Ray's commentary. "Do you have any idea where Keith lives? Or even his last name?"

Ray released a high-pitched giggle that sounded like air escaping a pinched balloon neck. "I've got you covered. Keith has a knack for sales, but he says his real love is finance. He's between jobs right now, so he's picking up bookkeeping gigs. He's going to help me out."

"Please, Ray. If you know where I can find Keith, tell me." I might have said it with the tension of a tennis racket strung too tight.

He pursed his lips like Grandma Ardith when we told her Edith Wentz stole her cream puff recipe and passed it off as her own. Without a word, he rose and reached under the counter to the cash bag. With jerky movements I was sure were intended to let me understand he was offended, he opened the bag and rummaged through the cash to pull out a business card.

"I'm sorry I didn't realize you were in such an all-fired hurry. But I've got what you need." He shoved the card at me.

I grabbed it and read the address. Someplace in Lakewood. I nearly pocketed it before I noticed the name.

Not simply Keith.

The basic cream business card on heavy stock belonged to Bradley K. Heimlich.

34

One of Elvis's best assets was his heater. He might not warm your seat or steering wheel, but he kicked out a steady stream of hot air to keep the cab comfy. He wasn't, however, terrific on icy roads. And now that the sun had set, the wet roads had turned into an obstacle course of black ice. I managed to steer us safely from the stock show complex across I-25 and into a quiet neighborhood of two-story and split-level homes circa 1960s or '70s, with tall conifers and well-maintained yards. At least, they seemed well cared for, but since they were blanketed in two inches of snow, it was hard to tell for sure. Lights from the windows and porches reflected on what looked like whipped cream. It might be cozy and idyllic, except a woman was dead and a man was being targeted by dangerous people.

We fishtailed around a few turns before I took the hint and slowed down. Sandi and Nanette sisters. Keith being fired for a crime he never committed. The scapegoat for Jefferson, career ruined by Blaine. And after he'd worked in Ray's booth for two days, Nanette was found dead with a SharpCo knife buried in her.

All the details clumped like sticky dough in my brain. Blaine and Nanette were together. Then she switched sides and joined Team Jefferson. Blaine swan-dived into an endless, bitter sea.

Keith appeared out of the blue at the stock show the same time as

Nanette and Sandi. And lucky for him, Gwen happened along to offer her services.

I followed Ms. GPS telling me to turn left in eight hundred feet and the destination would be on my left. She didn't lie. Keith's house was easy to spot in the darkness because the garage door was open, sending a shower of light to highlight the dancing snowflakes. I doused Elvis's headlights and pulled over, idling closer to get a good look.

A little white car, the kind you see everywhere that you'd never notice, was parked on one side of the double garage. Just the same kind of car that had careened into The Four Seasons parking lot to pick up Sandi.

A red Subaru Outback took up the other side of the garage with the hatchback open. Instinctively I ducked down when Keith hurried out with a large suitcase and hefted it into the back. A second later, Sandi appeared with a cardboard box that she slid into the back seat.

Yikes. They were making a getaway. Did that mean they'd killed Nanette? Revenge because she'd somehow contributed to Keith's ruin?

With no gun and no backup, it would be silly to traipse in there and stop them single-handedly.

I picked up my phone and jabbed at buttons. After two rings, a woman said, "9-1-1, what's your emergency?"

I didn't need to keep my voice low, but I did. "I'm watching a robbery in progress in Lakewood." I picked up Keith's business card and held it close to my window for light from a streetlight. I rattled off the address.

Typing was followed by her asking, "Is there physical danger to anyone?"

"No." Dang. I wanted to take that back because it would get less priority from a force busy with weather-related traffic accidents and who knows what kind of violence.

She asked for more details, and I explained I was a neighbor and the man and woman taking items from the house didn't live there. I was lying left and right and straight down the middle.

Finally, dispatch ended with, "Okay. Get in a safe place. Stay away from the scene. Don't make any contact. We'll send a car as soon as possible."

And there I sat. Watching as Sandi and Keith made more trips from the house to the car. My heart thudded in my chest. I kept checking my rearview mirror. As if I wouldn't see headlights or a cop's lightbar the second it turned the last corner. My fingers tapped Elvis's wheel. "Come on. Come on."

I called Aria. It kicked immediately to voicemail, and I hung up and texted her. "Keith is Bradley Heimlich. Waiting for cops."

She'd be with Jefferson. This would all be over soon. I'd probably need to hang around for a bit to give a statement to the cops. But then I'd be back at home, without Brodgar, since Craig McNeal had probably decided we weren't suitable for his champion if we couldn't even keep an appointment. But Fiona was still there. And Poupon. He'd never show it, but that ridiculous fluff would be happy to see me.

My phone vibrated, and I looked down to see a text from Aria.

Brodgar.

Huh? Did that mean she'd gone back to the stock show and made a deal with Craig? I had no doubt she could work that kind of magic.

Keeping an eye on the open garage door and the falling snow, I couldn't help a spark of excitement, so I punched in redial to Aria's phone. This time it didn't ring. An automated voice informed me the number I reached was out of service. I pocketed the phone. Must be the storm.

No lights in my rearview. I fidgeted. Tapped more on Elvis's wheel.

Keith appeared from inside the garage, this time wearing his puffy coat. He fitted a box into what seemed like the last available space, then stepped back and slammed the hatch down. He brushed his hands together and disappeared, probably back into the house.

They were done. In a matter of minutes, they'd take off, and I doubted Elvis could effectively tail them. For one thing, we'd likely slide off the road, and if we didn't, a 1973 Ranchero doesn't exactly blend in.

One more glance at the mirror to confirm I was on my own. Then I let myself out of the car and ran to the garage, kicking up snow and slipping on ice. No one was inside, and I took a moment to notice the shelves were tidy, with the gardening equipment separate from the outdoor gear. Container boxes with neat labels were stacked in order. Keith kept a tight ship. It didn't look like someone planning murder or extortion. Although I wasn't sure neatness counted in that way.

I slid a five iron from a golf bag. This would have to do.

The door to the house was up two wooden steps to a small platform. I snuck there and eased open the door, grateful that Keith was the kind of guy who kept the hinges oiled. I stepped into a small mudroom, with a bench along one wall. Two pairs of Crocs, a pink pair and a larger set in olive-green, nestled under the bench, along with two sets of snow boots. Men's jackets and coats on the hooks above, mingling with several women's jackets. White-and-beige vinyl flooring led the way to a kitchen well-lit with a brass ceiling fixture even I knew was woefully out of fashion.

Keith stood with his back to me, facing Sandi in her white puffy coat across a butcher block. "We can get to Cheyenne tonight. Stay at Little America. I know it's hokey, but I love that place." His voice was light, not like someone who had murdered a woman that morning.

Sandi's smile was something I'd never seen on her face. Genuine and open, it made her look young and almost innocent.

My movement must have registered with her because she stiffened and gasped, stepping back.

Keith whipped around, his eyes going wide as he fell back against the butcher block. It took him a second to recognize me. "What are you...? Is something wrong?"

Sandi wasn't taking the time to ask questions. She recovered from her shock and flew at me.

I raised the golf club, but she plowed into me before I could swing, and it clattered to the floor, along with the two of us.

"Leave me the fuck alone," she grunted as she pinned me to the floor and straddled me.

Keith stuttered. "Sandi. Hon. What's going on?"

I'd been raised in the middle of a feral pack, and if I could wrangle calves and plant fence posts, Sandi didn't stand a chance. It wasn't even hard to buck her off, yank both her arms over her head, and reach for the golf club before she could crab-walk backward to the corner of the kitchen. "Help me," she screamed at Keith.

But I was on my feet, wielding the club at both of them while Keith gaped at us, still not moving, standing next to the butcher block. I pointed to the corner of the kitchen next to Sandi and indicated the floor. "Down there. Now."

He shuffled over and plopped down.

The look Sandi gave him was full of affection and tolerance and about bowled me over. She didn't have that same softness for me. "What the f—." She stopped before she finished the word, and with a shift of her eyes in Keith's direction, she continued. "The hell is wrong with you?"

"The cops are on their way. So, let's sit tight until they get here. I don't want to have to clobber you with this nice five iron."

"It's not that nice," Keith said. "An old set my sister gave me."

Sandi shot him the kind of look long-time couples exchange at a dinner party when one warns the other not to tell *that* story. He said to her, "Sorry. I'm nervous." To me, he said, "Are you here to rob us? We don't have much, but there's a little emergency cash in the safe box upstairs."

Sandi dropped her head and let out a hiss like steam escaping.

That derailed my thoughts. "Why aren't you taking that with you?"

His earnest expression felt authentic. "Well, it's for an emergency. So, it'd be irresponsible to spend it on a getaway."

There it was, getaway. "Walk me through your thought process because I'm a little confused." I addressed Sandi. "If you wanted to get hooked up with Jefferson for the money, why would you hire Gwen to hurt him?"

She smirked at me. But Keith got steamed. "Wait a minute there. Sandi doesn't like Jefferson. Not like that."

"Then you tell me. What were you all doing together at the trade show targeting Jefferson?"

Keith turned a plaintive face to Sandi. "Tell her, okay? I think she's really trying to help."

Sandi snorted. "She's not trying very hard, or she would have figured this out."

Where were those cops? I'd had enough of this interrogation. "I know you and Nanette are sisters. That Blaine dated Nanette before she hooked up with Jefferson, and their marriage wasn't great. Keith got canned because of Jefferson and Blaine. Now I see you and Keith are together. You tell how that all fits together."

Her annoyance knew no bounds. "Okay, Sherlock. What's the common thread in all that? Unravel that and you'll know who's been harassing Jefferson."

"It lands on you and Keith, I'm afraid. I thought it was Nanette, but since we found her dead this—"

Sandi's inhale stopped me. "What? What did you say? You didn't. No. You didn't." As she spoke, her voice got louder and higher, ending in a shriek.

Keith was quieter but no less shocked. "Nanette? She's dead?"

Sandi threw herself at Keith, and his arms closed around her. She buried her head in his chest and repeated *no, no, no*, her hoarse voice taking up all the air in the house.

I wanted to rewind and stop myself from blurting that out. That was the second time I'd callously announced Nanette's murder to people who loved her. Somewhere Karma was setting up a banquet of misery for me.

I could do nothing but drop to the floor across from them with my back against the butcher block and duck under the wave of shock and grief.

Keith rocked Sandi and murmured words of comfort. When she'd gone limp, he gently hauled her up to sit next to him.

Her face was death-mask pale and her eyes a flaming red, along with her nose. Her blond hair was a tangle, and she slumped against Keith. In a voice roughened from her sobs, she said, "He finally did it."

Keith made an attempt to smooth her hair, but she shook him off. "Now, you don't know that," he said.

This was the first time I'd seen her lose patience with Keith. She pushed away from him. "No. You do not get to think the best of him. Not this time."

He looked like a dog who'd been slapped on the nose with newspaper.

Fresh grief bruised everyone in the vicinity. Of course, I felt bad that a young woman was murdered and how it obviously devastated her sister. But it picked at the scab of my own sister's death. And that sharp pain never lessened. Trying to cover up my own emotion, I might have sounded harsher than I intended. "You'd better tell me what you're talking about. Why were you at the stock show, and what were you doing with Jefferson?"

Sandi had lost much of her bluster, but she still burned with rage. "Damned Jefferson Hansford. It all starts and stops with him."

"And?" I urged her.

She sniffed and swiped at tears. "Nanette and I weren't raised in some ideal family with lots of clothes, a clean house, and a puppy dog. We pretty much lived in abandoned cars and went to school when Mom got sober enough to sign us up."

Keith's hand snuck up to her back, and he patted her. She allowed it. I wanted to tell her to skip her backstory, but she'd had a shock, and of anyone on the planet, I understood how she felt.

"So, when Nanette hooked up with Blaine, it was like hitting the jack-pot. He let us live at his house and bought us nice things. I was halfway in love with him myself." She glanced at Keith and landed a hand on his knee. "Not for real."

Sandi continued. "And then Jefferson came on the scene. I was a lot younger then, and he didn't notice me. But he had a thing for Nanette. And honestly, I think it was because Blaine loved her. Nanette couldn't see it, but I knew from the start Jefferson was a psycho. He started souring Nanette against Blaine right away, but not in a blatant way. Real clever, like she'd notice a bruise on his arm, and he'd pretend not to want to tell her and then eventually admit Blaine had punched him, or stuff like that. It took maybe a month or two and then all the sudden, Nanette is acting like Jefferson is the love of her life."

Keith shook his head.

Sandi kept going. "That's when I bugged out. I was too young, and I hooked up with the wrong crowd and had a few tough years. Did some things I'm not proud of."

"Water under the bridge, sweetheart." Keith shook her softly. "Everyone makes mistakes."

A soft smile formed on her lips and her eyes held gratitude before she turned back to me, and they hardened again. "But Nanette married that SOB. It wasn't long before things got bad. He wanted her to do some bad shit."

"Bad? Like what?" I wasn't sure I was buying all of this, but she sounded convinced.

She gave me a withering look. "Bad, like BDSM and kinky, gross things. Over the top, I mean."

Did Sandi's account sync with Blaine's? "If that's right, why didn't she leave before now?"

Keith kept his sympathetic attention riveted on Sandi.

Sandi's voice rose in temper. "Why does any woman stay? He threatened her. She had no money, no skills, no power. She stuck it out as long as she could, then she left."

She had a point. I'd left Ted, but it wasn't without a lot of internal debate. "Did she orchestrate the attacks on him to manipulate Eula into giving him his inheritance so he could pay her blackmail?"

Sandi stared at me as if I were insane. "That's nuts. How did you even come up with that?"

At least I didn't feel bad about questioning Blaine's explanation. "So she didn't go after Jefferson?"

She paused and considered. "Well. Nanette wanted to kill him for what he did to me." She touched her bruised eye.

Keith inhaled and closed his eyes as if what she said stabbed him. "You should never have been there in the first place."

"You'd better back up and tell me that story."

She acted annoyed. "Nanette decided to blackmail Jefferson because she felt she deserved more from the divorce settlement. I worried Jefferson would talk her into giving up on that because she's so stupid about him. So I decided to beat her to it. I'd do a little entrapment thingy. Not follow through with the sex or anything, but get pictures of him I could threaten to take to Eula."

This family. I was amazed at their plots.

Keith looked stricken, like he might throw up. "I tried to stop her. And when she got alone with him, he started to get violent. Thank goodness Sandi was smart enough to switch the drinks or it could have been so much worse." Keith looked near tears. "I'm so sorry, sweetheart. I should have never let you go."

She patted his leg again. "Not your fault. Nanette told me what he was like, so I knew what I was getting into." Suddenly, she slapped a hand across her eyes as the tears burst. She squeezed out the words. "Damn it, Nanette."

Keith seemed close to tears himself. "We told her she could stay here with us as long as she wanted."

"Wait." I pointed to them. "You were together before now?"

Keith hugged Sandi closer. "Nanette introduced us."

When I gave him a questioning look, he continued. "After I was fired, Nanette found me. She'd figured out what happened with the money and how they'd blamed me."

"Go on," I said to Keith.

With eyes locked on Sandi, he said, "After I was fired, Nanette helped me out, and we stayed friends. That's when I met her sister." He hugged Sandi to him.

I hadn't bought into Sandi's theory that Jefferson was the murderer. "Which brings us to now. If Nanette had her payoff and Jefferson and Blaine never had to confess to Eula, why would Jefferson kill Nanette?"

Sandi made an impatient click of her tongue. "Because after she got the money, Nanette decided she would still go to the board meeting and tell Eula not only about the embezzlement, but about Jefferson's lies and how he'd abused her. All of it."

Fear began to roll in my belly and grow like a snowball. "Did she tell Jefferson she was going to do that?"

Sandi cried and snickered at the same time. "It's Nanette. Of course she told Jefferson."

Keith sounded like he couldn't believe what he was saying. "Jefferson killed Nanette to keep her from doing that."

Of course he'd take the duffel of money from the hotel room. The smoking gun I'd told Aria about. On speaker phone.

35

The race across the city back to the stock show was more of a turtle crawl. The snow piled up and the black ice underneath made it a Slip 'n' Slide, and even the good citizens of Denver, who had experience driving in those conditions, were stuck on the sides of the roads. Getting involved in an accident would keep me from getting to Aria, so I was forced to take it slow.

But that didn't prevent my heart from pounding with my need to hurry. I'd left Sandi and Keith with instructions to call the cops and send them to the Highland pens in the stockyard across the tracks from the events center. I believed that last text from Aria was a message of her location.

As I exited the interstate toward the stock show complex, I called Jeremy. Big surprise, no answer. When his voicemail invited me to speak up, I shouted, "Come to the stockyards. The Highlands. Hurry!" He was my cavalry of one, especially if the cops didn't arrive in time.

The main parking areas were nearly empty. Not that it was so late, but people weren't hanging around to pet lambs and bunnies when winter had its fangs out. I took a jog to the west and wound around deserted roads, past towering new buildings from a major expansion to the stock show complex.

Streetlights cast orbs in the cloudy, snowy sky but did little to illuminate the area. A black Lincoln SUV was the only vehicle in this back lot, tucked at the outskirts of the new portion of the stock show complex, far away from the arena building and surrounded by steel-paneled pens, mostly empty now that the show was winding down.

Between the snow-hushing sound and the constant traffic of the interstate nearby, I didn't worry I'd be heard this far from the pens. I pulled Elvis next to the Lincoln, climbed out, and rummaged behind my seat. Being elderly, Elvis was prone to flat tires and any number of mishaps. Among a smattering of useful tools, I carried a tire iron. And, because you never know when an escaped calf might need to be rounded up and roped off a highway, a well-broken-in rope. Since I didn't have a gun, or even a golf club, these would have to do.

Indentations in the snow that led from the SUV were filling in fast as the snowfall piled up. These would be Jefferson's and Aria's footprints. At least the bumps appeared like two sets. They weren't easy to follow, but I knew the way to the Highland pens and prayed that's where I'd find them.

Cold burned my nose and cheeks, and I dug for the gloves I normally kept in my barn coat but they were, of course, now missing. My fingers would numb quickly in the temperatures that had to be dipping toward the negative side.

Pens were ringed by metal panels so the animals could be seen easily, and some had a three-sided metal structure with a five-foot-wide roof that provided protection from sun and rain. Since there wasn't much wind, it helped with tonight's snow.

Something banged on the metal wall of a shelter at the end of the pen where Baxter and I had petted Brodgar yesterday. A few furry Highlands milled nervously at the far end of the pen, snow sticking to their coats and making them look like four-legged abominable snowmen. They probably waited to be claimed by whoever had bargained the best with Craig McNeal. I'd mourn my loss of Brodgar when Aria was safe and warm, drinking mulled wine by a roaring fire.

As I snuck closer to the pen, the sounds of a scuffle grew louder.

"How does this feel, perfect little Aria. Our Turbo, whose slightest touch turns everything to gold." Jefferson's voice was snarky and harsh. No hint of the charmer he so easily adopted to get sympathy from his mother and most other women.

Aria responded with a growl of fury that sounded like she was exerting effort. "Why are you doing this? I was always on your side. I backed you up every time with Aunt Eula."

"Sure, until you didn't. We were always the best of friends, you and me."

She sniffed what might have been tears but was probably rage. "We still are. We can figure this out."

His voice sliced like a saw through a soft log. "You should have let it go, but no, you wanted to blow the whistle on me."

She shrieked into the muffled edges of the snowy night. "You killed Nanette!"

He sounded as if he struggled with Aria. "You never liked her, so why do you care?"

Bitterness filled her voice. "Blaine was right all along. You're a monster. And I never saw it."

He laughed, but it sounded unhinged. "You love me. And so does Mother. I love you, too. That's why what you're forcing me to do is so hard."

I shuffled to the edge of the shelter and squatted down to peer around the end.

Aria grunted, and she sounded itchier for battle than afraid. "So, what now? You're going to murder me, too? And go about your life? You're crazy if you think you won't get caught."

One arm banded around her shoulders and hugged her to him, only her toes on the ground. He hadn't looked that strong before, but it took muscle to control Aria. In a falsetto singsong, he said, "What were you doing out here in a snowstorm? Looking for a bull? We know you're a drinker. You might have been okay if you hadn't slipped and hit your head. And even then, you might have made it, but the damned cold. Hypothermia is no laughing matter."

Jefferson planned on killing Aria. In a million years I'd never have thought this could happen. Why hadn't I seen the clues? Why hadn't Aria?

He'd spent his whole life playing people, manipulating, scapegoating. A master at the top of his game. Until today, when he'd snapped and murdered Nanette. All that careful plotting over the years collapsed. Jefferson acted as though he believed he could wiggle out of this situation, walk away scot-free from Nanette's and Aria's deaths and continue to work

Eula to his advantage. But I figured he had doubts, and that made him desperate.

And a cornered animal is the deadliest. Aria and I were scrappy, but whether we'd be enough to stop Jefferson with the power of his delusion and fear seemed questionable, especially if Aria was injured. Even if tonight ended up being our last one, we wouldn't make it easy for Jefferson.

I really needed Jeremy with me, but there was no telling if he'd even get the message. I needed to act now.

Jefferson spoke to the top of Aria's head as she tried to wrench free. "What is hilarious is that you think you're so damned smart, and you never knew the whole time that it was me behind the break-in. And me who hired the hippies."

"It's you who's an idiot. You weren't quick enough with Nanette. She told me about the money," she said, her voice a mix of fury and fear. "And she told Aunt Eula, too. You're done."

Jefferson sounded amused. He rattled her, swiping her feet off the ground and making her stumble against him. "You're a good liar, Turbo. One of your best qualities. But Mother wouldn't believe Nanette over me. You wouldn't have either, if you hadn't seen the bag of money in my room."

Though she fought, it made little difference. "But I did see it. And Kate knows."

He laughed. "Now you're just making things up."

"No. I texted her. She's on her way now."

I wished Aria knew I was there and determined to save her, no matter what.

With a creepy lilt to his tone, he said, "Oh, dear, sweet Aria. I'm going to miss you."

Less fight and more desperation. "Don't make it worse. If you let me go, I'll find a way to get you out of this mess."

With an unexpectedly rapid move, Jefferson ran toward the shelter and slammed Aria against the wall, rattling metal. Her head bounced on a pole, and she lost her footing.

She must have passed out, because he slid her to the ground, propping her against the back wall. "I'd have made sure you had the beautiful, heart-felt funeral you deserve, but I'll be long gone by then. So sorry."

He stood with his back to me, arms folded, staring down at Aria. Maybe he was giving himself a moment before he'd bash her head into the side of the shelter.

Heart thundering and fear wedged in my throat, I snuck from the cover of the wall, tire iron raised. When I cleared the shelter, I sprang forward and swung the iron at Jefferson's head.

He must have heard me, because he spun around, throwing off my aim. The tire iron skidded off his shoulder, doing no damage. With a quickness that surprised me, Jefferson punched me, hitting me squarely in the nose. A bright burst of pain exploded, blinding me momentarily and sending me backward to land on my butt in the snow. A hot surge of blood splattered across my face, the salty, bitter taste hitting my lips.

I scrambled backward as Jefferson bent over for the tire iron. He found it and stood with his legs slightly apart, arm dangling at his side with the weight of the iron, heaving, though we'd not fought. "What is your deal? You couldn't mind your own damned business?"

"The cops are on the way. If you leave now, you'll get a jump on them."

He swished the tire iron back and forth like a musketeer with a sword. "Look at you, so devoted to Aria, like the rest of the world. You just have to save our perfect goddess." His voice got scary-sweet. "I'm not really like this. Everyone loves me. But you're forcing me. This is all your fault."

I swiped my arm across my nose, detonating another wave of pain from my frozen face.

He raised his arm to bring the iron down on me.

It took all of my discipline not to roll away too soon. I wanted him committed to the action before I skittered out of the way. When the iron was dangerously close, I rolled to my hands and knees, shoved up, and barreled into his stomach. The iron smacked the wall, metal on metal, a muted clang in the snowy night.

Jefferson stumbled a few steps backward, but I didn't have enough force to tip him over. He came up with an uppercut that caught my chin and snapped my head back as if my neck were made of rubber. It wasn't and felt as if all the vertebrae shattered. I choked and crashed sideways into the snow.

Jefferson drew his leg back, preparing to kick me into Kansas, and I tried to slide away. From behind Jefferson, Aria conjured up her own rebel yell. Somehow, she'd rallied, or maybe she'd been faking how bad off she was in an effort to buy time.

She now held the tire iron and brought it down but missed Jefferson's head when he leaned away, instead hitting his neck.

He grunted and staggered to the side. Before he lost his footing, he steadied himself with a hand on the back of the shelter. Shoving off, he came at Aria and grabbed her by the hair. As if she were a Raggedy Ann, he flung her aside.

She screamed and crashed into the wall, then slid to the ground. She didn't move.

I was already on my feet and lunging for the tire iron. Too slow. Too clumsy, with blood clogging my nose and slipping down my throat, making me cough.

Jefferson came after me, but before he could knock me away, my fingers closed on the icy metal and I shoved from the ground, tire iron arced for his head.

He bent backward, and the iron connected with his chin in a satisfying crack. He shouted in pain. In the gray light of the snowstorm, I saw a blossom of blood grow on his chin.

Sirens. Faint but real. Help was on its way.

But Jefferson wasn't ready to concede.

With a roar, he charged at me. I'm tough, but I'd been clocked, and Jefferson was so much bigger than me.

It wasn't hard for him to wrench the iron from my frozen fingers. While I punched, kicked, and batted, he swung and smacked me in the jaw.

Another white-hot blast of agony and splat of blood on the snow. My legs buckled, and I hit the hard ground on both knees, toppling to my side. The world turned fuzzy and even darker, like an old TV screen filling with static. I narrowed my eyes to slits to see through the blood.

Jefferson grunted and moved away, heading toward Aria.

She lay in a heap where he'd tossed her.

Jefferson approached her and stopped for a second. He spoke in a voice low and mumbling. "Look what you made me do."

I cried out, but it sounded as weak as a lamb's bleat. My brain sent signals to my arms and legs, but they reacted in slow motion.

Jefferson was going to kill Aria, and there was nothing I could do.

While he ruminated, giving himself the time to build up his nobility in murdering the one true friend he'd ever had, a shadow shot from the side of the shelter.

It flew with such speed and power it seemed like a phantom, but it hit Jefferson with enough force to knock him into the snow.

I struggled to my feet, slipping and falling to my knees. Whatever, whoever it was might need my help against Jefferson.

Grunting and sounds of struggle were muffled by the snow, but a smack of flesh followed by a yelp of pain told me what I'd suspected.

Jeremy. Our savior. My brother.

Sirens snaked their way in the night.

Jeremy's shouts.

Jefferson yelling.

I lunged forward on my knees, fingers searching frantically in the snow. Face slick with blood I had to keep wiping from my eyes. I finally grasped the tire iron.

By now, both men stood facing each other, getting ready to launch into another battle. I'd never be able to swing the iron and do any damage. But I wouldn't need to.

We're Foxes. We fight each other. We curse and complain. But there is something deep and true that connects us.

I yelled, "Jeremy!"

He didn't take his eyes from Jefferson, but his hand shot out in my direction, and I handed the tire iron to him like a race baton.

I didn't need to see the final blow. I could trust that to Jeremy.

He raised the tire iron, then paused and dropped it. Using both fists, he went after Jefferson, pummeling him until Jefferson curled into a ball in the snow. Jeremy would have bruised knuckles, but there wouldn't be manslaughter charges.

By the time the cops arrived, Aria, groggy and battered, had regained consciousness. Her face was swollen, and a gash across her cheek bled hard enough not even an Hermès scarf would have helped.

Jeremy stood over us both, keeping an eye on Jefferson to make sure he didn't crawl away. "I told you, Katie, I'm your brother. That means no matter how tough you think you are, I'm always here to protect you."

36

My suitcase was packed and waiting by the front door to load into Elvis for my trip home. Only a small scab marked my chin from tackling the thief three days ago. It seemed like a year since then.

Unfortunately, I now had a Frankenstein string of stitches along my forehead, a swollen nose, jaw three sizes too big, and my eyes didn't look so great, either. Bruises and contusions I'd sustained in my fight with Jefferson made me achy and sore.

The snow had stopped somewhere around two o'clock this morning, about the same time Aria and I finished up at the emergency room and with our initial reports to the police. Eula had arrived to take Aria home with her, already making arrangements for plastic surgery for the gash on her cheek. Whatever conversations they'd have wouldn't be easy.

Diane had arranged for someone to retrieve Elvis. Jeremy and Diane had stayed until I was released. He'd insisted on going back to the hotel room he shared with the others working the stock show, determined to go to work the next morning.

The cops took statements, and we'd probably have a few more interviews as they gathered their information on Nanette's murder. I doubted Eula would pay for lawyers for Jefferson, but you can't predict a mother's love.

Diane took me to her house, and I dropped into bed, hoping to grab a couple of hours of sleep.

I hadn't slept enough, though. My body ached. I worried about Aria and how she'd feel about Jefferson and his betrayal. She'd had a lifetime believing they were friends, family, and allies. And then to find out he was none of those things that she relied on.

She and Eula, and probably Blaine in his way, would be grieving and coming to terms with the reality. Not to mention having to deal with media and all that fallout.

I wanted to gather my family close. Maybe Louise had instigated a recall against me, and a contingent of brothers had sided with her, but we'd never resort to murder. And in a pinch, Jeremy had saved my life. The love for my family soothed my injuries.

But it couldn't do much for my heartbreak, and my mind kept ratcheting to Baxter. Was he happy with Aria? Was she happy with him? Above all, I wanted their happiness. But did I want it more than my own? What if I confessed to both of them how I felt? That I loved Baxter. I could wax poetic and say thoughts of him vibrated on low as I went through every motion of every day. And then, out of the blue, I was ambushed with longing so acute I'd miss a step or stop breathing.

But that was ridiculous, obviously. A reasonable person knows that relationships come and go. Even with devoted couples, if one dies, the other carries on, and maybe finds love again. Even Dad had moved on from a forty-year marriage that had seemed ideal.

Falling for all this maudlin crap was self-indulgent. And we Foxes are not given to that sort of romantic frivolity.

It had surprised me when I'd come downstairs after a shower to find Diane shooing her kids out the kitchen door with Marta on their way to school. Normally, on a Monday morning, she'd be at work.

An amused shine lit her face as she leaned back on the kitchen counter and assessed my face. "You weren't in the mood to tell me last night, but now I want the blow-by-blow."

I pointed at a bruise below her eye that, despite her makeup expertise, was still faintly visible. "You first."

She reached for a coffee mug in the cupboard behind her. "You know better than to ask."

I did.

"But I want your *whole* story." She went to work at her complicated coffee machine that produced a magical brew complete with froth. I'd thought I'd achieved appliance nirvana when I finally acquired a refrigerator with an ice machine and water dispenser in the door, but now I cursed Diane for showing there was a wider world of kitchen machines to covet.

Before I had more than one sip, I realized she'd set a tablet on the counter, and Louise appeared from the cozy comfort of her kitchen, in the house where we'd all grown up. A ten-pound bag of potatoes sat on the counter next to her, and she held a russet in one hand, a vegetable peeler in her other. "It's Teacher Appreciation Day, and I need to make Funeral Potatoes. So, you talk, I'll peel."

Funeral Potatoes could be as perplexing to folks not from rural Nebraska as the idea of chili and cinnamon rolls served together. The dish, served at crowded events, not only funerals, is a roaster full of potatoes doused in cream (not milk), butter, and sour cream—some recipes call for cream of mushroom soup—and topped with cheese and sometimes cornflakes or crushed potato chips. There are few humans who can resist this combination, so, unless you've tried it, don't be too quick to judge.

Lifting my hand where only Diane could see but Louise couldn't, I flashed a middle finger. "Good morning, Louise." I made my voice as pleasant as I could. Which still sounded tired and cranky.

She gasped. "What happened to your face? Did you have a car wreck? I knew it was going to happen. That city traffic is awful."

I glared at her, but Diane filled in. "Nothing serious. Just our Katie doing what comes naturally."

Louise huffed and scolded. "You need to be more careful. A woman your age shouldn't be wrangling cattle. Did you go to the fundraiser like that? What about Jefferson? Is he okay with you looking like you've been in a fight? I mean, he's around some pretty wealthy people."

I cradled my warm mug. "Jefferson isn't—"

From the tablet screen, she took in every bump and bruise. "I mean, city people...people with money don't expect you to look like you've gone five rounds in the ring and lost by knockout. I wish you'd take this more seriously. I read if you don't find a partner in your thirties, your odds go way down of ever having a long marriage."

I didn't explain that a person in their thirties had more years left to live than a person in their fifties. But I didn't want to go into how misleading statistics could be.

"If you don't stop with your bullshit, Louise, I'll hang up on you." Diane settled next to me with her own gourmet blend. "Kate is just about to tell us about her weekend." She raised her eyebrows expectantly at me.

It took a while to get through the details, ending with a substantially downplayed version of the battle in the cattle pen. Diane stayed quiet and sipped her coffee. Louise exclaimed every two sentences, slowing down the narrative.

When I'd finished and enjoyed the last of my coffee, Louise said, "I'm shocked. What is it about you that attracts the wrong kind of man?"

Diane had to hold a hand to her mouth to keep from spewing her coffee. "That's your takeaway?"

Louise was elbow-deep in potato peels and gave Diane a curious glance. "Why? What should it be?"

Diane set her empty cup down. "How about this, Jefferson is a psychopath and he managed to fool everyone around him. And also, Blaine is fucked up. Probably the whole family is."

Louise frowned. "I don't know why you need to use that language."

Diane winked at me. "I'm trying to acclimate you to the contemporary world. How are you going to relate to your daughter in college if you don't update your attitude?"

Louise banged a potato on the counter. "If you're trying to tell me Ruthie is gay, I'm going to stop you right there."

Diane and I both blinked at that lob from outer space. Diane said, "Is Ruthie a lesbian?"

Louise glared through the screen with a look of challenge. "I don't know. Does it matter?"

Baffled by the turn in the conversation, we both said no, and Diane went on. "So, what I'm saying is that a grown-ass person needs to quit letting people tell them what to do or who they should be or..." She slowed down to emphasize her point. "Who they can love or not love." And she turned to me with a pointed stare.

Louise's voice was stern. "Leave Ruthie out of this."

That didn't seem to me to be the lesson of Jefferson's story. Diane was twisting things pretty hard to make some point to me, and I thought I knew what it was.

I yearned to be with Baxter. And some part of me suspected he wanted the same. But honor and loyalty prevented me.

Diane held my gaze as if she knew exactly what I was thinking.

From the screen, Louise's combative voice filtered over us. "I'm not here to be best friends with my children. My job is to raise decent human beings."

Diane and I continued to gaze at each other, and I somehow felt her severing thick vines I'd let grow around me, imprisoning me inside the castle like Sleeping Beauty. Except, if I was really asleep, it wouldn't hurt like this.

Louise seemed oblivious of us. "Look at you, Diane. You do all you can to raise your kids right without being their playmate. It's the same thing. And Kate, you need to learn how to be firm if you ever have kids, because you let the nieces and nephews run all over you."

She paused and sounded out of breath. "Hey? Are you guys listening to me?"

We still hadn't moved.

Louise sounded irritated. "Okay. You do whatever it is you're doing over there. I've got to get these potatoes in the roaster." The screen went dead.

"You're right," I said to Diane. A bright light burst inside of me, sending champagne bubbles into my veins. Honor meant not cheating or lying. It meant being kind and protecting the weak. It did not mean giving up what I wanted without so much as a peep. "There's something I need to do. Someplace I need to go."

Diane looked only a little smug. "I know. There's a car on the way here. Your flight leaves for Chicago in two hours."

Oh, Diane. Tough, smart, focused...and devoted, observant, and sometimes my champion. I loved her. "How did you know?"

She rolled her eyes. "I know all."

Two more hours to Chicago. Then to his tower two blocks off the river.

The light inside me suddenly dimmed. "What about Aria?"

Diane stood from her barstool with a sigh. "There are three grown-ups in this situation. You're all going to have to figure it out. The first step is for you to be honest. See what happens from there."

Fear swooped in. "What if he doesn't want me?"

She raised her eyebrows. "What if? Then you will have done what you could, and you'll need to move on. It won't be this paralyzing purgatory you're in now. No. Not even that. You're living in hell, and I can see it, even if you can't."

A horn honked. And she gave a shooing motion. "Your ride. Get out of here."

If she hadn't jerked my arm and dragged me to the door, grabbed my suitcase and coat and rushed them to the car, I might have run back upstairs and hid under the bed.

The bright Colorado sun reflected off the fresh snow and stabbed into my swollen eyes. The thin air froze in my nose and scraped against my bruised face as I forced my feet to follow her down the front walk. The walk, by the way, that some service had come before dawn and shoveled for her.

If Baxter didn't want me, that meant there would be a finality I hadn't faced. I thought I'd dealt with it, but the hope creeping from the shadows of my heart reminded me I'd kept the possibility of us alive, believing that someday we might find a way.

As long as I didn't force the situation, there was hope. I would manage Aria's herd and see Baxter from time to time. He'd be in my life.

But if I declared myself to him. And he didn't want me...

It took my breath away to think of it. It would be a loss in the same stratosphere as Mom's betrayal. As wrenching as Glenda's death. I wasn't sure I had the courage to do this.

Diane hollered at me. "I'm freezing my ass off. Get in the car."

Still I couldn't move.

From down the block a car turned, heading toward her cul-de-sac. The tires made a splashing noise where the plowed street had melted already in the bright sunshine.

"Katharine." Diane's voice was as stern as when we were kids and she was in charge of me doing my chores. "Don't be a wimp."

The car slowed, and Diane and I both watched as it pulled in behind my ride.

My heart hit my chest like a Clydesdale hoof, and I feared it might end me right there. Though the windows were tinted, the back passenger window rolled down, and I caught the glimpse of brown hair with a slight sprinkling of gray.

Maybe I breathed and maybe I didn't. And maybe I'd never breathe again.

The back door opened, and Baxter stepped out, his feet landing in a puddle at the curb, but he didn't seem to notice.

His eyes, those lion eyes, locked onto mine.

I'll never know how I reached the end of the walk or how many steps he took coming toward me, but we collided with such force it made us both grunt.

He stepped back too soon and peered at my face. With gentle fingers, he traced a path around the bruises. I read the layers of emotion in his eyes. Concern, tenderness, and eventually a hint of amusement when he decided everything would heal. "There's a story here."

I felt no pain. Didn't care about the injuries or stitches. "Later."

Our arms twined around each other, pulling tight. But never close enough.

I wanted to climb inside of him and feel his pulse, hear his heart, breathe his air.

Still clutching each other, we leaned our heads back enough to connect with our eyes again.

"I love you," he said with a conviction that seemed to be carried through every molecule of his body.

I didn't bother with inadequate words. There would be time enough to talk later. I answered by falling into the first kiss of the rest of our lives.

KILLER FLOCK
Kate Fox #11

Seeking refuge from a relentless blizzard, a bird-watching group takes shelter in a high school—only to find that the deadliest threat is already inside.

Kate Fox has her hands full when her sister Louise and her father's latest ex-girlfriend, Deenie, show up at her doorstep just as a freak snowstorm comes bearing down. But when the sheriff—snowbound and stranded out of town—calls on Kate to assist a van of bird-watchers stuck along the road, she has no idea what she's signed up for.

With the help of Deenie and Louise, Kate settles the stranded group in the local high school gym, hoping they can ride out the storm together. But as the blizzard howls and cell service dies, Kate and the eight quirky tourists find themselves utterly isolated. What began as a refuge quickly turns into a nightmare when, by dawn, one of the birders is found dead—murdered.

Trapped by the blizzard, Kate has to single-handedly preserve the crime scene and discreetly begin her investigation, all while keeping the ruffled birders calm. But she soon realizes that each of the bird-watchers has something to hide...and more than one of them had a reason to want the victim gone. Secrets run deep, and as the snow piles higher, so do the lies. With the murderer still among them and no chance of escape, Kate must untangle the deadly truths beneath the snow to avoid becoming prey to a killer in this flock.

Get your copy today at
severnriverbooks.com

ACKNOWLEDGMENTS

This book might have pitched me fits, but it was fun to write and especially a joy to research because I got to spend time at the Western National Stock Show in Denver. So, a thank you to everyone who has followed Kate this far down the line and allowing me to keep going with her adventures.

I hope I gave you a taste of the energy and scope of the stock show. Thanks to Dave for venturing from our sunny Tucson home to brave the chill of Denver in January. And thanks for having even more fun than I did, particularly running into horse people from the past.

Thanks to Bob West of the Whiskey Belle Ranch for your enthusiasm and expertise about Highlands cattle. Any errors are mine. And extra gratitude for allowing me to use Brodgar's name. I met that particular gentleman a while back, and he's one gracious and handsome fella. Bob's okay, too.

To my friend Smith Leser, who may not know much about livestock, but knows and loves Denver, and is always happy to host me and share the best the city has to offer. As she says, we've known each other since before our first husbands, and our friendship has stood the test of time.

Thank you to Sharon Connealy, for all the amazing photos and for keeping me real about the Sandhills. And to Bob and Terry Rothwell for letting us hang out at your ranch to remember the beauty and peace of the 'hills.

For those in the know, you might have noticed this book refers to the old Casa Bonita. That's because the first book in the series began in 2016 and each book takes place on a varying timeline, usually with only months in the story world. That means, in Kate's world, Casa Bonita hasn't been sold and remade into a fine dining experience requiring a lottery to get a table. (And I've not been one of the lucky few to have visited.) As an aside, my weird timeline for the series means I haven't had to deal with COVID yet. Whew.

Books don't happen in the privacy of a writer's home, so I'm grateful to have an amazing team on my side. To Severn River Publishers, thank you so much for believing in Kate and me. A writer couldn't have better hands in the pasture than Andrew Watts, Amber Hudock, Mo Metlen, Julia Hastings, and Catherine Farrell to round up the strays and keep the herd together.

My agent, Jill Marsal, is smart and savvy, and never keeps me waiting. Jessica Morrell, dream editor, has ridden shotgun on every Kate book. Honestly, her name should be on the cover.

Here's the unvarnished truth: I would have quit writing and slunk away to a dark corner years ago if not for the amazing women, talented writers all, who sit in the saddle next to me on the darkest and stormiest nights. Jess Lourey and Erica Ruth Neubauer and the dreaming room keep me heading north when I might be tempted to veer off course. Susanna Calkins is unsinkable. Lori Rader-Day knows all the things. Wendy Barnhart never lets me get away with anything. And even though Janet Fogg can't be with us, she's always whispering in my ear holding me up and urging me on.

Not ever to be left out, I thank my amazing daughters. There are no words for the strength, courage, and humor, you drop into my life like atomic bombs of love.

For Dave. Every day.

ABOUT THE AUTHOR

Shannon Baker is the award-winning author of *The Desert Behind Me* and the Kate Fox series, along with the Nora Abbott mysteries and the Michaela Sanchez Southwest Crime Thrillers. She is the proud recipient of the Rocky Mountain Fiction Writers 2014 and 2017-18 Writer of the Year Award.

Baker spent 20 years in the Nebraska Sandhills, where cattle outnumber people by more than 50:1. She now lives on the edge of the desert in Tucson with her crazy Weimaraner and her favorite human. A lover of the great outdoors, she can be found backpacking, traipsing to the bottom of the Grand Canyon, skiing mountains and plains, kayaking lakes, river running, hiking, cycling, and scuba diving whenever she gets a chance. Arizona sunsets notwithstanding, Baker is, and always will be a Nebraska Husker. Go Big Red.

Sign up for Shannon Baker's reader list at
severnriverbooks.com